Make
It
Right

Also by Megan Erickson

Make It Count

Make It Right

A Bowler University Novel

MEGAN ERICKSON

WILLIAM MORROW IMPULSE
An Imprint of HarperCollinsPublishers

Excerpt from *Make It Last* copyright © 2015 by Megan Erickson.

EPub Edition SEPTEMBER 2014 ISBN: 9780062353498
Print Edition ISBN: 9780062353511

10 9 8 7 6 5 4 3 2

To my son and daughter, who I love with all that I am: As much as I want to shield you from all that's bad, I can't. You're human, so you'll make mistakes. Just know that I'll always love you, and it's never too late to make it right.

Acknowledgments

THIS BOOK. To take a character like Max, who made some pretty big mistakes in the first book of this series, and make him the good guy in his own book . . . well, let's just say that was a challenge. I hope my readers see past some of the mistakes he made and see that he's trying to be a better person. Because I fell in love with Max writing this book. I hope you do too.

This time, I'm going to first thank my readers. Because I love you guys. The response to MAKE IT COUNT was fabulous. You guys laughed and swooned and cried. I couldn't have asked for greater readers. You sent me messages and texts and, holy cow, I was overwhelmed. This book is for you. I write for you.

So many bloggers were amazing in getting behind this series: Books by Migs, Painful Reads, Owl Always be Reading, Amy's Reading Realm, Teacups & Book Love,

Hootie and Globug Need a Book, Crystal in Bookland, Allodoxophobia, Lovin' Los Libros, Too Fond of Books, A Bookish Escape, Lazy Book Lovers and more. I'm probably forgetting some. And I'm sorry. Know that I love you too.

Huge thanks to my agent, Marisa Corvisiero, who is my biggest champion. And thank you to Amanda Bergeron, who loves what I write and allows me to be me. You are so inspiring, Amanda. And I love working with you.

I couldn't write a single word without my amazing critique partners Natalie Blitt, A. J. Pine, Lex Martin, Lia Riley, and Lucas Hargis. Big hugs to you all. You are my everything.

Thank you to my Cool Kids Mafia, NAAU, '14 NA debuts and my BUB girls who have been with me before I ever wrote a word of a novel.

Thank you so much to Jennifer L. Armentrout for reading this book and loving it like I did and lending your name for the cover. I admire you so much as an author, so this was a real honor.

To every single person that read or reviewed or talked about MAKE IT COUNT, I love you. And I'm writing for you. Because you saw something in my writing and characters that made you want to read more.

To my family—thank you for understanding when I ignore your phone calls and retreat to my writing cave. Thank you to my amazing husband and my wonderful kids. Thank you to my friends for supporting me. And Andi—you still aren't one of the "little people."

Chapter 1

MAX DRAINED HIS cup of beer and closed his eyes to let the sounds of the party sink into his skin and down into his bones.

This usually worked—the alcohol in his veins, the music, the friends. The girls.

He fed off others' energy, always had. His favorite thing to do to unwind was to head out to a bar or party and just let loose.

So when his roommate Cam found him cursing and pacing his room like an animal after a particularly *delightful* phone call with his father—Max curled his lip in a sneer just thinking about it—he'd encouraged Max to go out. That's what his friends did. They knew him better than he knew himself sometimes.

But for once, Max hadn't wanted to. He'd wanted to go to the gym and sweat out all the anger, but Cam was persistent. So Max relented.

He knew now he shouldn't have.

Because the beer tasted skunked and the music hurt his head and even the girls weren't interesting.

The redhead beside him right now was still talking. He'd asked her one question about her major, and she was still rambling on about it five minutes later.

He'd said maybe two sentences to this girl, both questions about herself, but she was clearly still into him, pressing her chest against his folded arms. The lace of her bra peaked out the top of her neckline, and he could feel the textured fabric through her thin shirt when it brushed against his knuckles.

He hadn't even been in the mood to lay on the charm. He knew how to stand, how to smile with his eyes. *Smize*, one of his brother's ex-girlfriends had called it with a giggle.

Whatever it was. He knew how to do it. And knew how to get the girl. Too bad he didn't want her.

Fuck this shit.

He set his empty beer cup on a window ledge. "Um, Kelly," he said, cutting in when she finally took a breath. He remembered her name, because he always remembered names. Kelly blinked and peered up at him through her lashes, lips parted. She was hot. Big rack. A year ago, she would have been his type. Hell, most girls were his type. But lately, they'd reminded him of how much he'd almost fucked up his life.

Except that one girl . . .

He shook his head, and leaned down to speak into her ear. He heard a stuttered inhale and resisting rolling his eyes. "I gotta head out. I forgot I need to get home. Early morning." He leaned back and shot her a smile. Or smize. Whatever.

Confusion crossed her face, but he was over this scene. "Sorry," he said with a shrug and turned away before she could respond.

Max searched the sea of bodies for Cam. The guy was over in the corner with a girl, flashing his dimples while she looked up at him with pure infatuation. Max rolled his eyes and hollered, "Ruiz!"

Cam turned his head and Max gave him the sign he was heading out. Cam waved in acknowledgment and turned back to his girl of the night.

Max made his way through the crowd, feeling a couple of touches on his arms or shoulders, some "Hey Max" 's, but he kept walking because he wasn't in the mood and enough people already thought he was an asshole.

He wished Alec, his best friend, was around, but he'd decided to stay home with his girlfriend, Kat, tonight. Kat, who used to be Max's girlfriend. Before he fucked it up.

Life was complicated.

Once he stepped outside, he pulled up the collar of his jacket against the early October air and walked briskly back to the townhouse he shared with Alec and Cam. The phone call with his dad still rankled, the words poking him with their sharp edges.

He'd mentioned changing his major, had barely even spoken the words when his dad proclaimed *Paytons stick together!* and Max was expected to complete his business degree and then work at his dad's mechanic shop, helping with the books and business side of things.

Max didn't want to, but the obligation to work with his dad and two brothers weighed heavily on his shoulders. Plus, his dad said he wouldn't hesitate to withdraw his tuition help, and Max couldn't afford to cover it, despite his two jobs.

The bastard.

The lights of the convenience store near his house caught his eye and he changed direction, suddenly hungry for those super-greasy pizzas they made in the back and kept in a warmer on the counter.

He was still a little drunk but hopefully the cheese, dough and sauce would mop up the rest of the awful beer sitting like acid in his stomach.

He crossed the parking lot and then stopped beside the front doors, fumbling inside his pockets. His phone fell out and he cursed as it clattered on the sidewalk. He shoved it back in his coat pocket and then dug his wallet out of his back jeans pocket. He blinked at it blearily and tried to count his bills.

He kept losing count of his ones and had to start over. Fucking beer.

The bell on the convenience store door tinkled and he heard a voice—that damn musical voice that hit him in the gut every time he heard it. And he couldn't figure out why.

He looked up from his wallet and there she was, Lea Travers, talking to some tall blond guy, his arm around her slender shoulders.

Max must have made a sound or movement because Lea turned her head, her long, dark straight hair swirling around her shoulders. In the glow of the streetlights, her eyes were even bigger, rounder and darker than normal, staring at him from under her thick fringe of bangs.

She wore low-heeled knee-high boots and tight jeans and a thigh-length pink jacket that cinched at the waist. Her full lips were parted and her cheeks flushed, probably from the warmth of the convenience store she just left.

For a moment, he enjoyed the way she looked at him, a little bit of curious hope.

He'd met her last year, because she was friends with Kat. There was something about Lea, this power or strength that lurked below the surface of her small, fragile frame. He wanted to grab that strength, roll around in it like a cat in catnip.

Max looked to the guy who stood next to her, a proprietary arm around her shoulders—which Max glared at—and a pizza box in the other hand. The guy was tall and blond and had big blue eyes and looked like he just came from Wimbledon, where he had front-row seats because he was the heir to his dad's pharmaceutical business. He was the kind of kid whose dad drove some fancy BMW or Mercedes into the shop and then looked down on Max and his brothers, with their grease-stained clothes and fingernails.

He looked vaguely familiar but Max couldn't place him, and the guy's perfect hair and collared polo made him want to hurl.

So she had a boyfriend. And Max was done, absolutely

positively fucking done with girls who were attached. He'd almost lost his best friend over the last time he'd let himself get involved with one.

So, like always, he fell back on what he knew. He curled his upper lip into a smirk, opened his mouth, and let out the asshole. "Hey there, doll."

Lea's eyes narrowed and her lips pressed into a thin line. Well, it'd been nice while it lasted. His fault. Her lips parted one time to sigh. "Hi, Max."

He didn't want it to be this way between them. He wanted to saunter up next to her, wrap an arm around her neck and look down into those dark eyes while they filled with lust . . .

Shit. Fucking drunken daydreams. None of that was happening because somehow, around Lea, he turned into a six-year-old boy, teasing the girl he wanted the most.

And no matter how hard he tried, he couldn't curb the asshole. He jerked a thumb at the convenience door. "Might want to find a new boyfriend, there, Travers. Clearly Polo Boy can afford to take you to a nicer place." The words were coming, coming up like vomit, and with them came a heavy helping of self-loathing. He couldn't stop them. "Although, if a convenience-store pizza is all it takes to get a date with you, even I can afford that."

Polo Boy opened his mouth but Lea tapped his chest with the back of her hand, so he clamped his jaws shut.

Max's mouth just had a mind of his own now. "Oh, he replies to hand signals, too? Got 'em trained."

"Max, why are you always such an asshole?" The worst part about it was that Lea wasn't angry, her voice wasn't biting, it was dripping with disappointment and that was worse. He wanted her to be angry and stomp in a huff. He wanted a reaction.

He didn't want pity.

He spread his arms wide. "That's who I am, doll." It was a lie, but he'd perfected being an asshole to an art. Just like the charmer role. It was easier than trying to figure out who he really was or wanted to be.

Her eyes narrowed more, and then Polo Boy spoke up. "Look—"

Lea cut him off. "It's fine, Nick. Let's go."

They walked away, Polo Boy's arm around her shoulders, Lea's limp from a childhood car accident more pronounced in the cold weather.

Max gritted his teeth. For once keeping his mouth shut from calling after them to ask what would buy him second base.

He looked at his wallet again in his hands and shoved it back into his pocket. He wasn't hungry for pizza anymore.

LEA STARED AT her boots as she walked and curled her hands into fists in the pockets of her jacket. Nick was silent beside her, lost in his own thoughts.

She hadn't known Max long, and what she knew of him wasn't so great. He'd dated Kat and hadn't been a very good boyfriend. And everything about Max, from his swagger to his snug T-shirts to his cocky smirk, screamed confident asshole.

Which meant he wasn't for her.

But tonight, for a brief moment, those big, expressive brown eyes had showed a glimmer of hope before he blinked. Then the alcohol haze clouded over them, and that little sliver of another Max disappeared with one curl of his lips.

She wondered if he realized how much those eyes gave him away when he wasn't careful. She wondered if anyone ever tried to look deeper.

She wondered if he wanted anyone to.

Nick squeezed her shoulder. "You all right?"

She chewed her cheek. "Yeah, just thinking."

"You know I went to high school with him, right?"

Lea looked up at her cousin and saw his blond stubble catching the rays of the streetlights. "What? Who?"

Nick gestured behind them. "Max Payton. He went to Tory High School."

She frowned. "But—"

"I'm three years younger. I mean, I doubt he has any idea who I am. I only know him because, well, everyone knew Max when he was a senior. Popular guy."

"Why didn't you say anything just now?"

Nick shrugged. "What's the point? So he can say, 'I don't remember you?' I was just a freshman. Doubt he ever saw me." He picked at his shirt. "And he was glaring holes in my polo shirt like it personally offended him."

"He was just drunk."

"I don't know, maybe he hates horses."

Lea laughed. "I don't think that's it."

"But can you imagine him on a horse? Max is a big dude. Poor horse."

Lea elbowed Nick in the ribs. "Stop."

"He'd probably try to bench-press the horse."

Lea elbowed him harder. "Nick, stop!"

Nick chuckled and squeezed her shoulder again before dropping his arm. "So, that's kind of funny he thought we were dating."

Lea wrinkled her nose. "Ew."

Nick scrunched his lips to the side. "I mean, we're not actually related by blood, so . . ." he waggled his eyebrows.

"Seriously, ew. And you have a girlfriend."

"Threesome?"

"Nick."

He bumped her with his hip and laughed as they climbed the stairs to his place. When they opened the door, Nick's girlfriend, Trish, bounded up from the couch. "Finally! What took you guys so long? I'm starving."

She grabbed the box from Nick and immediately began to dish out slices onto paper plates. Lea took her plate and sat on the beanbag chair, tucking her legs under her. Trish sat across from her and when Nick sat down, he gave Trish a soft kiss on the forehead. They'd started dating sophomore year in high school, and the affection between them melted Lea's heart every time.

"So, Lea and I are together now," Nick started, "and my name is Polo, and I am a crappy boyfriend who takes her on convenience-store dates."

Trish froze with her pizza halfway to her mouth. "What are you talking about?"

"We ran into Max Payton and . . ." Nick turned to Lea. "Wait, how do you know him?"

"He used to date my friend Kat, who is now dating his friend Alec."

Nick blinked.

Lea picked off a slice of pepperoni and dropped it into her mouth. "It's kind of a long story."

"Alec Stone goes here too?" Nick asked.

"Oh yeah, I guess you know him, too. He and Max went to high school together."

"Small world," Trish said.

Nick shrugged. "A lot of kids from surrounding high schools apply here." He looked at Lea. "And can we talk about how he was flirting with you?"

Lea snapped her head back. "In what world was that flirting? He was an asshole."

"Wait, what happened?" Trish asked.

Nick held up a hand. "Okay, I admit it was a poor attempt. But he didn't like my arm around her shoulder, I'll tell you that," Nick muttered.

Lea rolled her eyes. "I don't think Max has a problem picking up girls, so if he wanted to be effective, he would have been."

Nick picked at the cheese on his pizza. "I don't know, maybe he didn't want to be."

"I'm really confused right now," Trish said.

Lea shifted on the beanbag chair. "Me too."

Nick looked up. "I'm not saying it's mature, but sometimes, when a guy wants a girl but knows he doesn't have a shot? Well, he's kind of a dick."

Lea narrowed her eyes. "Max has no interest in me."

Nick cocked his head.

"Seriously!" Lea threw up her hands. "There is no way."

"Why?"

"Because . . ." She pressed her lips together. Nick's previous girlfriend was Kat. Beautiful, effervescent, nothing serious—until she met Alec—Kat. Lea was . . . well, cynical and a little grumpy sometimes and wouldn't stand by while Max acted the asshole. She waved her hands. "I think I'm done with this conversation."

Nick's opened his mouth, but Trish knocked his knee with hers, so he rolled his eyes and took another bite of pizza.

But as they talked about classes and Nick imitated his professor's deep tenor, all Lea could think about was that hopeful glint she'd seen in Max's eyes for that brief moment.

No matter how much she tried to deny it to herself, she wanted to see it again.

Chapter 2

THE CAT WAS back.

Its left ear was shredded but healed, and that scar on
its chin a hairless C amid the black fur.

It was limping and Max could see a dark, wet spot on
its haunch. Small red footprints marked its path leading
to Max's back door.

He crouched down and held a hand out. "If you could
talk, bet you'd say, 'you should see the other guy.' "

The cat sat down ten feet away and licked its black lips
as if in an affirmative answer.

"I bet you got some good licks in, huh?" He said,
reaching behind him for the can of tuna he'd opened
when he saw the cat through the window of his college
town house.

The cat didn't move, just studied him, yellow eyes
glowing in the setting sun. From what Max knew of
cats—which was limited since his dad threatened to

shoot any potential feline pet when Max had been a kid—the cat must be hurting to let the injury sit without cleaning it thoroughly. So he quit the small talk, scooped out the tuna onto a small plate and shoved it toward the cat.

Then he waited. And the cat didn't move.

This wasn't their normal routine. Max always left immediately after supplying the food, like he was the cat's dirty secret and if its big cat-gang buddies found out it had a human on the side, it'd be laughed out of the alley.

But he didn't like the way the cat was favoring its leg. He had a massive hangover from the night before. And he was tired of being a dirty secret.

Next he grabbed a plastic bowl of water and shoved that alongside the food.

Then he waited. And still the cat didn't move.

"Come on, buddy," he whispered, hearing the concern in his voice. "I'm your friend."

The cat's yellow eyes never left Max as it dipped its head and slowly crept forward, body tense, clearly fighting the flight instinct.

Max didn't move.

The cat reached the plate of food and crouched, then scarfed up bits of tuna in between glances at Max. Max ran his eyes over the sleek, battered body and sighed. He didn't know if the cat was male or female. But it seemed like a big tomcat, so Max guessed it was a he. He didn't necessarily want to get closer to find out if he was wrong.

When the cat ate all the tuna, he gave Max a long look before lapping at the water.

He was close, only about two feet away, and if Max just stretched out his arm . . .

The screen door banged open behind him and the cat took off like a shot, bounding down the alley and disappearing through a hole in the neighbor's shrubs.

"Dammit!" Max swore, jumping up from his crouched position and whirling to face whoever interrupted the moment. "Could you be any fucking louder—"

Lea stared at him, an empty water bottle dangling from her fingers. She dropped it in the recycling bin and wiped her hands. "Didn't want to litter in your house."

He winced. He should apologize for swearing at her, but the words stuck in his throat. His head pounded, reminding him how he'd drunk too much last night. And hadn't he made some shitty remarks to her and that blond guy . . . ?

Lea cocked a hip. "What are you doing out here anyway?" Her eyes landed on the empty plate of food and bowl of water, then roamed past his shoulder.

The scrutiny unsettled him. Made him cranky. Okay, crankier.

It must have shown on his face, because Lea's pixie features hardened into an indifferent mask. He waited for her to leave so he could clean up after his cat—shit, *his* cat—and get to class.

She crossed her slender arms over her chest. "It takes time, you know?"

"What're you talking about?" he snapped.

Lea didn't flinch. She nodded toward the cat's dinner area. "Cats. Takes a long time for them to trust. And sometimes feral cats never trust humans."

Who died and made her an expert? He'd get that cat to trust him if it killed him. "Well thanks, Miss Veterinarian. Didn't know you were studying that on top of your Shakespeare and Dickens."

She dropped her hands at her sides, fingers curled into little fists. "Why do you always act like this?"

He didn't know. If he did, he wouldn't do it. But with her, the words he wanted to say never came out. Instead, all he was able to do was snark and snap. "Why are you still bugging me?" he shot back.

Those liquid brown eyes fired. "Grow up, Max." Then she turned around and walked back into the house, her limp more pronounced then he'd ever seen it.

He didn't watch the way her ass looked in her tight jeans. Or how her hair shone in the sun. The sight of her eyes—so alive and challenging, calling him on his bullshit—didn't linger in his mind.

His phone rang in his jacket pocket and he pulled it out, eyes still scanning the road to see if the cat came back. He glanced at the caller ID and sighed. "Yo."

"Max," Calvin's voice grunted in his ear.

"Who else would it be? You called me."

His oldest brother ignored the question. "Friday afternoon, you don't have class, right?"

As a senior, he'd had his pick of classes, so he'd made sure to keep his Fridays open. That was his day. A day for himself. One where he didn't have to attend class in a major he hated or work in his dad's automotive shop, doing work he hated. A constant reminder he was about to be stuck doing that same work he hated for the rest of his life. Unless he crawled out from under Jack Payton's steel-toe boots. Which he didn't see happening.

"You know I don't," was all he said.

Another voice murmured over the line and Max recognized Brent's voice—the middle brother. "That's what I'm doing right now, assface," Calvin's voice was muffled as he spoke to Brent, and Max rolled his eyes.

"Max," Calvin's deep voice came back on the line, clearer.

"I didn't go anywhere. You called me. What do you want?" Max growled.

Silence.

"What crawled up your ass and died?" Cal asked.

"Cal—"

"Can you drive to Dad's Friday? That big-ass dying tree in the backyard finally cracked under last week's ice storm. Dad wants it cleared out and if we don't do it Friday, he's going to do it over the weekend. And then he'll throw his back out and be even more miserable than usual. Brent and I don't want to deal with that shit, so we need to get this tree taken care of. You in?"

Max gritted his teeth and rubbed his eyes with his thumb and forefinger. His older brothers had to work with their dad every day at the shop. And sparing them from their father's wrath was the only reason he said what he did next. "Sure."

Cal's voice was muffled again. "Will you quit yapping in my ear? I asked him and he said he'd do it. Fuck, you're annoying . . . What? . . . Christ, fine, Brent." More muffled sounds and again the clearer voice. "Max?"

This time, he didn't even dignify it with an answer. Cal continued, "Brent wants some of your cookies."

He couldn't help but grin. "Last time I saw both of you, looked like you needed to lay off the cookies."

"Fuck you," Cal said, laughing, and Max grinned wider.

"I'll be there. With cookies."

"Later, bro."

Max ended the call, took one last look at the alley and then gathered the cat's dishes before trudging into the kitchen. As he washed the dishes, voices filtered in from the living room, Kat's laughter, Lea's quiet murmuring, Alec conversing with their other roommate, Camilo Ruiz.

Amazing how the voices of a full house made Max feel even more alone.

A breeze ruffled the back of Max's T-shirt. He glanced over his shoulder at the open screen door and frowned. He must have forgotten to shut it. He dried his hands, pulled the door shut, and then walked into the living room.

Lea and Kat sat on floor in front of the coffee table, books open in front of them, heads bent to their task. Alec sat behind Kat, his spread legs on either side of her.

Alec, his best friend since elementary school, turned his head when Max cleared his throat. Alec's face turned wary, and Max hated he'd been such a prick lately that even his best friend was cautious around him. "Hey, man," Alec said.

Max nodded. "What's up, Zuk?"

Alec smiled, clearly loving that Max used the old nickname. Max had given it to him years ago because of his pompadour hairstyle—like Danny Zuko from *Grease*.

Alec's fingers absentmindedly shifted through Kat's hair. "Cat let you touch it yet?"

Lea's eyes were on Max. He could feel them, like twin heat-seeking missiles. "No," he said.

Alec nodded encouragingly. "He will. Just give it time."

Max shrugged, playing it off like he didn't care.

"Wanna play?" Cam asked, tilting the controller to his video game system, eyes on the TV as his army guy dodged a grenade and took aim at a sniper.

Max chuckled at their roommate. "No thanks, man. Got some studying to do." Even though he didn't give a shit about his major, he was so close to graduating, he could smell it.

He took one step forward, when a black blur flew past him and raced up the stairs. "Holy shit!" Max yelped, losing his footing and crashing painfully into the coffee table. The girls screeched. Cam threw his remote control, and Alec joined Max on the coffee table, both of them clutching each other like it was some B-rate horror movie.

"What the fuck was that?" Alec's low voice vibrated in Max's ear.

"A raccoon?" Cam guessed.

"A dog," Lea said.

"A real big dog," Kat added.

"I think it was a bear," Max said.

Alec's nails dug into Max's biceps. "I don't think bears move that fast."

"Okay, so, like a freak bear." Max gently pushed Alec off of him before he could develop bruises.

Cam stood up slowly, eyes on the stairs. "I wish I had my gun."

Alec rolled his eyes. "We're not in a combat zone."

"I'm going to get a broom," Max declared, heading for the kitchen.

"A broom?" Alec called after him. "What's a broom going to do?"

Max grabbed the wooden handled broom from the corner of the kitchen and walked back into the living room, brandishing it like a sword. "I don't know, I'll poke it."

Alec narrowed his eyes. "I'm sure this freak bear is going to love being poked."

"You have a better idea?" Max retorted.

Alec was mute.

Kat tapped her finger to her lips. "Should I grab the fire extinguisher? That seems like something someone would do if this was a movie."

Alec laced his fingers with Kat's. "I'm thinking we don't need the fire extinguisher."

Max drew his eyes away from the couple to see Lea quietly climbing the flight of stairs. "Hey," he said, shouldering past her, broom held out in defense. "You don't know what that thing is. Don't just march up there alone."

Lea eyed the broom, then him, and raised an eyebrow. "You're going to protect me, then? With a broom?"

Max's cheeks warmed. "Well, I don't see your Polo Boy around to help you . . ."

Her eyes narrowed. "His name is Nick," she said through gritted teeth.

Again, a flash of recognition hit him, but he pushed it aside and focused on the petite spitfire in front of him. "Well, you wanna call him and see if he has any better ideas?"

He swore Lea growled under her breath before she waved him on. "Fine, you first then."

Max walked slowly up the stairs, broom handle out, while the caravan followed him, Cam bringing up the rear. Alec's room was at the top of the stairs and Max poked his head in, looking around.

"All clear!" He called out.

"Christ," muttered an exasperated Alec behind Lea.

"All clear!" Kat echoed, followed by a "Roger that!" from Cam.

Next was the bathroom, and Max used the broom handle to slowly push aside the shower curtain. The only creature in there was a wad of hair Kat had left behind. "All clear except for a Kat hairball!" Max called.

"Hey!" Kat protested.

"Roger that!" Cam repeated.

Lea laughed behind Max and he decided he liked that sound.

Next was Max's room, and the door was definitely open wider than he had left it. He held up a closed fist and Lea bumped into him. "Don't you know the hand signal for stop?" he whispered over his shoulder.

Those eyes pierced him. "Excuse me. Your massive head is blocking my sight and I can't see anything."

"Hey," Max said, affronted. "Cam, you gotta teach Lea the military hand signals or whatever."

"Roger that!" Cam called again with a laugh. He was in the Air National Guard and knew all that fancy stuff.

Max focused back on the task at hand—ridding their campus apartment of unwanted wildlife.

He motioned for Lea to stay outside his bedroom door and peeked in, broom handle at the ready to defend his person.

And right there, in the center of his unmade bed, was a ball of black fur. Yellow eyes blinked at him and a pink mouth opened to reveal white teeth and a chipped fang.

"Well fuck me," Max said, lowering the broom handle and releasing the tension in his shoulders.

"What's going on?" Alec called and Max turned around to survey his makeshift backup.

"It's him," he said, still in awe.

"Who?" Kat asked.

"Him," Max waved a hand toward his bedroom. "The cat."

Kat's eyes widened. "How the heck did he get in the house?"

Max bit his lip. "I left the back door open while I washed the dishes. I guess he crept in and hid or something, then we saw him when he ran up here." He shifted his weight. "And he's hurt, I think."

"You just going to leave him in there?" Kat said.

Max shrugged. "Sure. I mean, he could use a break from the cold and he seems to be loving my bed."

Alec slung an arm around Kat's shoulders. "All right,

well, we'll leave you alone with your cat, then. Let us know if you need anything." They walked downstairs, Cam at their heels. "I'm glad it's not a bear," he muttered.

Max stood in the doorway of his room, staring at the cat on his bed. He seemed right at home, lounging on the worn gray comforter.

"What're you going to name him?" A musical voice said beside him, and he looked down at Lea at his side. Her head barely came up to his armpit as she gazed at the cat.

Max looked around his room, at the shelf that held his favorite hockey stick and the game puck he won when he called into a radio show and had to belch the Ocean City Devils' fight song.

Then his eyes fell back on the cat. His scarred, chipped-toothed cat. "Wayne."

Lea's head tilted, and a soft lock of hair brushed his bicep. "Wayne?"

He nodded. "Yeah, after the hockey player Wayne Gretzky. The cat's kind of . . ." He almost said *scarred* but he remembered Lea's limp, and he stopped short. "He seems tough. You can take one look at him and see he's won his fair share of fights."

Lea pursed those lips, the ones he'd stared at many times, all lush and full with a cupid's bow. Her eyes searched his and he didn't know what she was looking for.

Then she hummed in the back of her throat and her hand fluttered at her left thigh. "Guess so," she said quietly. Then she turned and peered at him from over her shoulder as she left his bedroom. "I'll leave you two alone, since you have some 'getting to know you' to do."

Then, with a quick smile, she was gone.

Max turned to Wayne, whose eyes shifted from the door back to Max. "What you think of her, buddy?"

Wayne licked his lips, and Max laughed. "Yeah, me too."

Chapter 3

LEA BALLED HER fist and kneaded her left quad to ease the soreness out of the overtaxed muscle. Normally she worked behind the desk of the library, where she sat in a comfy chair, but like a dummy she'd volunteered to reshelve these book returns because Nick—who'd just gotten a job at the library with her—wasn't feeling well. So he sat behind the desk, coughing and infecting everyone with the plague.

She waved to him and he began to wave before he went into a coughing fit.

So maybe he would have been better off in her place.

"Hey Lea," said a voice, followed by a crunch of teeth sinking into an apple. She turned her head and looked into the bright green eyes of her roommate, Danica Owens.

Bright green, as in almost neon. "New contacts?"

Danica fluttered her eyes. "Yep. Like 'em?"

Lea shrugged. "I like your natural eye color."

Today—because Danica's look changed every day—she had a grunge thing going on. Black jeans, motorcycle boots, ripped Guns 'N' Roses T-shirt under a studded leather jacket.

"Rock on," Danica said, sticking her tongue out and making the devil horn gesture with her hands.

Lea snorted and went back to shelving books. "How's Monica?"

Danica toed a tear in the library carpeting with her boot, her gesture unusual. Uncertainty wasn't a look she normally wore. "Okay," she answered, that one word saying more than she probably meant it to about her on-again, off-again girlfriend.

Lea stopped what she was doing and turned to Danica. "What's going on?"

Danica shrugged, the leather of her jacket squeaking where she leaned against a shelf.

"Dan—"

An irritated sigh. "She wants me to go home with her over Thanksgiving break."

"Okay . . ."

The neon eyes narrowed as they honed in on Lea. "She wants me to meet her parents."

Lea opened her mouth and then closed it again. She needed to think before she spoke again, because even though Danica munched her apple like she like she was carefree, her eyes hadn't left Lea's, clearly gauging her reaction.

Danica was a rare creature. Like an albino deer. Everyone wanted her, but they wanted her to keep. And she didn't like to be kept. Pinned down. Forced into any sort of consistency.

Her loyalty was unrivaled, but it was hard-earned. Lea still didn't know how she'd managed to become part of Danica's inner circle. Which really only consisted of her and Alec.

Lea licked her lips, and even though she knew the answer, she asked anyway. "And how do you feel about that?"

Danica's black-manicured hand reached up and pushed Lea's bangs out of her eyes. "Why do I have to do meet them? Why can't she and I just be together without all . . ." Her hand fluttered as she pulled it away. ". . . without everyone else."

Lea took a deep breath. "That's not really fair to her, Dan. You can't live your lives in a vacuum."

"But—"

"You care about her."

Danica snapped her jaw shut and didn't deny it.

"She cares about you and if introducing you to her parents is important to her, you need to recognize that, you know?"

Lea liked Monica. And she understood her desire for Danica to meet her parents. Lea hadn't ever really dated seriously, never cared enough about a boy to want to meet his parents. But she got that it was a big step, the need to introduce your family to the important person in your life.

Danica focused again on that rip in the carpet.

"You'll think about it?" Lea asked.

She raised her head, a smile tugging at her lips. "Yeah. Yeah, I will."

A booming laugh caught Lea's attention. She turned her head toward the sound. Max Payton's deep voice blasted through the silence of the library as he talked to Cam Ruiz. Students sitting at nearby tables stared at the disruption.

She'd volunteered in libraries since high school, so a loud voice in a quiet room full of books made her react like Pavlov's dog. So without conscious thought, Lea raised her index finger to her pursed lips. "Shhhhh!"

Max jerked his head up and froze, those chocolate eyes zeroing right in on her finger at her lips. She dropped her hand and gripped her thigh.

And then he strode toward her, all long legs and wide shoulders and big hands. He wore a pair of worn jeans that hung just right on his hips and she clenched her jaw for even noticing. He was a jerk. A jerk with a nice butt and a rip in his jeans that strategically showed an inch of muscular thigh. She hated how the sight of him heated her skin. How his voice rumbled down to her bones.

The asshole.

He stopped a foot away and cocked his head. "Did you just shush me?"

Crap, she did, didn't she? She shushed him.

"Your voice has a high decibel level." That was the first brilliant thing that came to mind. She should have said, *I carried a watermelon.*

"Decibel level?" He raised an eyebrow, and the corner of his mouth twitched.

And it irritated her.

"This is a library. Students are studying so would it behoove you to keep your voice down?"

"Behoove?"

"Do you only speak in questions?"

"Do you only speak in SAT words?"

They went into a stare down. Lea glared as Max furrowed his brow. Out of the corner of her eye, Lea saw Danica's gaze ping-pong between the two of them.

Max took a step forward, resting a hand on the shelf beside her head and leaned forward, smelling infuriatingly good, like soap and man. She resisted breathing him in a like a lunatic and instead placed her hands on his chest to push him back. Except her hands met firm pecs and then she wasn't pushing at all. Instead her fingers curled into the muscle, and she relished the strength under her palms, surrounding her.

She raised her eyes and met his: long lashes surrounding liquid brown. Screw him and his attractiveness. She stiffened and dug her nails through his T-shirt as he grunted but didn't step away. "Back up, Max."

Why did he have to be so hot? With those eyes and long lashes and chin dimple? For God's sake.

"I don't know if I should," he said. "Need saving from anything today? I can get my broom."

If only he knew just how little Lea needed saving. From anything. "Maybe some other girls are impressed by the size of your . . . broom . . . but I'm not."

He threw back his head and laughed, then clutched her hand where it pressed against his chest. "Oh doll, you wish you could get a shot at checking out my . . ." he leaned close, his minty breath a promise on his lips " . . . broom."

She opened her mouth but before she could say anything, Nick went into another coughing fit at the front desk.

Max's head snapped up, and he looked in Nick's direction. Then he jolted away from her as if she were on fire, palms out. His eyes now icy cold to douse the flames.

His whole body radiated tension and discomfort. He ran his tongue over his top teeth, a gesture she'd seen him use before when he was uncertain. His one tell. Then he jerked his head in Nick's direction. "Never mind, you have Nick, huh?"

She blinked at the rapidity of his mood change. She should correct Max, tell him Nick was her cousin, the closest thing to her brother she had. She knew Max had a history with unavailable women. She knew what he'd done to Alec, almost wrecking a decade-long friendship. If he had learned anything from sleeping with his best friend's girlfriend, it would be to treat non-single women like the plague.

And the way Max was looking at her, she was infected.

Nick as her imaginary boyfriend was her shield. He kept Max at a distance and was her excuse for keeping Max there. She'd seen Max flirt, flashing his smile at girls and pouring on the charm until they were putty in his hands. But not with her. Oh no. He talked to her with a sneering curl to his lip. Well, screw him. She wasn't interested anyway.

But in the back of her mind, part of her wanted that challenge. She wanted to see what happened to Max Payton once all that charm had drained to zero and the real Max emerged. She'd caught a glimpse the other day when she saw him crouched outside of his townhouse, coaxing the battered cat to eat.

Max shook his head, and the cocky mask returned. He eyed Danica's shirt. "Hey Axel."

Danica ran her tongue over her teeth. "Hey Roid Rage."

Max smirked as he walked backward and raised his fist beside his head in a bicep curl. Then he laughed and turned around.

So Lea got a nice view of his tight butt in those jeans. Jerk.

She stared holes in his back until Danica stepped into her line of sight.

"Well, well, well," she drawled.

Lea tugged on the ends of her hair. "I know, he's such a jerk, right?" She smoothed her shirt and then brushed her fingertips over her warmed cheeks. "I mean, he can't just say, 'Oh, sorry for being a loud jerkoff while people are trying to study.' Noooo, of course he can't. He has to get all macho and up in my business with his big hands and minty breath and muscles. And what is up with those jeans? They are, like, molded to his body and stuff. I would be doing a public service buying him a new pair. Ugh!" She dropped her hands to her sides in a huff and stared at Danica.

Who wasn't rolling her eyes about the big jerk. Who wasn't commiserating. Nope. Danica was smirking.

"What's that look for?" Lea demanded.

Danica's smile grew until she curled her tongue along her front teeth. "I've never seen you this worked up."

Lea narrowed her eyes. "I'm not worked up."

"Uh, yeah you are."

"No, I'm —"

"Lea, you're close to fuming."

"Fuming?"

Danica tilted her head and raised her eyebrows.

Lea growled in the back of her throat. "Okay, I'm irritated."

Danica rolled her eyes. "Fine, irritated. I'm just saying. For a guy you profess not to like . . . well . . . the lady doth protest too much."

"You're quoting Shakespeare now?"

"If the seventeenth-century playwright fits . . ."

"Oh shut up," Lea said, turning around and slamming a book onto its shelf.

Danica raised a perfectly curved eyebrow. "That was some weird sexual banter."

"That was not—"

"You were talking about *his broom*." Danica practically shouted the last two words on a full-body shudder, and a student walking by jerked his head up and stared at them.

Lea tried to hold in the giggles because they'd already made enough noise, but the laughter couldn't be contained and burst through her lips. Danica watched Lea dissolve with a grin that proved she struggled holding it in as well.

When Lea composed herself again, Danica sighed. "Look, I just want to say be careful. He's not boyfriend material."

Lea bit her lip. Despite Nick's claim Max was flirting, Lea didn't believe it. Max wasn't interested in her. She wouldn't allow this weird fantasy about getting to know the real Max put her heart in jeopardy.

Danica shifted her weight. "And you know how he treated Kat."

Lea had heard. He hadn't been the best or most chivalrous boyfriend to Kat. Sometimes he'd been downright mean. But with help from Alec and Danica, Kat had learned last year she had dyslexia. Thanks to the diagnosis and getting the extra help she needed, Kat's grades were thriving.

And thanks to Alec's unconditional love, Kat herself was like a sunbeam.

"And you deserve the absolute best." Danica was saying. Her expression serious now, those eyes softer. "You know that."

Lea pursed her lips and nodded. She didn't want to have this conversation in the middle of the library. "I know, Danica. I . . . I need to get back to work now, though, okay?"

Danica waited a beat, then nodded. With a hug and a last lingering look, she clomped out of the library, the buckles on her motorcycle boots rattling.

Lea took a deep breath and then turned back to shelving books. She ran her fingers over the worn spines, smoothing peeled tape.

She knew she deserved the best. But the problem was she didn't trust anyone to give her the best. She'd dated, sure, but she was like a cat. Everything always had to be her idea—where they went, what they did, how soon they kissed and slept together.

Which was why she dated . . . meeker men. Beta men. Not alphas or aggressors like Max. She didn't want to have to fight for control. She wanted it all.

Max challenged her. Made her feel out of control. Not just his size but his domineering personality. And yet that's what drew her to him, attracted her, made her wonder if she could get her hands on that attitude and that flesh and mold him . . . *oh shit.*

She shook her head and slammed another book on the shelf. Screw Max with those warm eyes and big body and perfect smile. Screw him.

She'd never let him get the upper hand. *Ever.*

SHE FINISHED SHELVING the returns and leaned heavily on the cart as she wheeled it back to the front desk, where her cousin sat.

As an only child, Lea always looked at Nick Lawrence as her brother. He'd been adopted by her aunt and uncle as a baby, and looked nothing like the rest of her brunette family, with his bright blue eyes and thick mop of honey-blond hair. But she liked to think he was the sweetest of all of them.

Nick was three years younger and had attended a different school district from hers, but they'd always remained close. They hadn't planned on attending college together but it seemed natural when Nick applied and received his acceptance.

Getting a job together in the library was done on purpose.

Now, Nick sat behind the counter, head propped on his palm. His face was pale and he gave one weak cough.

His eyes narrowed as she approached. "Are you telling me Max still thinks I'm your boyfriend?"

Lea's steps faltered. "What?"

"I'd really prefer not to be caught in the crossfire between whatever the hell is going on with you two."

"Nothing is going on, Nick."

He raised his eyebrows. "Denial isn't just a river—"

She pointed a finger in his face. "Do not finish that sentence or I'll throw you in a river."

Nick didn't look concerned. "I'd love to see you a) find a river and b) try to throw me in."

"You're being a pain in the ass right now."

Nick sighed. "Look, Stone's a good dude, but Payton is bad news."

Lea ground her molars. Why did everyone feel the need to warn her? To protect her? Like she didn't have a brain and couldn't see or hear Max. Or judge him based on her own experiences.

"I really don't need a lecture—"

Nick held up his hand. "I know. You would probably chew him up and spit him out before he got your last name—"

"He already knows my last name—"

"*Anyway*, I didn't mean anything by it. I'm not trying to warn you. I know you can take care of yourself around guys. Just stating a fact."

"Okay, but what about him is so bad? He likes to sleep around? He's a jerk? I mean, what? And doesn't he get a shot at being able to change?"

Nick's eyes softened and his gaze traveled over her body, resting on her hips where he knew ink marked her skin beneath her clothes. She'd used a fake ID at sixteen. That was a rough period in her life which she'd come back from. Changed.

She stood before Nick as proof of it. And he knew it.

"I guess . . ."

"No, honestly. So because he was an asshole in high school, he's always an asshole now?" And that was the problem. As much as she wanted to hate Max and as much as she thought he *was* an asshole most of the time, she also glimpsed something else there. A kindness that made her want to dig under the cocky sludge of his exterior and get to his heart.

"Don't get preachy with me, Lea. Has he been anything other than an asshole to you? Some people don't change, you know."

"But some people do. And what, is there a statute of limitations on change? Like, if he hasn't changed now, he can't?"

Nick twisted his features. "What is going on with you? Why are you defending him?"

She didn't know. Why was she? Because the image of him taking care of that stupid cat, the turmoil that swirled in those warm brown eyes, flashed in her head. There was something more to Max than he let on. Another Max.

And she wondered if she'd ever meet him other than in fleeting glimpses.

But she wasn't going to admit that. Even to Nick. "Just playing devil's advocate," she muttered, fingering the sharp edge of the cart.

Nick squinted at her, and she knew he didn't believe her, but this conversation was over.

Lea glanced at the clock on the wall over his head. "Why don't you head out early? It's okay, I have this covered. You don't look so hot."

He looked liked he was going to argue but then sighed and rubbed his face. "Fucking sinuses. My head is killing me."

"Then go. Honestly."

"Yeah, but sometimes the library picks up now right before close and you'll be here by yourself . . ."

Lea propped a hand on her hip. "You're too nice for your own good sometimes. Go. Home. Nick."

He smiled, a weak smile compared to his usual bright grin.

Nick looked to the front doors at the darkening sky as the sun set. "Yeah, I guess you're right. Trish was going to meet me and walk home with me, but I'll just text her and tell her I'm heading home early and to head on over to my place."

"Yes," Lea said, helping to gather his things. "Shoo."

Bookbag over one shoulder, Nick slung an arm around

her neck and tugged her to him in a quick hug. "Thanks, Lea."

"Get Trish to make you tea and give you a scalp massage," she said.

He laughed softly. "Sure, I'll do that."

Lea watched him go and then glanced at the clock again. Another couple of hours and then she could go to the gym and relieve some stress. Maybe pretend Max's face was on a punching bag and beat the crap out of it. She smiled and chuckled to herself. Sounded like a plan.

Chapter 4

MAX DRUMMED HIS fingers on the desk of the recreation center on campus, counting down the minutes until he was off duty. He worked the desk in two-hour shifts a couple of days a week. He made minimum wage but every penny was worth it.

A girl walked up to the desk and handed him her student ID card. He scanned it absentmindedly and handed it back to her so she could head into the gym. She smiled and sauntered away, throwing a look over her shoulder. She was cute—with her blonde hair and hazel eyes—but lately, he'd been in the mood for dark hair, thick bangs and challenging brown eyes.

He rubbed his temples. *Shit.*

After the whole debacle with Alec's ex-girlfriend and Kat, Max had sworn off girls. Or at least, sworn them off when he was sober and could remember everything. And especially attached girls.

But from the first moment he saw Lea Travers last year—the pixie face, deep brown eyes, glossy hair—he couldn't get her out of his mind. He had no business flirting with her, but damn, it made him hard when she pushed back.

Everything about her made him hard.

"Payton."

His name focused him on the present, reminding him he was at work so thinking about his dick was inappropriate.

The portly frame of Bruce Shaw stepped in front of the desk. He was the recreation director, who managed all the comings and goings of the recreation center and was Max's boss.

"Yeah, hey Bruce," he straightened from his hunched position and smiled.

The man clapped him on the shoulder. "Busy tonight?"

Max shrugged. "So-so."

Bruce—he'd told Max he could call him by his first name during his interview, sophomore year—leaned on the desk. "You ever take any martial-arts classes? Self-defense?"

Max shook his head. "No, but I can do a mean tackle."

Bruce snorted a laugh, but he seemed distracted. "Yeah, all right."

"You need something? Or— " But before Max could finish his question, Bruce's phone vibrated on his hip.

He glanced at it. "Ah, gotta get this. Talk to you later, Payton." He rapped his knuckles on the desk and then walked away after barking a greeting into his phone.

Max watched him go, curious what that question was about, but figured Bruce could catch him later. He made his schedule, after all.

Ten minutes later, Max was off work, in his happy place at the leg-press machine.

He gripped the handles of the bench, took a deep breath and puffed out his cheeks as he exhaled while straightening his legs, raising the leg-press bar. His legs burned from the second set of five hundred pounds, but leg day was his favorite and he had a lot of frustration to get out.

But then the source of that frustration flashed in the mirror in front of him in a black and fuchsia vision and his knees buckled. As the weights clanged back into place, she jerked her head at the sound. Her dark ponytail whipped over her shoulder, and she locked eyes with him under her fringe of bangs.

How had he never seen her at the gym before? Granted, he rarely went at night, but this morning's routine got messed up when he had to make those stupid cookies for his brothers to take to his dad's tomorrow.

He didn't move, just held her gaze, like she was a rare, beautiful doe and if he moved, she'd bound off. He'd never seen her with clothes that snug. The pink tank top showed off her small breasts with just the right amount of cleavage. Her black pants were skin tight, ending below the knee, hugging her perfect ass and narrow hips. She was a tiny thing, but how come he never noticed the definition in her arms and the muscles of her calves as she shifted her weight from foot to foot? Some scars twisted out from under the hem of her pant leg, and he wondered if she suffered from pain, or if her limp was from destroyed muscles.

He wanted to hear her voice. He wanted her to give it back to him as good as he gave it. Anything to take his mind off of tomorrow, when he had to go home and see his dad, start his every-weekend sentence.

When he raised his eyes back to hers, she jolted forward, like she thought about walking over to him, but then she shook her head and turned around, walking back toward the free weights.

No. Fuck that. She wasn't walking away. Not after the attitude she threw at him in the library earlier.

He stood up, wiped down the machine with his towel, then threw it over his shoulder and walked toward Lea as he took a sip of water from his Camelbak bottle.

She was bracing herself on a bench with her left knee and hand, her right leg straight with her foot on the floor. Her back was parallel to the bench as she executed a pretty damn good tricep kickback with a fifteen-pound weight, keeping the upper half of her arm tucked to her side, bending and straightening her elbow.

But still, it was his job to mess with her, he decided. He couldn't have her, but he'd take what he could get, even if it was a battle of insults.

He stopped in front of her so the top of her head was about a foot from his thighs and he leaned back against the mirror, crossing one ankle over the other. A subtle shift of her body was his only indication she noticed him.

"Nice technique." He took another drink of water.

Lea completed two more tricep kickbacks and he heard her mutter "twelve" under her breath before she straightened, the weight hanging at her side, knee braced on the bench. "Gee, thanks. I didn't realize you were a personal trainer."

"I'm not."

She widened her eyes and looked around. "Oh! So this is free advice then. From . . . a random guy."

He straightened from the mirror. "Hey, I'm not some random guy." What was it about her that made him defensive? He could never get the last word with her.

She only smiled at him and rotated her wrist that held the weight.

He pointed with his head toward the area behind her. "You know, they have a machine for triceps. You don't have to use free weights."

She shifted now, straddling the bench, then knelt her right leg on the bench so she could perform the exercise on the other arm. "I'm aware of that. But I like using free weights, because it works out the stabilizer muscles."

He knew that. Fuck, he totally knew that but he was shocked she did. "How come I've never seen you in here before?"

She raised her eyebrows and bent over. He admired the dark rope of hair that curled around her neck, and the beautiful strip of toned back muscle exposed above her tank top. "I don't know. Either too busy looking at yourself or all the pretty shininess in here." She jerked her head toward the treadmills where a blonde was running. Pretty hot with a big rack. But Max's eyes went right back to that dark bent head. "Doll, my eyes are on the only thing in this room pretty and shiny." The words were out before he could tell himself to stop flirting with her.

Lea's free weight wobbled. She swore softly and placed it on the rubber mat by her foot. She put her hands on her hips, but not before he spotted her hands shaking. "Don't," she said, softly but firmly.

"What?" he asked, playing dumb.

"Don't," she repeated and grabbed her bottle of water at her feet—a pink Camelbak that matched his gray one.

"I don't—"

She took a drink, eyes on his. "Don't play games with me, Max. I'll win every time."

He frowned. "What games? I'm not—"

"Yeah, you are."

He clenched his fists. "Don't tell me what I'm doing, Lea. I'm not playing games with you. I don't lie."

Those dark eyes burned into his and fired a flaming arrow right between his eyes. "Oh, you just omit the truth then."

He knew what she was referring to—the fact that he'd slept with Alec's high-school girlfriend and kept it from him even after they broke up. Yeah, he was a shit, but he'd apologized. He was trying to be a better person. And who did she think she was? He leaned forward, his voice rumbling deep in his chest. "Don't talk about that like you know what really happened, because you don't. You don't know me. And you don't know how that guilt fucking ate at me every day. How I hated myself for being a coward for not telling the truth."

All the harshness from Lea's face drained and those hard eyes that had previously burned with a pain-inducing heat now smoldered with a soothing warmth. A slender hand rose. Fingers brushed his chest and his eyelids dipped as the touch shot sparks over his heart.

"I'm sorry," she whispered. "I shouldn't have thrown that in your face. I . . ."

But he didn't find out what she planned to say next, because a phone chirped and she blinked, the connection between them broken by a stupid piece of microchipped plastic.

She pulled her phone from a strap on her arm and glanced at it, frowning. She flicked her eyes up to him, like she was apologizing. "I'm sorry, but I need to answer this." She tapped the screen. "Hey, Trish."

A voice sounded on the other end, loud and slightly hysterical and Lea's face slowly paled. "What?" she said in a pained whisper.

Max stepped closer and she leaned slightly into him. Something was obviously wrong but he found a small bit of satisfaction that his presence seemed to comfort her. And that should weird him out. Because he didn't do this "damsel in distress" thing. He wasn't a white knight. He'd learned that the hard way. But something about Lea made him want to be.

Lea spoke into the phone. "Oh Trish, I'm so sorry. I'll be right there. The hospital in Maple Grove?"

More hysterical words.

"Okay, give me twenty. And tell Nick to hang in there."

Nick. The boyfriend.

Max clenched his fists. He should step back. Get away. Run as far away from this tempting, beautiful doe as fast as he could.

But her eyes were wet and her lip quivered and he couldn't leave her. So he waited, unsure if she wanted his words or not.

She looked up at him finally, her eyes dry but her lips trembling. "That was Trish, Nick's girlfriend, and . . ."

Her voice trailed off, maybe because his face was surely a riot of confusion. Nick had another girlfriend? What kind of sister-wives shit was Lea into?

She blinked and bit her lip. "Nick is my cousin. Trish is his girlfriend. I didn't . . ." She waved a hand. " . . . whatever. And, she just said he . . . oh shit." She yanked on her ponytail so hard her scalp shifted.

Max filed it away to deal with this Nick-cousin thing later. Because right now, something was bothering her, and everything in him screamed to root it out and make it better. He batted her hands away and placed his on her slender shoulders. "Doll, take a deep breath and tell me what's going on."

She looked at him with eyes no longer dry. Her hesitation was unmistakable. He could feel her trying to pull away under his palms so he softened his voice. "Hey, fight your flight instinct and talk to me."

He didn't know if it was his words or his voice but her muscles slackened under his fingers and her weight sagged into him.

"Trish said Nick was robbed or mugged right outside his apartment and . . . and . . ."

A tear slipped down her cheek, and he massaged her shoulders with his thumbs. She took a deep breath and her next words were said on a gasp, brown eyes pleading with him to tell a different truth. " . . . beaten up."

Max's breath left his body in a rush. "And he's at the hospital now?"

Lea nodded, her eyes welling up again, but she focused on his face, as if their eye contact was the only thing keeping her body from collapsing. He squeezed her shoulders and jerked his head toward the door. "I'll take you to the hospital."

She balked at that, the muscles again bunching, her face hardening, but he cut her off before she could protest. "Look, just let me help, okay? You're upset, and you'll be tired when you leave. Let me do this for you."

The muscles remained tense, but those eyes stayed on him. And with a jerky, reluctant nod from Lea, they were striding out of the gym, Max's arm around her shoulders.

Chapter 5

DESPITE THE HEAT blasting from the vents, the cold air in Max's truck clung to her bare legs and seeped through her thin exercise pants, but all Lea could think about was Trish's voice, so broken. *They hurt him, Lea. Bad.*

Because that flashed her back to another time, years ago, when she and Nick were rushed to the hospital. When her leg went from normal to broken.

When the sight of Nick's honey-blond hair resting on the white hospital pillow sent her heart plummeting into her stomach.

Because she hadn't protected him.

Max kept his eyes on the road, right hand on top of the steering wheel, the other arm propped on his door, fingers rubbing his chin.

He must have felt her eyes on him, because he glanced over quickly. His brows furrowed and he reached behind him into the cluttered cab. He pulled out a blanket and placed it on her lap. "Uh," he cleared his throat and shifted in his seat. "Sorry that blanket's kinda dirty, but you're . . . you know . . . not wearing much. So hopefully that helps."

She glanced down at the blanket, a sweatshirt material bearing Bowler University's logo. Crumpled, dried leaves clung to the fabric and some patches held cakes of dried mud, but she wrapped it around her legs, thankful for the extra layer because the cold was no friend to her left leg.

"Thanks," she said, wishing she could ease the chill in her bones. Although she knew it wasn't only from the cold, but the thought of Nick, battered and bruised.

She wanted to punch something.

He'd left the library early because she encouraged him to do so rather than work the rest of his shift and wait for his girlfriend. What if she'd just kept quiet? Would he have been at the wrong place at the wrong time? Or would he and Trish both be in the hospital as patients right now? She clenched her fists in the blanket that smelled so strongly of Max.

They pulled into the drive of the hospital and Max drove right to the front doors.

"You can't park here." Lea said, peering out the window.

He leaned back in his seat. "I know, I'm dropping you off."

"You don't have to do that." Although, the ache in her leg was killing her now, the result of not stretching properly after her workout, then sitting in a cold, cramped car.

"I know, but now you can get in there and find out where he is while I park. I'll meet you in there, okay?"

"I can get a ride back with Trish or something . . ."

He shook his head and nodded toward the door, his voice soft but firm. "Lea, please get out of the car. I'll be in as soon as I can, and I'll take you home."

This was weird, the way he looked at her. The bright lights of the hospital shone into the depths of his dark eyes.

Earlier today, she wanted to deck him, and in the last hour, he'd allowed her to lean on him, physically and emotionally. He'd provided a much-needed ride and even noticed she was cold and offered a blanket, for God's sakes.

None of that aligned with the brash, cocky flirt he usually appeared to be. She wondered which was the act, but she thought she knew. And when her mind was clear and not on Nick, she'd examine it further.

She realized she'd been sitting there, silently, staring at him as he stared back at her. "Um, okay," she mumbled, awkwardly trying to fold the blanket, which was stupid because it was dirty and it's previous home was in a heap in the back of the cab. She swiped her bangs out of her eyes and wrenched open the truck door. "See you inside."

Max nodded, and she lowered herself out of the truck, then slammed it behind her. He didn't pull away until she was past the security guard and inside the hospital.

Once inside, she texted Trish, asking if Nick had been admitted yet. Trish texted back the room number and Lea asked directions from the help desk before sinking into a stiff hospital chair in the lobby to wait for Max.

She didn't have to wait long. Max walked into the

lobby with purpose, his cheeks red from the cold, his chest rising and falling rapidly so Lea got the impression he ran from the parking lot. Or at least jogged.

He spotted her and walked over, hands on his hips. "You know where he is?"

"Room 428."

He made to walk to the help desk, but Lea placed a hand on his arm. "I already asked, we just have to take the North Tower elevators over there to the fourth floor."

"Good job, doll." He guided her forward with just two fingers on her lower back. And why did those three words, said in an approving tone, make her feel warmer than that stupid blanket? Since when did she care at all about what Max thought of her?

Since he was there for you, a voice in her head whispered, but she ignored that, too. Another item on her mental checklist to analyze later in private.

They were the only two on the elevator. Max leaned back, bracing himself with spread arms on the silver bar, legs spread, eyes on the digital numbers over the doors in front of them. He was a picture of placid while Lea's insides stormed. She tried to be inconspicuous as she leaned a little into his arm, the warmth of it like a comforting brand across her back.

When the elevator doors opened on the fourth floor, those fingers were back, barely there, just a brush of heat through her thin jacket.

They made their way down the hall to 428 and when they reached the room, Max's fingers were gone.

He jerked a thumb over his shoulder. "I'm just gonna

hang out here on the bench in the hallway. Take all the time you need."

She glanced at her watch. It was 8:30, so visiting hours were over in about a half hour. "You sure that's not too late for you?"

He sank onto the bench and stretched out his legs, eyes falling closed like he planned to settle in and be there a while. "Nope."

She bit her lip, eyes on those thick arms crossed over his chest. They'd been around her less than a half hour ago, holding her together when she threatened to crack apart.

One dark eye opened. "You going to stare at me or go see your cousin?"

She jolted. "Um, I'm heading in."

He closed his eyes again.

Not that she didn't like staring at Max, but she was also stalling, not too excited to head into the room and see her injured cousin.

But she'd promised Trish she'd come. So she took a deep breath and placed her hand on the door.

"Hey," a deep voice came from behind her.

She turned around.

Both Max's eyes were open now. "Just . . . uh . . . don't fawn over him too much, ya know? Visit with him, and tell him to get rest and heal fast and all of that, all right? Don't coddle him and make him feel weak."

As if she didn't know what it was like to be in a hospital bed. As if she hadn't been surrounded by coddling and fawning.

But it hadn't made her feel weak. It'd made her feel loved and cared for.

She churned Max's words around inside her head, twisting and pulling at them until the meaning between the words seeped out.

Max's jaw was tense, his neck and shoulders tight in a challenge. But his face still held a hint of vulnerability, like he hadn't meant to blurt that out.

Even though she didn't agree with what he said, she could tell he'd told her from a place of concern. About Nick and herself. He thought he was right.

She forced the annoyance down and said softly, "There's nothing wrong with showing him how much I care. How worried I am."

Max's arms were crossed over his chest, and his fisted hands clenched. "He's a guy and—"

"Max," she kept her tone low and nonthreatening. "He's my cousin, so I know him. And no matter how hurt he is, he knows he's a strong person. Nothing I say in there will change that."

Max's lips parted slightly and his tongue peeked out to run along the bottom of his front teeth. Once. Twice. And then he mumbled something under his breath.

"What?" Lea asked.

He exhaled roughly and ran a hand over his short hair. "I said, he's lucky to have you." Max said, his voice deeper than she ever heard it. Then a small smile curled his lips. "As his cousin."

And crap if that dam holding back her tears didn't crack just a little. Because there was still more to Max's words and no matter which angle she looked at them, she couldn't figure it all out.

"Thank you," she said, returning his smile.

Before her, his vulnerability faded. Max flexed his arms and then rolled his shoulders, the muscles shifting as he put his armor back into place.

"No problem." He closed his eyes again and leaned his head on the back of the bench.

She turned back around and walked inside.

Lea's eyes swept the room, first landing on Trish in a chair and then taking in Nick lying on the hospital bed, thin white sheet pulled up to his chest.

His nose was swollen and his eyes had that red, puffy look that would surely turn into righteous shiners overnight. The clear, kind blue of his eyes was watery and the whites bloodshot. His right arm was in a cast and Lea thought she saw a bandage around his ribs. His blond hair was a mess, sticking up every which way.

He smiled weakly and Lea wanted to cry. Instead, she said, "If you make a 'you should see the other guy' joke, I might hit you again."

He croaked a laugh and then winced. "Don't do that, my ribs hurt. No laughing." He tried to glare, but the puffiness didn't help and he looked so sad, Lea's heart cracked.

Trish sniffled and Nick tried to awkwardly pat her hand with the palm of his cast. It was heart wrenching to watch the injured care for his loved one and Lea slowly started to understand a little of what her parents went through.

"Hey Trish, if you're spending the night, you want to go get something to eat before the cafeteria closes?" Lea asked.

Trish looked up and Lea could see in her eyes, she was about to say no, so Lea urged softly. "Go on, you should eat."

She looked at her boyfriend and he waved her toward the door, so she rose stiffly. "Thanks so much for coming." Trish hugged her. "Be back in a jiffy." She waved to Nick and then walked out.

Lea sank down in Trish's vacated chair. "So I'm going to cut to the chase. What the hell happened?"

Nick sank his head back onto the pillows. "I don't even know. The cops already visited and asked me tons of questions. I was outside my apartment, which has shitty lighting, you know that. And there was a shove from behind. I landed on my face and that's when the blows started. I mean, fists and feet and . . ." He shuddered.

Lea squeezed her thigh, the bad one, and gritted her teeth against the pain. It was the only thing that kept her from screaming with rage.

"Anyway," he continued. "They ripped my book bag off of my back and that's when I pushed myself up with my good arm and fucking ran like hell." His eyes widened as much as he could make them and his voice roughened. "Lea, I was scared shitless. I had no idea if they were going to . . . I don't know . . . kill me or whatever. But I guess they just wanted my wallet and my laptop. Which they got."

"Crap, I'm so sorry, Nick."

He shrugged, then winced again. "I never thought I'd be one of 'em."

Lea shook her head. "I don't understand."

Nick cocked his head, his eyebrows pulled down over his swollen eyes. "Haven't you seen the campus papers?"

"No, I don't think so."

"Yeah, this is like a thing. These guys go around and rob people and beat them up. No one knows why they assault. I mean, they didn't say anything when they were kicking the shit out of me. Maybe they just . . . like it? Because they are sickos? I don't know."

Lea blinked rapidly, unable to wrap her head around how this was the first she heard of this. "How many times has this happened?"

Nick looked at his hands and twitched his fingers like he was counting. "I think I'm the third. The first one was a townie. Second was a college student. And now, with me, the police are starting to take it seriously."

"Did you get a good look at them?" Lea asked.

He grinned crookedly. "Well, Detective Travers . . ."

She laughed. "Shut up."

"I didn't actually. Well, they wore black masks and all black clothes."

Lea slumped in her seat. "Well fuck a duck."

"The cops asked a lot of questions, and they said this is taking priority now."

She patted his casted hand. "I hope so."

They talked a little about the library and a totally weird love note Lea found tucked in one of the books while waiting for Nick's girlfriend.

Lea wasn't sure how much time had passed when Trish walked back into the room, a coffee cup clutched in her hands. Her hair was smoother, her face clean of tears. Clearly, she had needed the break to pull herself together.

"People always say negative stuff about cafeteria food, but I just had a really awesome hot turkey sandwich," Trish said, smiling.

Nick chuckled in a gasping way and Lea smiled. "Well, I need to head out because my ride needs to get home, so . . ."

"Is that your ride out in the hallway?" Trish asked.

Crap, Lea had hoped to get away before anyone asked about him. "Um . . ."

"Isn't that Max Payton? Alec's roommate?"

Nick rustled the covers and if her boyfriend hadn't just gotten beaten up, Trish would have been on the receiving end of some Lea death glares.

"Max Payton? What the hell is he doing giving you a ride to the hospital?" Nick asked, anger evident in his tone.

Max really needed to work on his reputation. Lea turned to Nick. "I was in the gym when Trish called. I was upset and Max offered to drive me. Honestly, it was really nice of him, so I don't want to hear it."

Nick's facial expression was hard to read past the swelling, but his eyes blinked, like he was trying to figure her out.

Why she felt the need to defend Max was a mystery to her. "How long will you be here?"

"Probably only until tomorrow. They are worried

about some swelling in my brain or something and want to monitor me."

Lea scowled. "Well, get tons of rest and I'll bring you some guilty-pleasure food when you get discharged. Maybe a dirty magazine or two."

"Thanks for stopping by, Lea." Nick shifted his eyes to Trish, and Lea knew he was worried about her.

She hugged Trish and smoothed her hair behind her ears. "He'll be okay, all right?"

Trish nodded. "Thanks so much for being there for us."

"Anytime."

When Lea stepped outside of the room, her body sagged, her leg pulsing with pain from standing on it too long, keeping it tense and not stretching it.

But Max was there, like a silent, warm pillar. He didn't pick her up, which she appreciated, but let her cling to him as she hobbled down the hall to the elevator. And then he carefully lowered her to a chair in the lobby of the hospital, whispered that he would be right back, and then sped off to get the truck. She saw his headlights and as she made it outside, he was already out of the truck, opening her door and helping her inside. He covered her with his filthy blanket, apologizing for it again, but she snuggled into it. Because it smelled like Max and was given to her with care.

And then, to a low country song and the hum of his engine, she curled up in a ball, closed her eyes, and floated where there was no pain and no cousins in hospital beds.

Chapter 6

WAYNE'S PURR SOUNDED like a broken jet engine. It rattled from his throat on Max's face, where the cat sat, licking Max's hair while they both lay in bed.

Max tried to shove him off, but the cat probably weighed twenty pounds and didn't like to be budged.

"Seriously, asshole, get off me," he grumbled, pushing again, this time successfully rolling the cat onto his side on his pillow, his claws taking a chunk out of Max's chin.

Max rolled his head to the side and looked into the yellow eyes. Wayne's lids were half closed, and he licked his lips.

"You know that's weird, right?"

Wayne blinked.

"It's weird to eat my hair."

Wayne heaved a sigh and looked away.

A chuckle came from the doorway and Max raised himself up on his elbows.

Cam stood with his arms crossed, a grin tugging at his lips. "That sounded like really sweet pillow talk."

"Shut up," Max said and flopped back onto the bed.

"Hey, Zuk and I were heading to the diner to get some breakfast, you wanna come?"

Max checked the time on his alarm clock. "Nah, can't. Gotta head to my dad's."

Cam raised one dark eyebrow. "On a Friday?"

All the guys knew Max avoided his dad as much as possible. "Yeah, my brothers need some help clearing out a dead tree."

And that was the last thing he felt like doing. He was exhausted after spending a large portion of the night at the hospital with Lea.

And then his body heated under his covers when he remembered how peaceful she looked sleeping in his truck. How right it felt to help her stumble groggily to her apartment.

How he wished he could have crawled into bed with her. He'd stroked her hair on the pillow like a weirdo, just to see how it felt as she blinked at him hazily, half asleep already.

"Hey, where were you last night?" Cam asked, bringing Max back to present.

"I took Lea to the hospital because her cousin . . . hey, did you know about the thefts and assaults happening on campus?"

Cam unfolded his arms and braced the heel of his palm on the door frame. The wings of his Air Force tattoo peeked out from the hem of his T-shirt sleeve on the inside of his bicep. "Yeah, man, it's fucked up. The papers said one just happened last night on campus. Some dude got pretty beat."

Max blew out a harsh breath. "Yeah, it was Lea's cousin Nick."

"Shit," Cam said. "Who are these fuckers? Dare them to come at me."

Max pointed at him. "Don't start carrying your gun."

Cam huffed. "Weapons aren't allowed on campus. The only reason I don't wear my holster. So why did you take Lea to the hospital? I didn't think you two were buddy-buddy."

Max didn't know what they were. "We were talking at the gym when she got the call. She was upset so I offered to drive her."

Cam looked skeptical. "You? Offered to give up work-out time to drive some chick to the hospital?"

· Max glared. "Why is that so hard to believe?"

Cam shrugged.

Max's body heated again, but this time it was anger. "You know what? Fuck you, Cam." His voice rose and he didn't bother tempering it. "Can't people change? I'm not an asshole all the time."

Cam's eyes were wide. A scuffling sounded behind him, and Alec poked his head in.

Great, now there was an audience. Kat was probably out there, too, because she and Alec were attached at the hip.

Alec took a step into the bedroom. "Sure, Max, people can change," he said gently.

Max felt like a child but he held his tongue.

Cam cleared his throat. "Sorry, man."

Max waved his hand. "Nah, it's cool. Anyway, I need to get in the shower before I have to go to my dad's, all right?"

Cam waited a beat. "Sure. Later, Max."

"Later," Alec echoed, and Max gave them a small smile.

MAX PARKED IN his dad's cracked driveway and stared up at the house. The gutters needed cleaning and the winter hadn't been kind to the roof. He heaved a sigh. More work for him and his brothers to do come spring. Even though his dad would bitch and be unappreciative.

What else was new?

He grabbed the container of cookies from the passenger seat and stepped out of his truck. He walked into the house, gaze lingering on the dusty picture frames lining the hallways. Max in his ice-hockey uniform. His older brother Calvin in his football pads. The middle brother, Brent, pulling on his soccer-goalie gloves. And his mind flashed back to all the times he spent in the hospital as a kid, as a patient or a concerned brother. That bench last night held a familiarity he hadn't wanted to revisit.

Because they were always incurring injuries, especially because their dad encouraged the roughest play. Max had to check his opponent into the boards. Rip off his gloves and throw punches. Calvin had to tackle dirty. Brent had to slide cleats up or throw elbows.

That was what was expected of them by their dear old dad. The problem was, when you played dirty, others played dirty in return.

Which meant a lot of broken bones. Stitches. Concussions.

Max's eyes lingered longer on a picture of him taking a shot on goal on the ice and then shook his head. He needed to quit fucking around. There was work to do.

He dropped the cookies off in the kitchen and then continued out the back door to the yard.

The week's ice storm had wrecked the old, weakened tree in his dad's backyard. A large branch near the top had cracked in half, taking out its bare comrades below.

Max cocked his head. From one side it looked like a whole tree, but take a couple of steps to one side and it was . . . half a tree.

His brothers stood in front of it, arms crossed over their chests, and glanced at Max as he approached them, boots crunching on the dry grass.

Calvin pulled his beanie down over his ears. "Hey bro. Thanks for coming. We gotta get this shit taken down before Dad gets home." Cal was shorter than Max and wide, with a barrel chest he'd used to his advantage on the offensive line of the Tory High School football team. Like Brent, Calvin worked with their father at his automotive shop.

"Remind me why we're doing this again?" said Brent, the tallest of the three, at a lean six-three.

Cal flexed his fingers in his work gloves. "You know he'd try to do this all himself, then he'd throw his back out, and it would be all our fault. I don't want to have to be over here vacuuming his floors and making his meals and shit because he can't get off the couch. Now haul ass."

Brent grumbled as Cal fired up the chainsaw with a grin.

Hours later, Max was sweating buckets under his parka and his knees and hips were killing him from squatting to pick up fallen tree limbs. Cal had made it a game to try and drop branches on his head as he cut them off. Asshole.

The branches were bundled and the trunk lay in neatly sawed chunks on the grass.

Brent rubbed his forehead with the back of his wrist, leaving behind a smear of dirt. "Good enough for now, right? He can deal with this or we'll come back later."

"I'm starving," Cal said.

Both brothers looked at Max expectantly.

He sighed. "I'll see what Dad has in the kitchen."

He left his brothers outside to put away the work tools. He threw his coat over the back of the couch and rubbed his hands together. Funny how he could be damp with sweat but his fingers were still frozen.

He rummaged in the pantry and sighed. When he'd lived with his dad, he tried to keep the pantry full of ingredients easy to make into quick meals. Which his father ate with a grunt and then left the dishes on the table for Max to clean up.

Max pulled out a long-forgotten box of spaghetti and a jar of pasta sauce that was close to expired. In the freezer, he found a half-opened bag of meatballs. They looked a little freezer burned but the guys would never notice, so

Max plopped them in a pot with some sauce and started water to boil for the pasta.

Then he leaned back on the counter and looked around. The kitchen floor could use a mopping and a thin film of grime coated the windows, but at least the house wasn't covered in clutter. Cleaning had been Brent's job when they all lived at home. Brent and Cal now lived together in an apartment. Max missed that sometimes—a full house with deep voices arguing or laughing. Someone to eat meals with. Someone to watch hockey with.

It'd just been the four of them then, their mother bailing on the family shortly after Max was born. It had changed every couple of years, but she lived in California now with her musician husband. She sent him Christmas cards signed *Love, Jill*. Which he always found funny and depressing at the same time.

The back door banged open as Max dumped the pasta into the boiling water, and his brothers barreled into the house.

Brent stuck his head in the fridge. "Who wants a beer?"

"Spaghetti and meatballs?" Cal asked, dipping his finger into the sauce and then sticking it into his mouth. "Any garlic bread or salad or anything?"

"Seriously?" Max said. "You two probably live on pizza and chicken wings at your apartment. Don't get all uppity and demand garlic bread."

"Well, no beer for you, Mr. Touchy," Brent said, popping the cap on two bottles and handing one to Cal.

Max rolled his eyes and retrieved his own beer.

Once the pasta was cooked, he dumped in the meatballs and sauce, mixed it around, and then scooped the mess onto three plates.

"Thanks, Max," Cal said. Brent grunted his gratitude.

While they ate at the kitchen table, the only sound the clinking of forks on plates and slurping of noodles, the engine of a truck rumbled into the driveway.

"Old man's home," Cal said.

"How is he?" Max asked.

Brent shrugged. "A downright bastard."

Heavy footfalls sounded up the stairs from the garage to the living room and then the door creaked open. "Hello?" a voice called out.

"Hey Dad," Brent and Cal answered right away.

Max grunted and swirled the remaining sauce on his plate.

Jack Payton strode into the kitchen, greasy overalls covered by a heavy Carhartt jacket.

He threw his keys on the kitchen table and crossed his arms over his chest, widening his stance. "Saw your cars outside. Now you're in here eating my food. What's that about?"

Cal jerked his chin toward the back door. "You said the ice storm brought down your tree. We took care of it."

Jack's eyes flitted over his two older sons before landing on Max. "What are you doing here?"

He raised his eyebrows. "Cal just answered that, Dad."

"Don't give me attitude," he grunted, taking off his coat. He grabbed a plate from his cabinets and filled it with spaghetti and meatballs. He took a seat across from Max at the table.

Jack was a big man, six feet, twenty thousand inches tall. He smoked about a pack and a half a day, so his teeth were stained and the smell had likely seeped into his bones. Sometimes Max thought Jack's organs were nicotine ash by now.

As soon as his plate was clear, his dad pulled a cigarette out of his shirt pocket and lit up at the table. On his first exhale, he said, "Where'd you get the food?"

"Your kitchen," Max answered.

"You're welcome," his dad said.

Max didn't answer. He didn't expect his father to thank him for cooking dinner.

When Jack was finished with his cigarette, he rose from the table. "Clean this up," he said to no son in particular. When he passed by Max's chair, he tapped him on the shoulder with two fingers. "Cooking was good." Then retreated into the den with a beer.

Brent and Cal rose to take care of the dishes but Max sat frozen, the tap of those fingers echoing through his body. A weird sensation flitted over his skin and it took him a minute to realize the cause of it was his dad's compliment.

After the kitchen was clean, his brothers followed their dad into the den. Max didn't want to. He wanted to go back to his town house. Hell, writing a paper was better than this. But that would be awkward—to leave when his brothers didn't—so he sucked it up and joined his family.

The news blared from the TV and as Max sank into the couch, the anchor began to talk about the assaults on campus. A reporter stood outside the hospital, "reporting live" and Max zeroed in on the same doors he walked through last night.

Max fidgeted with a tear in the microsuede of the couch as the report centered on the injuries of the victims.

When it was over, his dad turned to him. "If those guys tried that with me, I'd take 'em all out."

There was no *Do you know anyone affected?* or *Be safe out there,* or *Watch your back.* Nope, his fifty-two-year-old dad just professed the ability to take on three young guys at once. "Sure, Dad."

"You have to fight back," he continued. "I think if I've taught you boys anything, it's that. Fight back."

That was the truth. It was ingrained in Max's brain. Like second nature to hit back when he was hit.

"Oh, and I don't need you Sunday," Jack said to the TV.

Max glanced at Cal and Brent. They looked back at him and shrugged.

"Who are you talking to, Dad?" Cal asked.

"All three of you," he grunted.

Max stared. He worked every weekend for his dad at his mechanic's shop. He hated it and he hated knowing he'd be working there after graduation. But his dad paid half his tuition and said he needed him to get his business degree so he could take care of the books. His brothers had never gone to college, so Max considered himself lucky he'd even had the opportunity.

Too bad his degree wasn't anywhere near what he wanted to do.

And a Sunday off? Unheard of.

"You sure?" Max asked, know as soon as he did, Jack would like to be questioned.

"Did I stutter?" Jack turned, his dark eyes pinning Max to the back of the couch.

He gulped. "Nope."

Jack faced the TV again.

Another half hour and Max was home free, climbing into the truck with an empty cookie container. He tapped his phone on his chin and thought about checking on Lea. But he didn't have her number. And if he did, he didn't know what to say.

In her mind, what did he do exactly? Just give her a ride? Is that all she thought?

Because that visit took a lot out of him. He hated hospitals. The smell alone made him nauseous.

But Lea's concern for her cousin reminded him of Alec's mom. When he was in eighth grade, he and Alec were climbing trees. Max grabbed a weakened branch and it cracked. He fell with a crash of rotted wood and dried leaves right on his arm, breaking it.

Alec's mom didn't baby him, but she showed concern. She allowed him to whimper in pain, she gave him ice and wrapped it on the way to the hospital. Alec rubbed his shoulder to ease his aching muscles.

And when Max's dad met them at the hospital, he thanked Alec's mom and told her he had it from there. And then they sat in the emergency room while his dad joked about Alec's mom "babying" Max.

He loved Alec's mom, but he'd been sure not to get hurt in her presence again.

His brothers might have shown him some comfort if

they'd all grown up in a different household, but under Jack Payton, showing concern was weak.

You took pain like a man, without complaining. Without flinching. And heaven forbid you cried.

But Lea didn't know that.

Before he could change his mind he dialed Kat.

"Hey," she answered cheerily. She'd never been that happy when they dated.

"You with Lea?" He thought it was a good chance, and he didn't have her number.

Pause. "No. Why?"

It was on the tip of his tongue to ask for her number, to hear that musical voice and make sure she was all right. But he chickened out. "I wanted to check on her. And ask how Nick is."

"Oh. Well that's . . . nice of you." Max fought to roll his eyes at her pause before *nice*. "Nick was released today and she's doing well. And . . . she really appreciated what you did."

That warmed him more than he thought it would, so he only grunted in response.

"You want me to tell her you called?" Kat asked.

Max knew he was chickening out before he said the words. "Nah, that's okay."

MAX WATCHED WAYNE scarf down his dry food. It looked gross—little star-shaped kibbles the color of red clay—and smelled worse. Like if a cow and a tuna had a baby and then a monkey farted on it.

Wayne didn't seem to mind. The foul-smelling food was probably gourmet compared to trash or flea-infested rats.

But just because his cat didn't mind eating trash didn't mean he had to, right? Max furrowed his brow and walked out to the living room, sinking down onto the couch and digging his laptop out of his bag.

He typed "homemade cat treats" in his Internet browser search bar and scanned the results. He clicked on a blog and scrolled through a woman's mile-long blog post featuring a dozen professional-quality pictures of her long-haired cat in various positions, in some sort of soft light. The cat looked like it was fed sushi-grade tuna and brushed with a comb made of solid gold and extinct rhinoceros horns.

Max glanced over at Wayne, who had followed him and sat in front of him licking his paw and running it over his shredded ear.

"You're just as good-looking to me," Max grumbled. Wayne deserved as much as this stupid cat in the pictures with its pink sofa. So Max would make him special cat treats. He was a good cook. As the youngest boy, he'd been relegated to kitchen duty most of his life. He perfected his chocolate-chip cookie recipe—the secret was to melt the butter and let it sit until it came to room temperature before adding it to the batter—and these cat treats didn't look hard to make.

Of course, on his rare Sunday off, he should have been writing a paper for macroeconomics—a class he hated with a passion—but his cat came first.

He grabbed a pen and jotted down the ingredients.

"Be back, buddy," he said, bending down to scratch Wayne under the chin, his favorite spot.

It started raining on his way to the grocery store, and his wipers were so rotted on his old truck, he could barely see anything. He made a note to buy new ones. Luckily, he could do basic car maintenance himself. That was one thing he could thank his dad for.

He parked and ran inside the grocery store, then grabbed a small cart. He realized halfway down the first aisle that his had a bum wheel and it rattled over the tile floor so it sounded like he was dragging about four chains behind him. The Ghost of Nine Lives. Fucking cart. He always got a bad one.

But he was tired and wanted to get back, so he kept pushing his obnoxious cart and ignored the looks from other shoppers. He needed some essentials. His dad threw him a couple of bucks for working on the weekends, but most of it went to his "debt" for his dad paying for his school. And he made some spare change at his job at the rec center. He grabbed some milk, bread, chicken breasts and frozen vegetables. Then he ran through his list for Wayne's treats and pushed through the aisles to gather what he needed. His cart held a random assortment of products—baby food, rice, eggs, and rice flour. The recipe called for parsley, which Max had at home. He used it to make chicken picatta, a recipe he gleaned from that Italian chick on the Food Network. He'd started watching her because she was hot and had great tits and always wore low-cut shirts. But then he started making her food and now he was a little bit in love with her.

But he did need salad ingredients, so he rattled his loud-ass cart over to the lettuce. A bag of chopped romaine went in the cart, then a container of grape tomatoes. Next were cucumbers. He grabbed one, threw it in and without looking up, reached for another. His hands closed around the width, but when he tugged, it didn't budge. He glanced at the cucumber, only to see a hand on the other end. A rather dainty, feminine hand. His eyes followed the thin wrist with delicate, protruding bones peeking out from the cuff of a pale purple sweater, up to a shoulder covered in a cascade of dark hair until he met the dark irises of Lea. He hadn't seen her since he dropped her off at her house two nights ago.

Her eyes, normally so round in her small face, were widened in surprise, as they both gripped opposite ends of a rather large cucumber.

"Umm . . ." Max mumbled. "Hey Lea."

She blinked, those long lashes fluttering over flushed cheeks. "Hi Max."

Neither moved, still gripping this cucumber between them like they were passing a baton in a race. A baton held at his crotch, which sorted his mind into one track. And because Lea made all his good sense and flirting knowledge fly out the window, he resorted to teasing her. In the library, he'd noticed the teasing coaxed Lea out of her shell. Instead of ignoring him or clamming up, she focused all that energy on him, even if it was to blast his ego to bits.

"You want this one?" He jiggled his hand, and her arm vibrated with the movement. His lip twitched involuntarily. "It's kind of big. You sure you don't want something smaller?"

One slow blink, and then those dark eyes flashed and narrowed. Her lips twisted in a wicked smile. "Oh, I like them big. Just so many more uses for them when there's some girth, you know?"

For fuck's sake. That smile. Those red lips, now wet from one swipe of her pink tongue. And he was hard. In a grocery-store produce aisle. While holding a cucumber.

Could he get arrested for that?

"Oh, of course, but do you know what to do with one this big? I mean, it can be a lot to handle. You don't want to waste any of it."

That tongue peeked out again. "Oh, I never waste cucumbers. I make them last a loooong time." She drew out the word, curling her tongue on her upper teeth on the *l* and emphasizing the shape of her mouth on the *oooo*. And then she chuckled, a deep sound that traipsed along his spine like fingers. "I'm not sure you're used to cucumbers this big, so why don't I just take this one? Hmmm?"

She tugged. And he tugged back. Through gritted teeth, he said, "Trust me, doll, I know exactly what to do with a big cucumber."

And that's when Lea lost it. She let go of the cucumber, threw her head back, shiny dark hair flying, and howled in laughter. She had a deep, husky laugh that settled into his gut like a cup of hot chocolate. He wanted to drink and drink and drink. Because he loved that he could make her laugh, especially in light of what had happened to her cousin.

When her laugh subsided, she eyed the cucumber in his hand and shrugged, giggles still escaping from her lips. "You can have that cucumber. There are plenty other big ones I can use."

Then she winked.

And he wondered if he had stepped into some alternate universe and this was a porno, because he wanted to say, *the only big cucumber you'll be using is mine*, and grab her and devour her mouth. But that was corny, and creepy and probably illegal in twenty-four states. So instead he threw his cucumber in his cart and bit the inside of his cheek.

Lea carted another cucumber—which was smaller than the one he had, he noted with a silent grunt—and looked at his cart.

"Baby food?" She raised her eyebrows.

He looked down at his cart. "Oh, uh, that's for Wayne."

She blinked. Then shook her head. "You're feeding your cat baby food?"

"Well, kind of? I'm, um, making him cat treats." Was that a bad thing to confess to a girl you wanted? At least his boner had gone down.

"What?"

He took a deep breath and plunged in. "Well I saw pictures of these fancy cats on the Internet with homemade food and thought, why can't Wayne have that? Just because he's probably eaten junk all his life and is okay eating junk doesn't mean he has to. So, I'm making him some treats."

Her lips softened, the smirk morphing into a smile.

She cocked her head and said quietly, "You're making your cat treats."

He nodded. Didn't he just say that?

She peeked into his cart again. "What else goes in the treats?"

He pointed to the ingredients as he listed them. "Well, I have some ingredients at home already, like eggs, water, oil and parsley. So I bought rice and baby food and some rice flour. The recipe said it makes a thick paste and then I spread it on a pan, bake it, and then cut it into bite-sized pieces. They are chewy treats, which I thought would be good for him. He eats dry food, which I read is best to control tartar. But I want to give him a treat, you know?"

Lea stared at him. Fuck, he was rambling like a nut job about his cat.

"Tess eats dry cat food, too. I give her canned tuna as a treat. She hears the drawer open where I keep the can opener and comes running."

The gears in his head clicked into place. "You have a cat, too?"

"Well, at home. Not at my apartment because Danica is allergic. I miss her though. She's a little tortoiseshell I got at the shelter. Her mom was brought in pregnant so she was born there and I picked her out as a kitten. She's completely kooky. But I love her."

He smiled. "Tess?"

"From *Tess of the d'Urbervilles*. By Thomas Hardy. One of my favorite books."

It didn't ring a bell. He shook his head. "Never read it."

She laughed. "Not everyone is a Hardy fan. But I like him."

"I'll have to look him up, I guess." He didn't read much, but if it was her favorite book, maybe he could make an effort.

She pursed her lips. "Well, he died in 1928."

Oh. "Oh, so, this is an old book?"

She giggled. "Yeah, the language can be hard to get through."

Well, fuck that.

"So, uh, I called Kat last night to ask about you . . ."

Lea's lips quirked but she didn't say a word.

"What?"

"I didn't say anything."

"I know, but you gave me a look."

She widened those eyes, all innocence. "What look?"

He didn't answer, so she laughed. "Why didn't you ask Kat for my number?"

"I didn't want to be pushy."

She studied his face. "Oh."

"So, how are you doing? And Nick?"

"Nick was released yesterday. I'm picking up some food to take over to him now. And I'm okay. Glad he's on the way to recovery now."

"Good, I'm glad."

She didn't look away, those eyes boring into him until he squirmed. "What?"

Lea pursed her lips. "Just trying to figure out which Max is the real one."

The real one? "I don't understand."

"The cocky flirt or the guy who drives me to the hospital and warms me with his blanket."

He still couldn't tell what exactly that meant to her. "Can't I be both?"

She cocked her head. "I guess you can." Then she lowered her gaze to the floor. "Thanks again. For the ride to the hospital. And for taking me home."

"Anytime," he said softly.

Lea grabbed her cart. "Well, I need to run. Talk to you soon."

She pushed away, her cart running nice and smooth, unlike his. Her limp was slightly more pronounced, and he wondered if her injury was affected by the cold, rainy weather.

He pushed his cart to the checkout and made his purchases.

The rain let up slightly on the way home. He gripped the steering wheel and thought about what Lea had said. He knew he was a flirt. Always had been. But that caring guy? A boyfriend? Nah, he'd never really been that.

With Lea he'd slotted into that role easily. She needed a ride, he drove. She needed a pep talk, he gave it. She was cold, he provided a blanket.

But did she see him as much more than a joke? The thought irked him. Normally he didn't care. He wasn't looking for anything serious so he didn't want the girl getting any ideas. But Lea thinking he wasn't more than a crass jock didn't sit well with him. It slid under his skin like a splinter.

Did he want to be more for her? And most important, could he be?

Chapter 7

LEA KNOCKED ON Nick's door, a plastic grocery bag clutched in her hand. He lived in the on-campus apartments Kat had last year. There were two bedrooms with two guys in each room and all four of them shared a common room.

Shuffling sounded on the other side and then the door swung open. Trish smiled wide. "Hey."

Lea took a step inside and hugged her friend. "How's everyone doing?"

Trish's smile faded slightly. "Okay."

That was a loaded word.

Nick sat on the couch, casted arm in his lap, wearing sweatpants, thick socks, and a thin white undershirt. "Hey you," Lea said walking over to ruffle his hair. He looked up at her and she was pleased to see the bruises had faded so they weren't as angry anymore.

She held up the bag. "Got you a treat."

His eyes brightened and a smile flashed. "What am I, a dog?"

"Have you been a good boy?"

"I chased the mail truck and got hit by a car."

Trish sank down beside him and nudged his shoulder gently. "That's not funny."

He nudged back. "Really? I thought it was. Lea's the tiebreaker."

She scrunched her nose. "Not funny."

Nick huffed in exasperation. "I need a more diverse sample size."

Lea rolled her eyes. "Do you want your ice-cream sandwiches?"

He stuck out his tongue and panted like a dog.

Lea laughed and dropped the bag on his lap. "Here ya go, Rover."

He grinned as he dug into the box and ripped open a wrapper. He took a huge bite and moaned, his head falling onto the back of the couch. "So if I get beat up, it means ice cream delivery service."

"It's not worth it," Lea said.

He wrinkled his nose. "Yeah, you're right. Arm itches like a bitch."

"Bitches itch?" Trish said. "I never understood that saying."

"Well female dogs are bitches and—"

"Enough with the dog stuff, Nick," Lea threatened. "Or I take the sandwiches."

He glared at her as he took another bite and hunched over his box. But he stopped talking.

"You need anything else?" Lea asked Trish. "I should have called before I left the store, but I saw these ice-cream sandwiches and grabbed them because they made me think of Nick."

"Nah, we're good." Trish smiled.

"So you're healing all right?" Lea asked.

Nick shrugged. "I guess so. I got this cast for another month or so and it's awkward as hell."

She hated to see him in pain and irritated. They'd been best friends as kids, playing cops and robbers in his parents' treehouse.

"I wish there was something I could do," Lea said.

Nick tapped his fingers on his knee. "You know, I was thinking about that, actually."

"Yeah?"

He nodded. "What if you called Jackie and asked her to help you with some sort of self-defense class on campus?"

Jackie Banner was Lea's karate instructor. Lea had been a martial student of hers since she was five. She loved everything about it—the discipline, the feel of the crisp fabric of the *gi* on her skin, the firm commands of her instructor.

And it was the one activity she could maintain after her injury. It focused her and she was able to participate and block out the pain in her leg with the moves, which were like instinct. Jackie also taught her how to alter them to relieve the muscles in her leg.

She hadn't been able to attend a class in years but she kept in contact with Jackie and visited her at the dojo sometimes.

Lea hummed. "I guess it's worth a shot. I'm sure once she hears about the assaults, she'd be willing to volunteer her time."

"I think it's a unique situation. I mean, these are guys but they aren't attacking just women. I think only one was a woman, right?"

Trish nodded. "Yep, mid–thirties, in town."

"Right," Nick said. "So these are a group of guys, attacking men and woman and, so far, this isn't a sexual-assault situation. This is an I'm-going-to-beat-the-shit-out-of-you-and-steal-your-shit situation."

Lea's mind whirled as she thought of all the ways she and Jackie could teach this class. "That's a good point. We'll have to make sure the class reflects this specific situation."

Nick picked at a loose thread in the couch cushion. "I mean, this is no joke. And I'm worried they're gonna . . . take it too far and really hurt someone."

"You were really hurt—"

Nick's eyes shot up at Lea, his brow furrowed, blue eyes flashing. "Yeah, and I got away. What if someone else doesn't get away?"

Lea sucked her lips between her teeth because yes, she did know what he meant. She just didn't want to think about it. Especially when she thought about that person being Nick.

She didn't talk about how much worse it could have been and Nick didn't either, but she knew they were both thinking it. And she knew Trish was, too, because she practically trembled on the couch right now, looking at Nick with red, wet eyes.

And then Nick broke eye contact with Lea and looked at his girlfriend. He smiled weakly. "Quit looking at me like that. Eat an ice-cream sandwich."

"But Nick—"

"I'm here and you're here and Lea's here and it's all okay."

Trish blinked rapidly.

"Okay?"

She nodded. "Okay." Then she stood. "I'm going to run and grab a soda from the machine. You two want anything?"

Lea and Nick shook their heads.

When Trish left, Nick crumpled his wrapper. "Thanks again, for the treats."

"You did the same for me after . . . the accident."

Nick smiled and she did the same, remembering when he brought her packs of Starburst and she picked out the orange and pink, so he had to eat the yellow and red.

His smile dimmed. "So, I want to talk to you about something. About Max."

His name sent a shiver down her spine and warmed her limbs. She'd never flirted like that in her life, joking about a cucumber's girth. And the man was making treats for his cat. It warmed her inner cat-lady's heart. Lea exhaled and focused on her cousin. "Look, Nick, he just offered me a ride—"

Nick held up his hand, silencing her. "I know. I actually want to apologize for getting on your case about him. I . . . he's not a bad guy. He gave you a ride to the hospital to see me and I have to give him credit for that. And

I know you can handle yourself. In fact, if anyone can handle Max Payton, it's probably you."

She pursed her lips, and thought about Max's soothing voice, his blanket, his hand on the small of her back. The way he rambled on about making cat treats. She looked down at her hands in her lap. "Whatever, we're just friends ... I guess."

Nick nodded. "Okay, but I'm sorry. Because you're right, people can change. Or they might not really be who we think they are."

LEA HADN'T BEEN home for five minutes from Nick's place when her doorbell rang. She peered through the peephole and then laughed when staring back at her was the close-up of one big, dark eyeball.

She opened the door. "Hey, Dad."

"La-la," he said in greeting, leaning in to give her a wet kiss on the cheek, his ever-present stubble scratching her skin. His familiar aftershave conjured up sleepy nights in front of their fireplace, a half-finished blanket over her father's knees as his crotchet hook flipped and twisted in a blur.

She wrapped her arms around his neck and soaked him in, love and comfort and safety in a five-foot-ten pudgy package. His nickname, bestowed on her when she called herself La-la as a toddler because she couldn't pronounce Lea, settled her.

He ran a hand down the sheet of hair on her back. "How's my girl?" he said, his lips moving at her temple.

She leaned back in his embrace. "Great, now that you decided to surprise me."

He hiked the nylon straps of his bulging cloth bag higher on his shoulder, then grabbed a grocery bag she hadn't noticed from off her stoop. "Well, let me in, then. We're letting the cold in."

She moved out of the way as he walked past her and shut the door of her townhome behind him. "So what's the occasion?"

"Just in the neighborhood. Thought I'd drop off some things. And I wanted to see your smiling face."

Lea ducked her head to hide her blush. There'd been years when she was a teenager that she hadn't smiled much. Answered her parents with grunts or rude answers. But thankfully, she'd outgrown the insecurities that came with her new body and mended her relationship with her parents. Her father never let her forget how grateful he was they were close again. "You don't have to buy me groceries. I just went to the grocery store."

He dropped the bag on her island counter. "I know, but I worry my La-la doesn't keep herself fed well. Look at you. So skinny."

"I'm not that skinny."

He sniffed and pulled out a pie. An entire shoofly pie. Her favorite.

"Dad . . ."

"Your mother said the ingredients were on sale."

"Oh really? Imagine that, just the ingredients for shoofly pie on sale."

His lips twitched.

"You're such a liar," she said, opening up her flatware drawer to pull out utensils. She cut them each a generous slice, then she sat down on a stool at her island to eat. Her dad stood with his back to the counter, plate below his chin.

As a kid, she'd fallen in love with the sweet, sugary Amish concoction when they visited relatives in Pennsylvania. The thick, wet molasses filler coated her tongue and the dry sugar topping clung to her lips. This pie was laughing cousins and napping under a maple tree and playing tag with two normal legs.

And that's when she realized the date.

"Thank you for the pie, but you didn't have to do this," she said, the mass of calories now lying in her gut like sludge.

He placed his plate on the counter. The fork clattered on the blue ceramic. "I know," he said quietly. "But I also wanted to ask about Nick."

Her aunt and uncle had visited yesterday and wanted to take Nick home, but he'd refused, worried about getting behind on assignments.

Lea cringed. "You guys are going to smother him."

"I know, but I told your aunt and uncle I'd at least check in."

Lea sighed. "I just left there, actually. He's okay. In good spirits. And probably sick from eating all the ice-cream sandwiches I bought."

Her dad laughed. "He probably thinks they have magical healing powers."

Lea smiled.

"So how are you with everything that happened?"

Lea bit her lip and chasing a crumb around her plate. "I'm okay, I guess. It hurt to see him like that. And I'm just thankful it wasn't worse."

She looked at her father, pleading silently to change the subject. She wanted to talk about something else. Because she wanted a reprieve before she was alone again, worrying over Nick.

And as always, her dad understood her silence. He bent to his bag sitting at his feet and pulled out a blue-and-brown blanket, crocheted in a chevron pattern. "Here, this is to match your couch pillows."

She and Danica had had a great time shopping at Pier 1 to decorate their apartment, because they didn't want it to look like just any college crash pad. Although Danica had tried to buy a pillow with a pattern that looked like a giant vulva.

"Oh Dad," she said, reaching out her hand to feel the worsted-weight yarn he always used, a mix of merino wool, mohair and silk. "I have like twenty blankets already."

"I know, but one can always use more blankets."

She laughed softly, cradling the softness and rubbing her chin over it. "True. This one is beautiful. I love the colors and pattern." She hopped over her stool, landing none too gracefully on her bad leg, before walking to her couch and laying it over the back. She ran her fingers over the ridges as her father's scent closed in behind her.

"How do you feel?"

That meant—how's your leg? What's your pain level?

She should have known her father would make an unexpected visit on the anniversary of the day her body became less than perfect. But for years, he hadn't been able to mention it, or get close to her, or give her blankets. She'd been an angry teenager. And she knew that he was grateful every day she'd come back from that and learned a little self-acceptance.

But not happier than she.

"I feel okay," she answered noncommittally, knowing he'd let it go. "You want something to drink? Coffee?"

He shook his head. "No, I want to sit down and talk with my daughter."

She sighed.

"Oh, don't act like it's torture to talk to your father."

She rolled her eyes and rounded the couch to sit. Her father claimed a recliner nearby, rocking gently, each forward motion a squeak.

"Your mother sends her love."

"Please tell her the same."

He paused. "So you were okay, going to the hospital?"

He knew the sight of Nick injured would slay her.

"It was okay. A friend offered me a ride, and he was really sweet about it."

Her father's face cleared. "Oh?"

"He lives with Kat's boyfriend."

"What's his name?"

Lea hesitated. "Max Payton."

He furrowed his brow and tapped his chin, like he was searching his internal Rolodex.

"Dad—"

"Is he nice?"

"I don't—"

"What's his major?"

"Um—"

"I want to look out for you, especially after that"—he lowered his voice to a whisper—"asshole Jason."

Lea rolled her eyes. First, because her father still couldn't swear like a normal adult, and second, because he acted like a young man offering a ride was some form of courting. At least the name Jason barely made her wince anymore. Her dad opened his mouth again and as much as she loved her dad, she didn't want to hear what he said next, so she held up a hand to cut him off.

"*He gave me a ride*, Dad. That's it. We're not getting married or even dating. And I'm a big girl now. So even if I did decide to date him in some alternate universe, that's my decision."

Her father blinked, wrinkled eyelids closing over wet eyes. Then he nodded. "You're right as always, La-la. When did you get so wise?"

"I'm not wise."

"Could have fooled me with all that talk, telling your old man what's what."

"Your influence, Dad."

"Phsaw," he said, waving her away, but his grin and red cheeks told her he was flattered.

LEA SAT IN bed later that night, reading over her e-mail to Bruce Shaw. After talking with her dad about Nick, he'd agreed that volunteering to teach self defense classes was a great idea. So she'd called Jackie and they discussed the situation. Jackie was understandably angry and concerned about the assaults. She said she had some ideas on the best way to teach the class, and she'd be happy to do it as long as the school provided a room.

So Lea composed an e-mail to the recreation-center director, proposing the class and asking to use a room. She hoped he'd be on board. She'd already designed some quick flyer examples to print out and paste around campus.

Satisfied with the e-mail to Bruce, she clicked SEND. Hopefully, she and Jackie could help students be more aware of their surroundings and confident in the wake of these assaults.

She asked for an assistant, though, someone she could practice on. She hoped Bruce had someone in mind.

After she sent the e-mail, she leaned back on her pillows and stared at her ceiling. Her thoughts drifted to Max. The blanket he'd placed over her legs. The light in his eyes. The openness of his face as he gave her advice, no matter how misguided.

The situation was so incongruous with what she thought of Max. He was just some arrogant jock who saw girls as disposable, right? The type of guy she stayed away from.

She pulled up her pajama leg and ran her fingers over the scars on her left leg. There were several, which arched from mid-calf over her knee to mid-thigh. Glass and metal from a scrunched-up car don't care about the soft tissue and blood and bones of the passengers inside.

The scars and often-gnawing pain reminded her what happened when she let her trust override her sense.

When she was thirteen, she'd been playing with Nick at his neighbor's house. They'd gone over to the play with the neighbor kid—same age as Nick—several times a week that summer. She'd grown to love and trust the mom, who fed them homemade snacks and peanut butter and jelly with the crusts cut off.

Lea had noticed the too-bright eyes, the trembling hands, the slurred words. But at thirteen years old, they hadn't meant anything to her.

She'd been told by her parents and Nick's parents never to get in the car with anyone but them. Ever.

One day, the mom piled them in the car, telling them she had to run an errand. Lea knew the rules and was responsible for the ten-year-old Nick. But she trusted the mom and buckled herself in the backseat, ignoring the uneasy feeling in her gut.

That was the day she became familiar with hospitals, pain, and the sick feeling of seeing Nick injured.

And that's when she learned what happened when you trusted others. When she didn't keep her guard up.

There were plenty of times she cursed her injury. Tried to hide it under baggy clothes. Cried about the bullying and mocking from her peers about the scars and her limp. Went through bouts of depression that put her in months of therapy as a sullen teen. When she wore all black. Lied about her age to get piercings and tattoos. The pressure to be a beautiful woman in society was too much, so she made the rest of herself unique to match the leg.

But all she'd managed to do was look like every other angsty teen, rebelling against their parents' rules, whining about how hard life was. So in the end, she still looked like everyone else except with a scarred leg and a limp.

So that was teenage bullshit. By the time she entered college, she'd come to terms with her appearance, became comfortable in her imperfect skin. She grew out the crazy colors she dyed her hair. She bought clothes that made her feel comfortable. Wasn't much to be done about the tattoos and piercings. She still liked most of them anyway.

And she didn't put herself in a position to be scorned. She didn't give anyone the power to make her feel less confident about herself, particularly men. Sure, she'd had relationships, but finding a man who was okay with her from the mid-thigh down was hard. She'd been asked to leave the lights off and the covers on when things began to get intimate. Well, screw that. Everyone had scars once they were naked. Hers were just a little more noticeable.

From what she knew of Max Payton he was the perfect example of a guy she wouldn't let close. A guy who would curl his lip up at her leg and suggest maybe she wear pants rather than the pencil-length skirts she was so fond of.

Sure, she'd noticed his eyes and cute butt and long legs, but men who didn't have the personality to match the looks didn't hold any interest to her. She'd tease and throw back any sexual innuendos he threw her way. But no way would she take it any farther.

But now . . . she wasn't so sure of her feelings. She was

guilty of judging his appearance and the act he put on in public as she'd been judged so many times. And that made her feel like a hypocrite.

Shaking her head, she shut down her laptop and picked up her YA literature textbook. But thoughts of Max kept slipping in. And by the time she drifted to sleep, all she thought about was his arms around her as he helped her from his truck, and how his lips would feel on hers.

Chapter 8

MAX TOSSED HIS book in his bag and stood up when he saw his replacement at the rec desk walk toward him.

He greeted the guy, Charlie something, and slung his bag over his shoulder. He retreated to the locker room to get changed to work out, and was two steps out the door and on the way to the weight room floor when Bruce called his name.

Max waited as Bruce jogged over to him. "Payton, you off your desk shift?"

"Yeah, just about get a workout in."

Bruce stopped in front of him and heaved a sigh. A bead of sweat ran down his temple. "I hate to ask you this, but I'm in a bind."

Max straightened. "What do you need?"

Bruce wiped his forehead. "Well, we're starting a self-defense class because of the . . . ya know." He waved his hand and Max nodded. "And it's kind of last minute, but my volunteer bailed. We need someone—like a big guy—for the instructors to practice on. Could you do that for me?"

How hard could it be? As he agreed and followed Bruce to the wrestling room where the class would be held because of the mats, his finger itched to text Lea about the class. It'd be something he thought she'd like. But he hadn't seen her for two weeks, since the chance meeting in the supermarket. He'd been busy with classes and every time he thought about contacting her, he wussed out.

A tall woman with dark skin and natural hair tied back with an elastic band stepped out of the classroom as they approached. She eyed Max. "This the volunteer?"

A female instructor? Really?

Bruce clapped Max on the back. "Max Payton. Good kid, treat him kindly."

Max didn't like the wink she gave Bruce.

He stepped into the room where about ten women and fifteen men stretched. His eyes swept the area until he landed on a familiar back. He'd seen those shoes and tight pants before. That dark hair swishing down the center of her back. And that tank top, too, except this one was royal blue.

And when she turned around, dark eyes locked on him. He stepped toward her.

"What are you doing here?" she asked, sweeping her hair into a messy bun on the top of her head. The effortless way she did it was hot, but he wanted to ruin it, rip out the elastic band and ruffle her hair, get it messy. That'd be even hotter.

"Max?"

"Oh, uh, my rec center boss asked me to volunteer. I thought about calling you. Glad you're here for the class. I mean."

She hummed under her breath.

He leaned in and jerked a thumb discreetly over the shoulder at the instructor. "I just have to avoid getting poked in the eye by some chick. Can't be too hard, right?"

Lea's jaw clenched and her eyes narrowed. If looks could kill, he'd be on the ground without his nuts. What did he say that was so bad?

But before he could ask, the instructor clapped her hands and brought their attention to the front of the class.

"Thanks for joining us. I know we organized this rather quickly, but in light of the crimes in the community, we wanted to give you some tools to improve your chances of staying safe or escaping relatively unharmed."

She introduced herself as Jackie Banner and talked about her background in karate and her experience teaching martial arts and self-defense for two decades. Max didn't think she looked old enough to have that much experience.

And then she turned toward Max and Lea. "Helping me today . . ." Max stepped forward. " . . . is my longtime student and black belt, Lea Travers."

And Max's heart plunged to the ground. At least the mat was padded. Black belt? Martial artist? Oh shit, this was bad, oh so bad, because what did he say? Something about a chick poking him in the eye? Oh fuck.

Lea stepped forward, her back muscles tight, and then turned around to face the class.

But her eyes were on him, and she still had the death stare.

Oh fuck.

Then Jackie said his name and introduced him as the volunteer, explaining to the class that Lea would be performing the moves on him, and he began to sweat.

Lea bent down, picked something up and shoved it into his chest. He looked down. It was headgear and some sort of weird padded thong. Like a sumo wrestler or something. And a bunch of other pads, but he had no idea where they were supposed to go. Hell no.

He handed it back to her. "I don't need this shit."

She clenched her jaw but didn't take the pads. "Are you sure?"

He tossed them to the side and rolled his neck. "Yeah."

He could handle this. He grew up with two older brothers. He'd broken five bones as a kid, including his nose during hockey. Fuck, Alec had run over him with a golf cart.

How bad could a couple smacks by little Lea be?

Twenty minutes later, he learned it was really fucking bad, as he lay on his back at Lea's feet, staring at the ceiling, stunned.

He'd been instructed to come at her as if to grab her shoulders. And then she'd taken the heel of her palm and with one well-place smack, hit his carotid artery in his neck. And it was like he'd been standing one minute, and on the ground the next. Standing over him as he waited to get feeling back in his shoulder and his head to stop spinning, she explained to the class. "A blow to the carotid artery isn't something to mess around with. It is dangerous."

He grumbled and she nudged his shoe with hers and shot him a look to shut up.

"But it's very effective, because it interrupts the blood flow, is very painful . . ." Max grumbled again but she ignored him " . . . and can even temporarily paralyze."

He didn't remember a warning. Was there a warning about this before he agreed? There should have been a waiver to sign. Like his will. He hoped Alec would take good care of Wayne when he died from a blow by a five-foot pixie.

He rose to his feet slowly, and Lea eyed him, but kept talking. "Remember, the purpose of self-defense is not to stand your ground and fight or inflict as much injury as you can on your attacker. Your purpose is to create a diversion and get away to call for help. Also, most of these assaults have been by multiple attackers. Life isn't a Jason Statham movie. You can't take on five guys at once. Okay?"

The class nodded, eyeing Max. He saw sympathy in those eyes. And that straightened his back. He was fine. Pain was temporary.

For the next exercise, Jackie instructed Max to grab Lea from behind and try to drag her away. Max wanted to laugh evilly and yell, "I will take you to my lair, fair maiden," but he didn't think Jackie or Lea would be amused, so he cleared his throat and stepped back toward the wall.

Lea stood with her back to him, that messy bun untouched, perfectly round ass in his line of vision.

Lea was supposed to try to stomp her heel down on his foot, so his job was to evade her heels. So he wrapped his arms around her and her ass snugged up against his groin. He danced backward, shifting his feet to avoid her stomping heels and it was all too much. He was only human. And a horny male. Her ass in her tight spandex and her coconut smell and her hair tickling his nose and her breasts resting on top of his arms.

All of it led to his dick perking up. During a violent self-defense class. What was *wrong* with him?

He shifted his hips back as far as he could, thankful he wore baggy mesh basketball shorts. He hoped to God she couldn't feel he was hard. Awkward.

But then Jackie called a halt to the exercise and the next words sent a chill down his spine. "Lea and Max demonstrated stomping on your attacker's feet when he grabs you from behind is not the most effective method to get away. Mainly because he's not going to stand there. His plan is often to grab you and take you somewhere. So, if your attacker is male, then you'll want to reach back and grab his groin. Pull, squeeze, whatever. It's all going to hurt and cause him to let you go so you can get away."

She turned to Max and Lea. "Let's show the class."

Lea shot a look over her shoulder and the spark in her eye told him this would not end well. And his stupid dick still loved the shape of her ass and back and hadn't gotten the memo it was about to get mauled. Or maybe, it had gotten the memo and wanted said mauling.

He took a deep breath and lunged forward, wrapping his arms around her slender waist again. He knew what was coming, but it was near impossible to avoid her hand while still keeping her in his arms. And then her hand brushed his hard dick and he released her immediately, taking a giant step back.

Lea didn't turn around, but stayed facing forward. There was no way she didn't feel it though. No way. And how was he going to explain that?

Jackie droned on in the background, addressing the class, instructing them to perform the exercises, but without physical contact. No injuries on her watch. Max wished she'd cared while he was lying on the ground.

They went through another couple of techniques before Jackie instructed everyone to buddy up to practice what they'd learned.

Lea finally turned to face him and beckoned with her hands. "Come on," she said.

"Come on, what?"

She placed her hands on her hips. "Don't you want to practice the moves?"

What he wanted to do was go home and take a cold shower. Or a hot one and jerk off. "I can fight."

Those eyes spit fire at him. "Seriously? Were you even paying attention? This isn't about fighting, this is about—"

"Yeah, yeah, creating a diversion and running away." Max flapped his hand.

Her voice lowered to a whisper. "This isn't a joke."

Shit. Her cousin had been assaulted and Max was making a joke out of her trying to do something right. He deserved her venom for that.

"Sorry, you're right."

Her face softened. A fraction.

She motioned for him to step closer and he did. When she spoke, her tone went into "teacher mode," slightly stern and very articulate. He imagined it was the one she planned to use in the classroom when she graduated.

Lea pointed to the side of her neck and tilted her head so he could see the thick cord under her skin. "The carotid artery runs here. Go ahead and feel it."

Max shifted his weight and looked around the room. Jackie was focused on two women in the back, so she wasn't watching them. He turned back to Lea. The heat rolled off of her body and her chest rose and fell with deep breaths. A steady pulse beat at the base of her neck and that beautiful stretch of skin begged him to latch on, kiss and suck until he'd marked it.

"Max," she prodded and he licked his lips and ran his fingers lightly down the side of her neck where she had indicated. Goose bumps trailed in the wake of his touch and he met her eyes. Her pupils were dilated, her pulse and breaths fast.

They held gazes for seconds, minutes, hours. Max didn't know. He was lost in those knowing eyes and didn't come to until Jackie clapped her hands near their heads.

"Next position!" she hollered.

So he'd been out of it for a minute tops. But if the flush in Lea's face, neck and upper chest was any indication, he hadn't been the only one.

"Hey, can you two walk around and make sure everyone is working on these correctly and show them if they aren't?"

Max nodded, unable to find his tongue or voice. Lea cleared her throat. "Sure, no problem."

Max followed Lea as she circulated the room. When she saw a mistake, she was kind but firm, never ridiculing the student or acting above them.

They reached two girls who were practicing defending themselves if an attacker tried to grab them by the throat. Jackie had instructed them not to try to break the attacker's arms or hands, but instead hit the attacker in the face. The tall blonde simulated smacking her partner, a petite redhead, on the cheeks.

Max stepped in. "Hey, umm . . ."

"Casey," The blonde said breathlessly, catching her breath from the exercise.

"Right, Casey. You want to focus on the most sensitive areas of the face, okay? Remember, Jackie said, 'eyes, ears, mouth, nose'?"

Casey nodded and looked uncertainly at her partner.

"Hey, it's okay, but I noticed your hands were on her cheeks. The most effective would be to use the heels of your hands and thrust into your attacker's eyes."

He gestured to Lea. "Here, she'll show you. She'll probably like blinding me again." He played off a joke, because Casey had begun to look a little embarrassed at being called out.

Lea smiled easily and they simulated an attack. He took a shot to the eyes for it, because Lea didn't do so well "simulating," but it was worth it to see the light dawning over Casey's face.

"Oh, I get it! So, like this." And when her partner

grabbed her throat, Casey's palms connected softly with her friend's eyes.

Both came away smiling and Max returned it. "Perfect, you got it."

"Thanks, Max," Casey said, turning back to her partner to continue the exercises.

Max moved on, scanning the room, eager to help out another student. He wasn't an expert like Lea, but he'd paid attention, despite Lea's ass as a distraction, so he felt justified in helping everyone out.

The hair on his neck prickled and he turned around. Lea was watching him, leaning a shoulder up against the wall and rubbing her bad leg. He jerked his chin toward it. "You need something?"

Her jaw clenched, then released. "Nah, I'm okay. You were pretty good with Casey."

He stepped toward Lea. "Thanks. I liked helping her out. It's really cool to see when that switch flips in their head, you know? When they just 'get it.' And that I helped them."

Lea smiled, a brilliant one, with all her teeth. "Oh, I totally get that feeling. Why do you think I want to teach?"

"You want your summers off?"

She laughed and smacked his arm. "Shut up."

He rubbed the reddened area. "I think you hit me enough today, doll, geesh."

"Sorry. But you were the one who challenged me. Acted like all you had to do was avoid getting poked in the eyes. Which, for the record, hurts really badly."

He shrugged. "I guess a well-timed punch works just as well. Those fucking shitheads try to beat me up and steal my shit, they won't know what hit them. I bench two seventy-five."

Lea's smile faded. "What, you think this class is only for girls?"

"Well . . ."

She wasn't pissed. Or at least, she didn't look pissed. But he knew a lesson was coming.

"What do you think *weak* means? You think a skinny guy, like, five-five, weighing a hundred and thirty pounds, is weak?"

Max shrugged. "I don't know, I met a lot of little guys that are pretty strong."

She shook her head. "You look at me and you think I'm physically weak, right? I mean, I weigh a little over a hundred pounds and have a permanently disfigured leg that is painful every single day."

He opened his mouth but she kept talking.

"And you think you're strong because you can bench a lot of weight and can hypothetically take on three guys at once if they attack you?"

Is that what he thought? Because now that she said it, it sounded pretty fucking stupid.

She shook her head. "It's not all about physical strength, Max. You know that. I know you do. It's about technique. It's about courage. And most of all"—she tapped her temple—"it's about what's up here."

Max mulled that over, his mind flipping between his father's words and Lea's. "Wouldn't it be courage to fight back? Hurt them? Make them pay for what they've done to others and to Nick?"

She took a deep breath and shrugged, then let her eyes roam the room. "Sure, I guess. But there's also something to be said for being smart. Knowing you're outnumbered. To have the courage to ditch all the pressure society puts on men to fight back, to man up, and protect yourself, get out and call the authorities."

Pressure of society? His dad was a whole fucking society of pressure on his own. Fuck everyone else. Max had been raised with "an eye for an eye."

But Lea had a point, too. Because how much would he be called a hero when three attackers overpowered him and kicked his head in? Who would care that'd he'd bloodied a nose or blackened an eye? Who would visit him in the hospital like Lea did with Nick?

"Hadn't thought about it that way," he mumbled.

Those all-knowing eyes again. They bored into him as he stared at the floor. "I know," her musical voice said.

Chapter 9

Max slammed the drawer of the register shut as the last customer of the day left the tiny shop office.

He looked down at his nails, caked with dirt and grease, and rubbed his eyes with the heels of his palms. A loud metal clang rang out in the attached garage, followed by his dad's husky curse and a mumbled apology from one of his brothers. Probably Brent.

Cal walked into the office and flopped down on the couch, propping his booted feet on top of the coffee table covered in outdated and coffee-stained magazines.

Another clang. Another curse.

"What's going on out there?" Max asked.

"They're cleaning up and Brent keeps putting the tools in the wrong place. I think he's doing it on purpose because he's pissed Dad made us stay late today."

"I hate when Brent does that."

Cal laced his hands behind his head and leaned back. "Why do you think I'm out here?"

Max turned off the Open sign and locked the door, then returned to the register to begin running the reports and closing it out for the night.

"What's with the . . ." Cal pointed to his eye and twirled his finger in a circle.

Max reached up and prodded the bruised area. "Oh, uh, I was in self-defense class."

Cal frowned. "I thought you wore pads and shit so you don't get hurt. And what are you doing in a self-defense class?"

Max concentrated on counting the bills in the drawer before turning to his brother. "I was the . . . volunteer attacker. The instructor performed the self-defense skills on me."

Cal smirked. "Big bad fighter dude hurt little Max?"

Max grabbed the credit-card slips and shoved them into a file folder. "More like a five-foot doll," he muttered.

Cal dropped his boots to the floor with a thunk. "What'd you say?"

Max sighed and rested his fists on the counter. "It was a girl. A . . . friend of mine. She's a black belt and she hits hard. Now don't tell Dad."

Cal threw back his head and howled. "A girl beat you up?"

"Well it's not like I was allowed to hit back." Max didn't explain that he probably couldn't have hurt her too badly. Her techniques were effective as hell.

"So who is this badass chick?"

Max felt the heat rise into his cheeks. "None of your business."

Cal stood up and leaned on the other side of the counter. "You like her?"

Max didn't answer, checking off the spreadsheet with the cash register totals.

Cal slapped his hand on top of the clipboard. "You haven't dated since Kat. You gonna change that anytime soon?"

Max glared at him. "Since when do we do this?"

"Do what?"

"This heart-to-heart bullshit. You really give a fuck if I date?"

Cal winced, a barely discernible wrinkle between his brows. "Hey, calm down. We all noticed you've been a little miserable. You got all flushed when you talked about her and acted like I was stealing your toy when I asked about her." Cal took his hand away and shrugged. "I figure you should ask her out."

A date? Max hadn't really dated in . . . well, ever. He'd picked up Kat at a party. He didn't think they ever actually saw a movie together or something date-like.

But that's what Lea deserved. A date. But not from Max.

"Nah," he waved it off. "She's a nice girl."

Cal didn't answer and when the silence stretched on, Max looked up. Cal stood with his arms crossed over his chest. "This pity party getting old yet?"

"What're you talking about?"

"You fucked up with Carrie and you fucked up with

Kat. That doesn't mean that's who you are. That doesn't mean you don't deserve a nice girl."

Max didn't answer. The Max of the last three years didn't deserve a nice girl. But maybe . . . well, maybe he could be a different Max.

Cal unfolded his arms and rolled his shoulders. Truth time was over. "Whatever, just think about what I said."

Another clang. Another curse.

"I better get out there to help. Finish the register."

Max watched Cal's retreating back and then returned his eyes to the spreadsheet in front of him. But he didn't see numbers. None at all. He saw Lea's hair and her smile. The determination on her face when she had to face her hospitalized cousin.

Lea was the real deal. And Max didn't know if he knew what to do with something real.

LEA STOOD OFF to the side of the class, listening to grunts and thuds as the students practiced the self-defense moves they'd learned today.

There'd been another assault and theft the previous day. So the class had almost doubled in size.

Max stood with a man and woman, pointing out the strengths and weaknesses in their technique. He met her eyes over the tops of their heads and then dropped them quickly, like he was embarrassed at having been caught. Lea smiled, watching her students again. But her gaze returned to Max like a magnet. And this time, those warm brown eyes of his met hers. He held her stare for a moment and as her smile began to drop, he tilted his chin up so she could see his grin. She returned it and then looked away with a blush.

This was only the second self defense class and Max had taken to it with vigor. He said he enjoyed coaching the students because it gave him a total high when they completed something correctly.

He moved away from the couple and looked up, meeting her eyes. A grin split his face and Lea couldn't help but return it, flashing a small wave. He walked toward her, his handsome face full of brightness and charm. He only wore a pair of wide-leg sweatpants and a tight T-shirt and she wanted to reach into the elastic waistband to see if he was commando.

Oh God, what was happening to her?

"Hey doll," he said, removing the padded helmet she'd made him wear today. Without thinking, she reached up and fingered the fading bruise she'd left on his face last class.

He didn't flinch. Instead, she could have sworn he leaned in to her hand. His thick lashes fluttered and she thought, not for the first time, how he had the prettiest eyes of any man she'd ever seen.

"Hey Coach," she said.

He cocked his head. "Coach?"

She waved her hand to the students, who had just begun to scatter as class ended. "Yeah, you seem to fit right into this. Coaching people through something physical."

He watched the trickle of students walk out the door.

His mouth worked, like he chewed the inside of his cheek. That charming, easy mask he wore had slipped just a little.

He turned back to her. "Kind of always wanted to be a coach."

Lea grabbed a mat and began folding it. "Of what?"

His movements faltered. "Hockey."

"Yeah? Why don't you, then?"

The mask rose when Max shrugged and didn't answer.

Before Lea could prod, Jackie called her name and she spoke to her for a couple of minutes while Max continued to fold the mats.

After Jackie left, Lea returned to his side. "You don't have to help me clean up."

"I want to," he said, then glanced at the clock on the wall. "Shit, I have to get to class though—"

Lea waved him on. "It's fine, I got this."

"You sure?"

Lea nodded. "Of course."

Max hesitated, then grabbed his coat and left.

Lea continued to clean up the room. That was one of the agreements for her to host the class, she had to clean up afterward. She didn't mind. Jackie usually needed to run to get back to her studio and Lea liked the peacefulness of being alone, doing something physical.

Although, today, her leg was killing her.

She hauled the mats into the supply closet and stacked them up in the corner. Then she placed the pads Jackie had loaned them on the metal shelving for next class. The room was lined with metal shelves, full of wrestling gear, jump ropes and other exercise equipment.

Lea glanced up and saw that someone had placed a footpad on one of the topmost shelves, separated from the rest of the loaned gear. Not wanting it to get lost in the shuffle, she grabbed a chair, dragged it in front of the shelves and stood on it.

The chair, however, had other plans. As she hoisted herself up and reached for the pad, a front leg of the chair buckled, sending her careening into the shelf. The chair leaned precariously forward as she gripped the top shelf with one hand and braced herself on the shelf below, a knee on the same shelf and her other foot on the worth-less chair. It had seemed sturdy but on second thought, that was probably why this chair was stuck in a supply closet. It was broken.

"Um, this is not good," she muttered to herself, while contemplating how to get out of the situation without killing herself or knocking down a whole four-shelf cabi-net full of jump ropes. She imagined getting twisted in them, doomed to spend days trapped in this supply closet, bound in rope and probably contracting cauliflower ear.

She examined her predicament as she clung to the shelf. She could jump, but that would be painful and a slight shift of her weight made the chair threaten to com-pletely collapse. She had visions of smacking her face or chin into the shelf in front of her so she would have to walk around campus with a bloody nose and chipped tooth.

As she thought about risking a nighttime of alternat-ing between ice and a heating pad for her leg caused by a jump to the floor, an arm wrapped around her lower back. Another arm slipped under her legs and she was hauled up and off the chair, then turned and pressed against a strong chest.

Legs dangling in the air, hands flat on his collarbones, Lea looked into Max's face from beneath her fringe of bangs. His eyes squinted and his lips tipped up in a wicked grin.

"That was neat trick there, doll, getting yourself tied up so I had to come save you."

Lea squinted her eyes back. "I could have gotten down myself."

"Yeah?"

"Yeah."

"And how did you plan to do that?"

She pursed her lips. "I was going to climb down."

"You were going to climb down."

"Yep."

He looked pointedly around her at the broken chair, which had collapsed completely forward, its back resting on the lowest shelf.

"Right, that looked safe."

"Well, thank you for being the white knight to my damsel in distress but you can put me down now."

His eyes glinted. Definitely *glinted* with amusement. "I'm your white knight?"

The hollow of his throat dipped as he swallowed, that small bit of skin beckoning to her to touch. Kiss. Lick. She curled her fingers to keep them where they were.

"What are you doing here? I thought you had class?"

"Forgot my water bottle. My Camelbak is my best friend."

She smiled. She felt the same way about hers. She carried it around everywhere.

"Well, fine, I guess I can admit I'm glad you came back."

Max beamed at her.

She rolled her eyes. "All right, now put me down, Coach."

And then, Max honest-to-God started swaying, his eyes closed, lips pushed out, while singing in a high-pitched falsetto, "Put me down, Coach. nah nah. I'm ready to stand . . . bop bop bop . . . todaaaay."

She couldn't help it, he looked so hilarious and he sounded so awful, that she burst into laughter and clapped her hand on his shoulder. "Please! Please stop singing. I'll do anything!"

Max stopped singing, and he slowed the swaying so that he gently rotated his hips from side to side, still holding her tightly with both arms wrapped around the bottom of her butt. Those eyes, so warm and playful focused on her face. There was a little bit of wickedness in them too, which filled her with an anxious dread.

"Anything?"

She didn't like this look in his eye. "Wait—"

"Go out with me," he blurted.

She snapped her jaw shut, then licked her lips. "What?"

His gaze darted back and forth between hers. *He was nervous.* "Lea Travers, will you go on a date with me?"

"I—"

You said anything—"

"Okay, but I might have some caveats."

His dark eyebrows dipped. "I don't know what caveats are but they sound fancy."

She giggled. "I mean, I might have some stipulations . . . or . . . amendments to my blanket *anything*."

He finally stopped swaying. "State these caveats and maybe I'll agree."

She tapped her fingers on his shoulders, enjoying the feel of his muscles on her palms. "No wine."

"What?"

"I don't like wine. The smell makes me gag. So no wine. I'll drink beer. Preferably IPAs."

He blinked. "I agree."

"And no movie theaters because those chairs are really uncomfortable." The *for my leg* went unsaid.

Max nodded immediately.

"And—"

"Geez, more?" he rolled his eyes dramatically and sighed.

She wanted him to keep saying yes, but she wanted to see how far she could push him. How many demands would he put up with? "Aaand," she continued, "I want to do something I haven't ever done."

Max's muscles stilled under her hands. He didn't say anything, but his eyes roamed her face, as if he could look through hers and see inside.

"Are you going to ask me how you'll know I haven't done something before?"

He didn't say anything for a moment, but his arms tightened around her. She couldn't stop herself anymore and ran her hands down his shoulders to rest on his biceps. He'd taken off his coat, so he only wore his thin T-shirt, and that vein along the top of his bicep bulged as he held her. She took her right index finger and ran it over the pulsing skin.

There was something about this moment. He was so alive against her, so real. She didn't want it to end.

Out of the corner of her eye, his chest moved with deep, rapid breaths. And she felt something against her thigh. Something hard and getting harder. When she raised her eyes back to his, he shook his head, the movement a little jerky. "No," he said.

What were they talking about? "No what?"

"No, I'm not going to ask how I'll know."

She smiled. "Confident?"

He huffed out a breath and said softly. "Not at all."

She sucked in a breath. "You still want a date with me?"

His chest hitched. "If a date with you means I get to look into your eyes when you smile and smell your hair when I'm close and feel those fingers on my skin when you laugh, then yes, doll. Yes, I want a date with you."

It was too much and not enough all at the same time. Because he was all around her, he *was* her—supplying her legs and providing her heat and giving her breath because she inhaled him every time he exhaled.

It wasn't enough because she wanted the liberty to run her fingers through his hair and kiss those lips and feel more of the hard heat of him currently pressing against her thigh.

But this was inappropriate on so many levels because

what did she think she was going to do? Hump him while surrounded by smelly gym mats?

"Okay," she said breathlessly. "You going to put him down now?"

Slowly, ever so slowly, he let her drop. She didn't know if it was so she could feel all of him on her way down or if he wanted to ease the pain in her leg. Or maybe it was a little bit of both. But either way, when her toes touched the ground, part of her mourned the loss of weightlessness.

He didn't unwrap his arms from around her waist and he bent down, so all she could see were those kind eyes. "We both know, doll, that you could have gotten down if you really wanted to."

"You caught me, then," she whispered.

His eyes blinked slowly and then he bent closer. His lips brushed hers, just the faintest touch and delicate taste before he pulled away. "Yeah, I did."

He let her go and backed away, reaching down to pick up his coat where he'd dropped it on the floor. "I'm already late for class, but it was worth it."

Another flashed smile and then he was gone.

She licked her lips, tasting him on her tongue and inhaling his scent with every breath.

Chapter 10

MAX STARED AT his third list of possible dates. He slashed a big X through them and tossed the paper in the trash.

He stared at his phone. He didn't want to have to do this. Nope. Nope. Nopetown: population infinite.

Danica Owens hated him, and he didn't much like her, but Kat was no help and Danica was the only other person who knew Lea well enough to help him with this date.

He wanted to curse Lea, but when he thought about those dark eyes and the feel of her in his arms, all warm and soft and vibrating with a nervous energy, he started daydreaming about them both being naked—then he didn't want to curse her anymore.

But he had no chance of getting her naked if he couldn't come up with a knockout date.

So, Danica was his pinch hitter.

Fuck.

He dialed her number, which Alec gave to him with a

clear warning to be careful with Lea because Danica had no use for balls and would mount his on the walls with staples.

He crossed his legs.

The phone rang three times before Danica's confident voice came on the line. "Yeah?"

"Hey. Danica. This is . . . uh . . . Max."

Silence.

"Max Payton."

More silence, then a rustling on the other end and a muffled, "Give me a minute, Mon, okay?"

A feminine voice muttered something in assent, then giggled.

He couldn't help himself. "Who you got there?"

"Why are you calling me, Payton?"

"I'm going to need you to describe exactly where you are, who you're with and what you're wearing. Feel free to talk in a breathy voice."

"Payton—"

"I ask everyone that when I talk to them on the phone."

"Fuck you, Payton." It sounded like she was walking. "I'm going to ask one more time before I hang up. Why are you calling me?"

Damn it. "It's about Lea."

The sounds on the other end stopped and then an ominous voice. "What did you do?"

"What do you mean what did I do? I didn't do anything!" His voice cracked. He cleared it.

"Why are you asking about Lea? And you have about five seconds before I drive there and staple your balls to the wall."

Shit, Alec wasn't kidding.

"Put down your stapler, office-supply psycho," he took a deep breath and stated his case. "I asked her out on a date. She said she wants to do something she's never done before, and I need help with what I can do."

The sound on the other end of the line sounded suspiciously like the grinding of teeth. "You asked Lea out on a date." That was definitely said through gritted teeth.

"Yes."

"She's way too good for you, Payton."

"I realize that, Owens."

A pause then. "How'd you get my number?"

"Who you think? Alec."

"Why'd you ask her out?"

"None of your business."

"Hey, asshole, you called me—"

"She's not like anyone I've ever met," he blurted. Then took a deep breath. "I mean, she's beautiful, but it's not about that. She's strong and confident and smart and gives as good as she gets."

A tapping, like long nails clicking on a hard surface. Then her reluctant voice came over the line. "In her room, she has a picture of the rink at Rockefeller Center during the winter, with the lit Christmas tree in the background. She went to New York shortly after . . . well, she couldn't skate then. She told me she always wanted to go and skate in New York at Christmas."

He chewed his lip on that. "It's November, they don't have the tree up yet and I can't afford to take her to New York."

A heaving sigh. "I know that, dumbass. That's something she's never done and always wanted to do. Figure it out. Be creative. That's all I'm giving you."

"Okay."

"You. Are. Welcome," she drawled.

"Sorry, I wasn't thinking. Thanks, Danica. For real. I'll figure something out."

A soft laugh. "I never thought I'd say this, but I have faith in you, Max."

"Thanks, Danica."

"One thing. You screw her over, and I'll show up at your door with a stapler."

HE'D SAID TO wear warm clothes. So Lea donned her thickest jeans, magenta-and-orange crocheted socks her father had given her for her birthday last year, and a pair of black low-heeled boots. Then she stood at the door of her closet, hand on her hip, upper body clothed in only her lavender lace bra.

She didn't want to be cold, but she wanted to be cute.

In middle and high school, she'd been so self-conscious of her limp and scars. She'd hid behind loose, dark clothing and a scowl.

Her first boyfriend seemed to use her as a public service announcement. *Oh, I'm dating the cripple girl, look what a great guy I am!* Jason gave her flowers and gifts and compliments when other people were around. But in private? He hadn't been interested in her at all. He liked to kiss with his eyes closed and roughly fondly her boobs.

Careful not to touch anywhere she was scarred, like it was contagious.

She'd been young and insecure and clingy and shared all her fears with him. He'd turned around, written a college admissions essay on her and her experience. He was lauded for his courage writing it, so much so that he read some of it at graduation. The day he was accepted into his dream university, he dumped her.

After Jason broke her heart, she realized she hadn't treated herself with any worth. Why did she expect someone else to do what she couldn't?

It had woken her up, and Lea vowed never to let someone make her feel like that again. She mended her relationship with her parents and took control of her appearance.

Shopping became her vice. Instead of arguing with her parents about her attitude, she argued with them about her meager bank account.

But it was worth it to value herself. She didn't dress to cover her leg or limp or to impress anyone else. She wore the latest styles and the best brands, matching colors and styles because it gave her control to match her appearance to how she felt on the inside.

She grabbed a fuchsia camisole off a hanger and slipped it over her head, then walked over to her dresser. Out of the second drawer, she pulled a loose-knit dolman-sleeve sweater and pulled that on over her cami. So, it wasn't super warm, but she looked cute and then she could shiver so Max could put his arm around her. Surely, he'd appreciate the hint.

After last-minute application of lipgloss, she walked out to her kitchen to down a pain killer to get her through the night.

Then she leaned back against the counter and waited.

Maybe it was a bad idea to issue this challenge to Max. Because more than ever, she wanted this date to be special. She hadn't dated in a while. And despite wanting to keep her distance from him, she couldn't. Every time Max looked at her, with a warm gaze that coated her like honey, she wanted to let herself be caught in the weight.

Why did she have to put this pressure on him? It was like she was unconsciously testing him. That wasn't fair to him, so she would have to lower her expectations for this date. Just enjoy Max's company and stare at that chin dimple she wanted to prod with her tongue.

Was that weird? Was there a chin-dimple fetish group?

A sharp knock on the door in a distinct rhythm. *Rap rap-rap-rap. Rap. Rap.*

She wiped her damp palms on her jeans and walked to the door.

When she opened it, Max stood in front of her, one big hand braced on the doorway, the other holding a . . . mini Christmas tree. With tinsel and glass balls. Bulging burlap wrapped around the base.

He held it out to her. "Hey, doll."

She wrapped her hands around the scratchy fabric and pulled it to her chest, watching the glass balls clink against each other and the tinsel flutter.

She loved the holiday—everything about it from the weather to the food to the charitable spirit. But this was

November. Even if some department stores hadn't realized it yet. Still, the little tree filled her soul.

"A Christmas tree?" she asked.

He shoved his hands in the pocket of his worn, camel-colored leather jacket, which looked so soft, she wanted to pet it.

"It's . . . uh . . . part of the date. You'll see." His voice shook a little, the muscles of his mouth twitching like he was unsure what to do with them.

She knew there was one thing she wanted to do with her mouth. Stretching her neck up, she puckered her lips, too short to do anything but wait. Max's brows dipped, then he haltingly lowered his head. She brushed her lips over his cheek, then whispered, "Thank you, I love Christmas and this tree is so cute."

He leaned back, face pinked. "Welcome."

WHITE LIGHTS FRAMED the swinging door onto the rink and two decorated trees in terra-cotta pots guarded the entrance like little pine sentries.

On the bench to her right sat two pairs of skates—one a white, figure-skating rental pair and the other black hockey skates—and two Santa hats.

A spotlight on the ceiling illuminated a small round table draped in a white tablecloth and two mismatched chairs. In the center of the table was a poinsettia plant, the pot wrapped in gold foil.

Emotions coursed through Lea like a multicolored strobe light. Happy. Nervous. Excited. Scared. Overwhelmed.

She clapped her mittens on her cheeks, speechless.

Max shifted beside her. "I heard you always wanted to skate in New York at Rockefeller Center. But A, it's November and B, um, the city is kind of expensive, so . . ."

His voice trailed off and once his words penetrated her pulsing, taxed brain, her body knew what it wanted to do.

She whipped off her mittens, grabbed Max by the lapels of that coat she'd wanted to touch since he showed up at her door, raised up on her tiptoes and tugged.

His head dipped easily and when their lips connected, her body stopped flipping through its catalog and focused on one emotion—desire.

She didn't worry about her lipgloss rubbing off on him or the crescent marks her nails were surely making on his coat or the twinge of pain in her battered knee.

His lips were soft and his stubble grazed her skin and his teeth scraped along her bottom lip, tugging gently. So she opened her mouth and melted into him as his strong arms enveloped her in an embrace and his tongue delved into her mouth. The kiss wasn't perfect, probably because she surprised him. But it was perfectly imperfect because it wasn't planned and she had wanted this for so long.

She'd had a lot of first kisses in her life, but none was even close to the sensation racing across her skin at the taste of Max. At first, their noses mashed together, but when Max's tongue touched hers, he made a sound in the back of his throat that she echoed in her own.

And then the Max she always knew was in him, but the one she'd never thought she'd see for herself, unleashed.

His fingertips slipped under her shirt at her back, teasing the skin above her waistband. His other hand rose, cupping the base of her head, kneading her scalp until all she could feel were the three points on her body he touched—mouth, head and back.

He took possession of her and in that moment, she let him, as he licked at her mouth and nibbled her lips and sucked on her tongue.

She didn't want it to end.

When he pulled away, his mouth was still open and his eyes still closed. He blinked them open a couple of times until the haze of lust cleared and he could focus.

"Um . . ." he mumbled.

She smiled and loosened her grip on his coat. Then grimaced at the scratches she'd left behind on the soft leather and smoothed her fingers over them. "I'm sorry, I, uh, might have marked up your jacket."

He didn't even glance down, those eyes boring into hers. "Good. A souvenir. Because I'm going to want to remember that."

His lips glistened with her leftover lipgloss, so she raised her thumb to wipe them off.

He yanked his head back and gripped her wrist. "What are you doing?"

"You have shiny pink lipgloss on your lips."

He smacked them together. "Yeah? Is it a good color for me?"

Lea laughed. "I don't know. You might be more of a deep red kind of guy."

"Well, too bad. This is my favorite now."

"You don't want me to wipe it off?"

He shook his head. "Another souvenir."

She lowered her heels to the ground. "I can't believe you did this. How did you know?"

He touched his lips, one corner of his mouth lifting. "You have that poster in your bedroom."

"You've never seen my room." She frowned.

"Nope, but your roommate has."

"My roommate? You mean . . ." she widened her eyes. "You talked to Danica?"

Big grin. "I called her."

"You, Max Payton, called Danica Owens."

"That sounds really dramatic when you say it like that, but yes, I did."

"She actually answered the phone?"

"Well, she didn't recognize the number."

Lea scrunched her lips to the side. There was no love between Danica and Max. It was a mutual dislike, really. So Max braving a call to a woman who surely put him through his paces was impressive.

But not as impressive as this recreation of Christmas in New York.

"So," he said, rocking back and forth from his heels to his toes. "If you're hungry, we can eat first. I mean, we don't have to skate—"

"Let's skate first!" she all but shouted.

Max chuckled. "Really? Well, okay." He led her over to the benches and pointed to the white figure skates. "I texted Danica for your shoe size and she said six. Is that right?"

Lea nodded, slipping her boots off, but froze when her brightly colored socks contrasted sharply with the black rubber floor.

Max snickered while slipping on his right skate. "Those are some socks."

She touched the seam on the inside of her ankle. "My dad crocheted them. Gift for my birthday."

Max finished lacing up his skate and stuck his foot in the left one. "Seriously? Wow, that's awesome. The last thing my dad gave me was a new muffler. And I had to do a day's worth of oil changes for it."

His head was bent, face hidden between outstretched arms tying his laces. But when both of his skates were tied, the laces of the left one were tighter, the knot sloppier. He stood above her as she tugged on her skates, now even taller with an additional five or six inches of steel and sole.

She took her time lacing up the skate while Max stretched. She hadn't skated since before the accident. She'd been taking lessons, had a birthday party at her local ice rink. Loved the sound of blades slicing the ice and the clomp when she landed a jump. Dreamed of being like Kristi Yamaguchi or Johnny Weir.

Asked to go skate at Rockefeller Center for her next birthday.

But then she trusted the wrong person, who crossed the wrong intersection at the wrong time, and Lea was forced to dream new dreams.

Skating was never mentioned again. When she'd packed for college and found that forgotten poster hidden in her closet, she'd tucked it into her luggage. And then displayed it behind her bed. Her parents pretended not to see it when they visited.

Max shook out his legs and gripped an elbow to stretch his tricep behind his head. With Danica's help, he'd found the biggest item on her bucket list, checking it off in the best way he knew how. He hadn't asked her about whether she could skate, hadn't treated her like a cripple or a broken doll.

He'd shown her the choices and let her choose.

She chose this. She chose skating. She chose dinner on the ice with a handsome man.

She chose him.

When she finished lacing up her skates, she straightened and leaned back, bracing her arms on the bench and clicking her skates together. "When I was thirteen, Nick and I were at his neighbor's, playing with her kid. I didn't know it at the time, but she was an alcoholic. One day, she said she had to run errands. So we all got into the car, the three of us in the backseat. We passed through an intersection, and a truck hit us. Or, really, hit my door and subsequently, me."

Click. Click. Click.

The sound of her skates reverberated off the walls of the vacant rink. Max's black skates in front of her didn't move. And she didn't look up.

"The details don't really matter, but I broke a lot of bones and needed surgery. I have a lot of pins to keep everything in place. But there are a lot of scars, and it's pretty obvious my leg isn't the same and never will be."

Click. Click. Click.

She stared at a scuff mark on the toe of the white leather of her skate.

Max took a step forward. "Do you still have pain?" His voice was a low rumble.

She stilled her feet. Couldn't someone have buffed out that scuff? "Sometimes."

Still staring at that scuff, she took a deep breath and told him about her lessons, her birthday party. Her dreams that could never happen. "You know, when I was sixteen, I thought I'd always be bitter. I thought I'd be a sarcastic bitch. Turn everyone away before they could turn me away. But then I came to college and now that I'm a senior, I've grown up a little. I've accepted myself." She shook her head. "I finally understand I can't predict how I'm going to feel twenty years or ten years or even five years from now. So I live my life in the moment how I see fit. It's been going okay."

When she finished, he took another step closer and knelt down. She raised her head as the weight of one large hand warmed her knee. The left one. "I'm glad you're choosing this moment. With me. In an ice rink covered in gaudy Christmas decorations in November."

The relief of trusting Max with her story and this moment washed over her. She threw back her head and laughed. The sound ripped from her chest and out her mouth in a torrent, unable to stop until tears were streaming down her face. At some point, the tears changed to sobs but she tried to hide them as best as she could, holding her face in her hands, not wanting Max to see this odd breakdown.

And then Max's hand wasn't on her knee anymore.

Now it was cradling her head to his chest and she was soaking his leather jacket with the salty river and she couldn't stop. Her hands gripped him as she burrowed into his chest. His other arm wrapped around her back and all she smelled was leather and soap and sweat and all she felt was Max's heat and shelter.

When the tears dried and she could breathe without a hitch, she pulled back, head down, furiously swiping her eyes, her hands now coated with ruined mascara and black eyeliner and gray eyeshadow. She didn't cry in front of anyone, let alone a man who wasn't her father.

She didn't know what to say, because that breakdown came out of *nowhere*. Didn't she read somewhere how extreme emotions are linked? Because that laughter *had* been normal at first, then turned maniacal and then took the highway at ninety straight to Sob Town.

Awesome first date, Lea. Bawl all over the guy.

She dried her face as best she could and raised her eyes to Max's, expecting to see his face etched with *holy shit, what have I gotten myself into?*

Instead he lifted up the hem of his shirt and wiped her cheeks and around her eyes and she really must have been a mess, because he even wiped her forehead and chin. The whole time, those brown eyes concentrated on her face, tender and strong. When he dropped his shirt back down, the cream-colored fabric was a sodden, gray mess. She opened up her mouth to apologize, but he shook his head, straightened and held out his hand. "More souvenirs. Now come on. This is our moment, and we're going to skate."

Chapter 11

MAX WATCHED AS Lea stumbled slightly on her bad leg when she stepped onto the ice. She didn't blush with embarrassment or apologize. She took a deep breath, a muscle ticking in her jaw and clenched her hands into fists. Then took another, steadier step.

Her strength was beautiful and inspiring. He wanted to bottle it up and rub it into his skin like lotion.

It'd taken an act of God to reserve the ice rink all to himself. The manager owed him a favor from back when Max used to work there in high school. And it was a matter of chance that the club team who called this rink home had an away game, and there was a figure-skating competition going on in the next town, so those athletes weren't practicing.

He'd still had to cough up a pretty penny, but it was worth it for Lea.

When she stumbled again, he spun in front of her and

skated background, holding her hands in his. She didn't acknowledge the help but didn't pull away either.

His hands dwarfed hers and his thumb found a raised scar on the webbing between her thumb and index finger on her left hand. He rubbed it, back and forth, back and forth, and they skated slowly in silence.

The colored lights he'd draped along the boards earlier that day cast a rainbow on the ice and flashed in the residual wetness of Lea's eyes.

He'd never throw this jacket away. And he was never washing this shirt. Because they both held parts of Lea she'd chosen to share with him. With *him*. She'd allowed him to provide support and comfort in what he suspected was a rare show of emotion. No one had ever let him do that for them.

Now he was addicted to being that man for her. He wanted always to be the one with Lea's nail marks in his jacket and makeup stains on his shirt. Lipgloss on his lips and taste of her in his mouth.

He hoped she'd see he could be.

When did he become the man who fell this hard this quick?

"Tell me about your family," she said, taking him out of his head.

They'd made one loop around the track. He wanted to ask if she was okay to keep going. Her hair on her temples was damp and her hands gripped his tightly, but her face was lined with determination, so he didn't question her.

Although the last thing he wanted to do was talk about his family.

"Uh, I'm the youngest. I have two brothers, Calvin—er, Cal—is the oldest and Brent is the middle. They work with my dad at his car shop."

"You get along with your brothers?"

He shrugged. "Sure. They are five, six years older than me. I came along because there were swimmers left after my dad got snipped."

Max continued rubbing the scar on her hand.

"You get along with your dad?"

"Not really." The truth was out before he thought about the questions that would follow in its wake.

She cocked her head. "Why not?"

Jeez, like a dog with a bone. But the wetness of her tears on his shirt clung to his stomach and he couldn't be anything less than honest. "He never wanted more than two kids. I think I could cure cancer and I'd always be an irritation, a reminder that his wife left him soon after I was born."

Pause. Then in a quieter voice. "Your mom?"

Now he looked her in the eye. "Jill."

Her brows dipped. "What?"

"That's how she signs her cards she sends to me on Christmas and my birthday. Jill."

He hoped that said enough so he didn't have to explain further. He waited for the grimace of pity, the whispered, *I'm sorry.*

But instead her lips tightened and eyes hardened. She tugged on his hands and he stopped skating. As they glided to a stop on the ice, Lea craned her neck and brushed her lips along his jawline. His eyes drifted shut as she muttered into his neck, "Her loss."

He wanted those lips everywhere all at once and he wondered how he was going to get through the rest of this date. His clothes were tight and his skin itchy. His body was covered in goose bumps, so he was aware of every hair. He would have let someone pluck them out one by one if it meant she'd keep kissing him.

But she pulled back and he suppressed a whimper.

"Tell me how you learned to skate."

He opened his eyes. Her lips were wet and her face was flushed and he had a modicum of satisfaction that she was as affected by him as he was her.

"Um, I played hockey as a kid."

She cocked her head. "You still play?"

"I wish. I thought about finding a men's league or something."

"What do you like about it?"

He thought a minute. "I like to skate. I like playing on a frozen surface and at the same time I'm sweating bullets. I like how much skill it takes. The sounds. Everything really."

"So do you plan to stay involved in the sport somehow?"

His mouth moved before he could communication to his brain to stop talking. But Lea had a way of dredging up all his feelings and ripping them out of his throat. "I thought about maybe volunteering to help out a high-school team . . ." He bit his lip as his voice trailed off and he looked down, watched their skates glide slowly over the ice.

"Why don't you?"

He blew out a breath. "I don't have the time now and

after graduation . . . I don't know. I doubt Dad would let me take time away from the shop to coach, even though he lives for sports. He lives for his business more." He didn't want to talk about this. He didn't want to get into all the reasons he felt trapped in a future that hadn't even begun. He didn't want to admit all the reasons he admired her for pursuing her dream of teaching.

Her brows furrowed. "But—"

"Want to eat?" He hated to cut her off but he'd spilled enough of his guts tonight.

She paused, then nodded hesitantly and they shuffled to the table. She plopped into her chair gracelessly across from him and bent forward, rubbing her knee with a wince.

He scooted his chair to her left side, picked up her leg and placed it on his lap. As he unlaced her skate, he jerked his chin to the cooler on the table beside the poinsettia plant. "Would you open that? I made sandwiches. I hope that's okay."

She watched him as he pulled her skate off, then scrunched her sock down so her ankle was bare. He pressed his fingers into her flesh and massaged, just like he'd been taught when he was in high school and worked as an assistant to the physical trainer.

When he looked up, her dark eyes were on his fingers, her lips parted. He kneaded up her calf and she moaned.

Well, shit, if she made noises like that, he wasn't sure how he was going to get through this. Thank God they were sitting on ice or he'd be busting out of his jeans.

She took a deep breath and said, "sure," reaching for the cooler.

He continued to work on her leg as they dined on the

turkey sandwiches, cranberry sauce and red potato salad. He ate with one hand, using the other to caress her leg under her jeans. She shifted in her seat a couple of times and winced once or twice but didn't ask him to stop.

After she swallowed her last bite of sandwich, she leaned back in her chair. "That was delicious, and your hands are magic."

"Yeah?"

"Yeah."

He grinned. "They can do other tricks, too."

The lashes swiped her cheeks as she blinked. "Is that so?"

Fuck, the cold wasn't suppressing his . . . situation . . . anymore. "You want to skate some more or are you ready to get off the ice?"

She shifted her leg in his lap, like she was testing its strength. "I think I'm ready to get off the ice."

He smiled. "Me too."

Before she could reach for her skate, he stood and scooped her into his arms. She squealed and clasped her hands around his neck. "Are you seriously going to carry me?"

"It's stupid to put your skate back on just to get off the ice. Plus, I kind of like looking at your sock."

She giggled. "I didn't know we were going to do anything where you'd see them."

"I was hoping I'd see more than your socks," he muttered.

"I heard that."

"I wanted you to."

She pulled her head back, eyes searching his face. He

went for his most charming grin. She pursed her lips to hide a smile.

LEA AND DANICA'S apartment was small, but unlike his bachelor-pad town house, her place looked like people lived here—from the pale yellow walls to the braided area rug to the beige couch with blue and yellow afghan.

The scent of the apartment—a mix of Lea's coconut scent and something else spicy and warm enveloped him. He wanted to curl up on the couch like a cat and never leave.

Lea didn't ask him if he wanted something to drink, just handed him a bottle of water and took a gulp from her own. He washed down the taste of German apple pie they'd had for dessert and wondered how it tasted on Lea's lips.

"I like your place," he said, and thought he was losing his touch if that's all he could say after a great date with a pretty girl while alone in her apartment.

Her lips curved into a smile. "Thanks. Danica and I had fun decorating it."

Max walked over to a table alongside the couch. A framed picture sat on the scratched surface. Behind the glass, a family of three smiled at him, a mom, dad and a little Lea with big eyes. They looked happy and loving. He wondered if his dad even had a picture of all of them.

When he straightened, Lea's eyes snapped up from his ass.

He cocked his head. "Were you looking at my butt?"

Lea blushed but met his eyes. "Do I have permission to look at your butt?"

He raised his eyebrows. "Seriously? Doll, you never have to ask. Look your heart out." He turned his back to her, bent over so his butt stuck out, then air-kissed at her from over his shoulder. He wiggled. "How's that?"

Lea bent over with laughter and this time, her tears of laughter remained happy tears.

When she tapered to chuckles, she began backing slowly down the hallway, beckoning him with a finger. He followed slowly. "You gonna return the favor?"

Lea bit her lip and nodded, that finger crooked in front of her face.

Fuck, he wanted her. Like he hadn't wanted anyone in a really long time. Her dark eyes shone in the dim light under her bangs and her hair hung in glossy sheets on either side of her head. Even with all her makeup rubbed off her face, she was still the most beautiful girl he'd ever seen.

When they reached the doorway of her bedroom, he made his move, grabbing Lea around the waist and hauling her against his body. It was a move he was familiar with—setting the pace, deciding when to move from kissing to the heavy stuff—since he'd lost his virginity at sixteen. Women saw his size and his muscles and expected him to take charge. And Max always tried to live up to expectations.

But when he lowered his head to take her mouth, she clapped her hand over his lips. He froze and raised his eyebrows, breathing heavily through her fingers, nostrils flaring. *Did he fuck this up already?*

Lea's face was in shadow, the only light provided by

a slice of moon through her bedroom curtains. "I'd like you to take off your shirt and pants and lie on the bed."

That musical voice, quiet but firm with an unmistakable undertone of dominance, seeped into his skin, entered his blood stream and plunged straight to his pulsing cock.

He didn't think, he just listened. His shirt and jeans were off in seconds and then he collapsed on the soft sheets in only his boxer briefs, eyes on Lea as she stood at the end of the mattress.

"Don't move," she said and he almost laughed because his whole body was one stiff divining rod and it was pointed right at her, the only well of water for a thousand miles. He wasn't going anywhere.

She circled an arm over her head, then swiped her hair over to one shoulder. She removed a necklace and then slowly, with a knowing grin on her face, removed her sweater. His breath caught as she tossed it to the side and placed her hands at the bottom of her tank top.

And then her hips moved, undulating to music that beat with the thump of his heart. He didn't know where to look, at her dark eyes, her wet lips, the swell of her breasts or those sexy, hypnotizing hips.

Then her tank top joined her sweater on the floor and with one hand, she reached behind her back and unclasped her bra.

And his heart stopped.

Her breasts were small and round, surely enough for a handful but it was the metal glinting off her nipples in the moonlight that sent his body into shock. He couldn't look away from those matching rings as she bent over to slip off her jeans, then stood before him in only a scrap of purple lace. "Holy fuck," was all he managed to say as he sat up and reached for her.

But she shook her head and didn't come closer. "Lie back, raise your arms and grab the spindles on the headboard."

Did she—? Did she tell him to grab the headboard?

He didn't move, seated with his arms braced behind him, one leg bent at the knee. That firm voice beckoned to him, but this wasn't anything he'd done before.

"Do you trust me?" she said.

He tried to talk but his throat was dry. He needed her like water. He tried again. "Yeah."

She took a step around the bed and that's when he saw the dark lines etched onto her hips, ink twisting and curving on her skin. His eyes snapped up when she started talking.

"Just lie back down and let me take care of you. You try so hard to impress everyone and live up to what they expect of you, right?"

All he could do was nod because *how was she in his head?*

"You've already exceeded my expectations, Max. So now let me do this for you. Just turn it off, Max. Turn off all that pressure and let me take care of you."

It was amazing how clear his lungs felt, the pressure of a lifetime of trying *so fucking hard* easing as her palms caressed his chest.

"Lie back, Max," she whispered. "Close your eyes."

Like his muscles had liquefied, he collapsed on the

bed, raised his arms over his head, grasped the wooden spindles of the headboard and closed his eyes.

The bed dipped near his hip and then warm, soft thighs closed around his hips, knees nestled at either side of his waist. Hair—soft, thick hair that smelled like coconuts—brushed his head and then lips that smelled like her cherry lipgloss brushed his temple, nibbled his nose and teased his lips. She licked the seam and the corners until a whispered, "open" had him parting them for her in an instant. And then she was inside, soothing his parched throat, rehydrating him until his skin swelled with her flavor.

He drank. And drank and drank and she gave it to him, gave him everything she had. He wanted to weep, hoping she wasn't some mirage and he'd wake up tomorrow dying of thirst.

Before he could flood, she pulled away. He opened his eyes and she stared down at him, those glossy pupils reflecting his need back at him. He'd never been this naked.

Her lips were wet and swollen and she quirked them in a grin before raising her hand and closing his eyelids. "I didn't say open," she whispered. He didn't protest.

A tongue dipped into the indent in his chin and who knew that was some kind of erogenous zone, because his dick twitched where it was nestled in her heat.

Then her lips traveled down his neck and across his collarbone. A nail scraped over his right nipple and his brain melted. "Oh my God," he moaned and her chuckle came with another scrape along his left nipple.

"Men have sensitive nipples, too." Lea's voice came from above but he didn't dare open his eyes because then she might take this delicious feeling away. Her fingers rubbed his lips and he stuck out his tongue and licked them. She giggled and then fingers returned to his nipples, this time wet with his saliva.

"Christ," he whispered, fingers tightening on the bed slats. "That feels fucking awesome."

Then her hands were on either side of his waist. Her weight shifted and two points of cool metal scraped along his body.

"Please, please let me open my eyes." He'd never begged in his life but he felt no shame.

"Since you asked nicely," she said.

When he opened his eyes, her face was near his waist, eyes wide under long lashes. Then oh so slowly she slid her body up his, the rings on her nipples running along his skin and chest hair.

When she reached his head, she lined up her right nipple with his lips and lowered. He opened immediately, sucking that ring into his mouth, swirling his tongue along the edge and through the hoop and then pushing it aside to get that swollen bud in his mouth.

She tasted delicious, hot skin and cool metal and Lea. He closed his eyes again and tugged the ring with his teeth while she writhed above him, her breath in pants on his forehead, his name on every exhale. He let go of her nipple with a pop and she shifted so he could give her left one equal attention. No Nipple Left Behind.

When she pulled away, he was drunk. Completely drunk on Lea and his moment and feeling weightless for once in his life.

There was the sound of a drawer, a crinkle of plastic

near his ear and then cool air hit his aching cock and heavy balls as she slipped his boxers down his legs.

A hot hand wrapped around his shaft and stroked and he arched his back off the bed.

"Open your eyes."

He did, looking into those dark eyes he craved, like an aged Scotch. "Lea." Her name was a plea on his lips and her returned, "Max," was his granted wish.

She ripped open the condom wrapper by his head and slid the condom down his length. At some point, she'd removed her underwear and now straddled him, gloriously naked. Her nipple rings beckoned to him and those tattoos on her hips tempted him.

"Touch me," she said, and sheathed him with her heat.

He came apart, like his bones flooded and ligaments dissolved. He never wanted to dry out and be pieced back together.

Lea leaned down, her hair in a curtain around his head, hands braced on the bed, and rotated those hips on him.

Back and forth. Back and forth.

So slowly. Giving him enough to make him crazy but not enough to drive him insane.

"Lea." His brain had one mode. And that was it.

"Max."

"Lea."

"Max."

She sped up, her hips not just rising and falling, but rolling and he knew he didn't have much more time.

He gripped her hips just so he had somewhere to put his hands, because she was in charge. She changed her angle and then cried out after a few more thrusts. Once her muscles clenched him, he went over the edge, shouting out his climax in a Lea waterfall.

They lay together, a tangle of limbs and sweat and heavy breaths.

Lea was on her side, the sheet wrapped around her knees. He ran a hand over the skin of her right hip, fingers tracing the ink, just dark lines in the moonlight. "What is this?" He spoke in a whisper, worried anything louder would make him wake up and he'd be back in his bed, cuddling with his cat.

"A devil."

He lowered his face to her hip and could make out a horned head, hooved feet and pointy tail. "A devil?"

She shifted onto her back and pointed to her left hip. "This is an angel."

He ran his fingers over the angel, naked with outstretched wings, and felt bumps under the surface. Scars.

"Why?" he asked.

She rolled back onto her side and cuddled closer. "The devil, on my good side, tells me I can do anything, take any risks, dream any dream. And the angel, on my scarred side, reminds me life is finite. Risks and decisions have consequences."

Max wrapped his arm around her and kissed the top of her head. He didn't know what consequences this night would have. But he did know that for a brief moment in time, Lea had given him peace. A moment in time where he'd given it all up to someone else.

And that was the best souvenir of the night.

Chapter 12

A SEARING PAIN, like daggers carving into her flesh, penetrated Lea's brain and jolted her from sleep to wakefulness.

She blinked at the early-morning sunlight glowing through her thin curtains. She turned her head to the clock on her nightstand. 7:32 A.M.

She turned to face the other way but was stopped short by the bulk of Max's head, shoved into her neck. His breath heated her skin, and the vibration of his soft snoring tickled her nerves.

His arm was thrown over her stomach while she lay on her back, his elbow bent, hand curved around the side of her breast.

Her leg screamed again, and she shifted out from under his weight. He made that soft, sexy sound in the back of his throat as he rolled away from her, and she was glad he hadn't opened those eyes, the ones that sucked her in every time. She threw her legs over the side of the bed, and took a deep breath, stomach churning with the anxiety of a pain-filled trek to her medicine cabinet.

She reached under her bed for the cane she kept just for mornings like these. And quietly, so as not to wake Max, she hobbled to the bathroom, the door only fifteen feet away but feeling like miles.

Tap. Thunk. Shuffle.

Tap. Thunk. Shuffle.

She focused on the sounds and hummed a made-up tune to take her mind off of her leg. She'd known all along last night would lead to this. Max had her makeup on his shirt and nail marks in his jacket.

Her souvenir was pain.

By the time she reached the sink, her whole body was shaking and sweat dampened her brow. She fumbled for her bottle of pain killers and swallowed the pills dry. Then she sat on the edge of the shower tub until she didn't want to die anymore.

Half an hour later, Lea stood at her kitchen counter, sipping hot coffee from a Bowler U mug her mother had bought her when they visited the campus in high school.

Her brain was so scrambled about what happened last night, she didn't know what to think about first. There was the lovely date, her rare breakdown, Max's confessions and tenderness and then there was what happened between her sheets.

She'd always enjoyed the upper hand during sex, conscious of only wanting to show her good side and requiring positions that were easy on her leg.

But last night was new. All night she'd looked into Max's eyes, occasionally glimpsing behind them the utter yearning to please. To make others happy. To avoid disappointing.

And she wanted to give him a couple of hours where he didn't have to think about what he was saying or what he was doing. He could just feel. Feel her and their bodies and a connection she was wholly unprepared for. Because while she gave him that peace, he'd given his surrender and it was now wrapped around her heart, keeping it beating.

"Shoot," she muttered.

She hadn't felt like this . . . ever. Even though Jason had broken her teenage heart, he'd never made her pulse beat like Max did, never made goose bumps race across her skin. This wasn't okay. She'd almost been ready to give Max everything last night. She couldn't let that happen. Couldn't show him he'd gotten to her. That he had more control than he thought. Because while he might trust her, she didn't return that trust. Or rather, she didn't *want* to return that trust.

A shuffling in the hallway announced Max's arrival into the kitchen. He stood in the doorway, one hand braced on the frame just like he'd done when he arrived to pick her up for the date. It's likely he knew how well it showed off his biceps and shoulders and muscled pecs. She'd never dated a guy like Max, someone who looked like he belonged on a romance-book cover or action-movie poster.

His full lips were parted slightly, his cheeks flushed

from sleep and hair mussed. He'd pulled on his jeans, but left them unbuttoned, giving her a glimpse of that trail of hair leading to that beautiful part of Max she'd so thoroughly enjoyed. His eyes were warm and content, his body loose. Part of her wanted to grab him and take him back to bed. Forget the day and just get lost in Max's eyes.

She needed to slow this down. This was all so fast. Her leg still hurt, the pain barely dulled by her pills, souring her mood. She opened up the top cabinet to the side of the sink and grabbed a mug. "Coffee before you go?" She winced because her voice was brusque. Cold.

When he didn't answer, she looked back at him. His eyes had shuttered, those relaxed shoulders now bunched with tension around his neck. "Sure," he answered, just as icily. "One sugar."

The one cup of coffee she'd already drunk sat in her stomach like acid now, and she hated that look on his face, hated herself for not reaching for him like she wanted to. Her hand shook so badly that the packet of sweetener slipped out of her hands when she tried to rip it open, the white powder coating her pristine, cobalt-blue-tiled counter.

"Damn it," she said, slamming her fist down on the counter, tears building in her eyes. What was it about Max that made her some sort of weepy, wilted woman?

She reached for a paper towel to wipe it up, but arms slipped around her, pinning her arms to her side. One hand rested on her lower belly and the other below her neck.

"Lea," he whispered into her ear. That same voice that

chanted her name like a prayer last night as she moved over him, around him.

"I'm sorry," she whispered back, head dropped between her shoulders. "I'm sorry."

He turned her around in his arms and gripped her head in his big palms, searching her face with wary eyes. He smelled like the leather from his jacket and sex and why couldn't she have greeted him this morning with a smile and a kiss?

Because that wasn't who she was.

She took a step out of his arms. And then one, two, three deliberate steps away from him, each one feeling like she was swimming against the current. Max's hands dropped from her head, his face falling, clearly showing a brief sting of rejection. But then his jaw and eyes hardened, the cocky smirk returning in the tilt of his lips. She wanted to slap it off of his face, because she knew how fake it was now. Then she wanted to slap herself for putting it there.

"You know what? I'll stop and get coffee on my way home. No biggie, doll."

He grabbed his T-shirt off the couch where he'd dropped it on the way into the kitchen, then grabbed his shoes and slipped them on, not bothering with socks. Like he couldn't get away from her fast enough. Right there on his shirt showed all the souvenirs he'd take him with him. But he could wash them off of that shirt. She couldn't wash Max off of her heart.

As he walked to the front door, she didn't protest. Didn't say a word, just stood there holding her coffee like a mute and absorbing the irritation rolling off of him in waves, no matter how much he tried to hide it.

He snatched his keys off of the table, knocking over the mini Christmas tree in the process. And last night came back to her in a rush. She almost staggered from the weight of it. From Max's kind eyes, his big hands massaging her leg, his eyes closed and mouth open in orgasmic bliss.

She shut her eyes, but the images replayed behind her lids.

The front door opened and she snapped her lids open. His lip was a sneer but the hurt shone through in his eyes. Max wasn't that good of an actor.

"Thanks for a good time, doll. See ya around."

She flinched as the door slammed shut, then walked woodenly to her Christmas tree, lying on its side on the floor. One of the balls had broken and she picked up the pieces carefully, then threw them in the trash. A couple balls had fallen off and rolled away. She crawled across the floor to pick them up, then righted the Christmas tree and gingerly hooked the ornaments back on the branches.

It wasn't until she carried the tree into her bedroom and placed it on her dresser that she realized her cheeks were wet.

MAX SWORE LOUDLY and dropped the hot pan on the counter with a clatter.

"Shit. Fuck. Shit," he said, throwing the worthless oven mitt in the trash and sticking his burned fingers under cold water.

He drooped his head between his shoulders as the sting began to fade. He glanced at the spot on the kitchen floor where Wayne had been, watching Max make his treats.

But he was gone now, probably scared off by the pan and Max's swearing.

"These are for you, so the least you could have done is stick around!" he yelled after his cat.

He'd been at work with his dad all day, so why he thought it was a good idea to come home and attempt to cook was a mystery. He turned off the faucet and wrapped his now numb fingers in a paper towel. He had to wait for the baked mush in the pan to cool before he could cut it into pieces. So he left the kitchen and sank into the couch out in the living room, head leaned back, eyes closed, feet crossed on the coffee table.

It was now Sunday, so two days after he woke up next to Lea and was then kicked out of her house for a walk of shame.

He'd been pissed all day Friday, spending most of the day at the gym, sweating out his anger. Then he got plastered Friday night, threw up a lot of rum and spent all day at work Saturday hungover.

His dad wasn't amused and shouted extra loud whenever he was around Max.

Jackass.

And the fact that Max *was* pissed made him even *more* livid. Since when did he care if a girl kicked him out the next morning? Since when did he sit around like a love-sick teenager waiting for a phone call?

He asked himself those questions in his head but his heart answered. Because when he closed his eyes at night, he still felt her lips brush his. He still smelled her skin, with just a faint hint of coconut. He felt her fingers on his face and her voice in his ear.

He jolted his eyes open as a key sounded in the front door. Cam walked in, shut the door behind him and then stopped when he saw Max on the couch. He looked around and then quirked an eyebrow. "Uh, dude, what're you doing sitting here in the dark and quiet by yourself?"

"I'm not alone. Alec and Kat are upstairs," Max grumbled.

Cam dropped into the recliner and unlaced his boots. "That doesn't change the fact you're sitting here by yourself." He paused after shoving one boot off. "And why the fuck does it smell like a chicken's asshole in here?"

"How do you know what a chicken's asshole smells like?"

Cam shoved off his other boot and leaned back. "I have an active imagination."

"I made Wayne treats."

Cam blinked, not moving for a moment, before his head jerked forward. "You made food for your fucking cat?"

"Is that really so weird?" Max snapped.

"Hell yes, it's weird. Why don't you buy pre-made food like a normal person?"

"I don't know. I guess I felt bad. He's probably been eating trash most of his life."

Cam smiled then, his dimples cutting into his cheeks. "Maxi's going soft."

"Shut up."

"So what's going on? I haven't talked to you since your date. How'd it go?"

Max clenched his jaw. It was the best date of his life until he woke up. "It was . . . great. We got along and she kisses like a dream. I spent the night and then she turned Ice Queen on me in the morning and kicked me out. Haven't talked to her since." Normally, he would have given Cam some details. Hell, those nipple rings deserved to be talked about and Max had always been one to kiss and tell. But what happened with Lea had been . . . private. Absolutely private and precious and talking about it out loud felt like sacrilege.

Cam waited, like he expected Max to keep talking, but he remained silent. Cam held his eyes, in that direct way he had, waiting him out, probably some stupid thing he learned in the military. "Are you going to say anything?" Max asked.

"You spent the night." Cam said.

"Yes."

More silence. More direct eye contact that made Max squirm. He hated when Cam did this.

"Okay," Cam said, drumming his fingers on the arm rest of the recliner. "Since you aren't even throwing me a fucking bone and telling me how hot she looks naked, I'm assuming shit got real."

Max cleared his throat and confirmed. "Shit got real."

"And then the next morning, she froze up."

"Like Elsa."

Cam rolled his eyes, "You and that fucking movie."

His roommate did not appreciate the genius of *Frozen*. Max had never watched animated movies as a kid. He'd been raised on *Mighty Ducks*. But he'd watched *Frozen* with Kat when they'd been together, and Max had been hooked. He'd never admit that to his family though. Max pointed at Cam. "Elsa's dress is hot—"

"Anyway," Cam talked over him. "Do you think it was as . . . intense for Lea as it was for you?"

Max pictured her eyes, heard his name slip from her lips in a chant, felt the warmth of her body as she snuggled into his side like she belonged there. "Yes," he answered.

"Yeah? Well then she kind of pulled a Max," Cam said. "She probably got freaked out. I mean, this was your first date, you previously hated each other—"

"Hate's a little strong—"

"And so she froze up. Acted out. Pushed you away." Cam shrugged. "Classic defense strategy."

"So . . ." Max's head spun. "You think—"

"I think she might feel the same way you do. But she either got scared or decided to push you away before you pushed her away."

Max hadn't known Cam before he'd already been through basic training and showed up at Bowler a semester late. They'd met in the dorms. But as long as Max could remember, Cam could read people like a freak.

"You should be on a talk show or something and tell fortunes," Max said.

Cam laughed. "I can't tell the future. But I can tell when people got fucked-up shit going in their heads."

"You always been like that?"

Cam thought about that a minute, his face losing all humor. "No, no I haven't. And there are some people I'm not sure I could ever read."

Max wanted to ask more but Cam stood and picked up his boots. "Gonna go take a shower and then get some studying in. I don't know if you and Lea can make it work but if she does apologize, hear her out, all right?"

Max nodded, and Cam trotted up the stairs.

Based on what Cam said, it all came down to trust, right? He thought he'd gotten somewhere on the date when she opened up about the accident. When she'd broken down in his arms. He'd let her hold her, comfort her, be a man for her. And he wanted that again. For once, he'd felt necessary and he'd felt he'd been right where he was supposed to be.

With her. By her side. He was going to have to figure out how to get her to trust him again.

Soft footfalls drew his attention to the stairs. Kat smiled as she reached the bottom. "You okay? I heard a crash—"

Max waved his hand. "It's fine."

She walked past him on her way to the kitchen, and Max's mouth moved before his brain caught up. "Can I ask you something?"

She cocked her head, then walked around the coffee table, sitting on the edge across from him. "Sure. What's up?"

Max bit his lip as he floundered for the words.

"Spit it out, Max."

He huffed. "How . . . do you think it takes a lot of

strength to . . . to . . . trust . . . someone?" His words came haltingly, and he flushed red because this was such an odd conversation to have with anyone, let alone his ex-girlfriend.

Kat looked down at her hands twisting in her lap.

"You don't have to answer—"

"Yes," she said firmly. "Yes, it takes so much strength." Her blue eyes were open and clear and so full of heart, in a way he'd never seen them before. It hurt a little that he'd never seen that side of her, and a part of him flared with jealousy that Alec got to see it. But more than anything, he wanted dark chocolate eyes under a fringe of bangs to look at him like that.

She took a deep breath. "I thought I was being strong, keeping everyone at a distance, but when I met Alec, I realized I was just hurting myself. It took so much out of me to trust him, but the reward for that strength is incredible."

God, he wanted that reward. "I don't mean to be negative but do you worry what would happen if . . ." He let the sentence trail off, but she nodded in understanding.

"I can't think like that anymore. I did and I was miserable."

Max winced, and she smiled wryly. "No offense."

He shrugged. "We weren't right together, and that's okay. I'm glad you and Zuk found each other."

She smiled. "Me too. But Max, it's worth it. It's worth every hurt and misunderstanding and leap of faith. It's all worth it."

Wayne chose that moment to jump up on the couch

turn in two circles and plop down on a cushion in a dramatic sigh.

His eyes on his cat, he said softly, "Thanks."

She rose and gave him a hug. Her citrus shampoo surrounded him but he longed for the coconut scent of Lea. "Take care."

"Yeah, you too."

Kat retreated to the kitchen. Max looked down at Wayne beside him.

"I'm sorry," he said. "Dropping the pan was an accident. And so was the swearing."

Wayne shifted his front paws.

"Treats will be cool soon and then I'll cut 'em. A little snack tonight. What d'you say?"

Wayne blinked, licked his lips, and then his broken-engine purr started. He crept forward, nudging Max's outstretched hand with a wet nose. Then he curled up to Max's thigh, and Max leaned back and closed his eyes.

Chapter 13

LEA HAD VISITED three grocery stores, one market, and two bakeries, until she finally found a tiny, shack-like roadside stand that had a shoofly pie.

Because ever since Friday morning, she had felt off balance. She wanted to do that morning over. Except this time, she'd kissed Max good morning. They'd had coffee and waffles and crawled back into bed, where she let Max take control—this time.

But she hadn't done that. She'd turned on him and then let two days go by.

So the only thing she could think of to make her feel better was a load of molasses and sugar in a piecrust.

And now that she had it, she wasn't even hungry. What a waste.

When Lea walked in her front door, she smelled something sweet and heard pans banging, followed by a few cuss words. "Dan?" she called, dropping her coat on the couch and heading into the kitchen.

Danica stood at the counter, her purple hair streaked with white blonde pulled into a messy knot on top of her head, wearing her hot pink apron that said, in bold letters, I DIDN'T WASH MY HANDS.

She furiously stirred a bowl of batter, face scrunched.

Lea set the pie on the counter and peeked into the bowl. "I ... uh ... think it's well mixed now."

Danica turned to her, blew a strand of purple hair off her face and plunked the bowl down on the counter. Her shoulders slumped. "Yeah, I guess so."

Danica stress-baked. It was to the point that Lea barely liked cookies anymore because they reminded her of a pissed-off roommate.

Lea took the bowl from Danica and began pouring the batter into the lined cupcake tin. "Sit down. What's going on?"

Danica eyed her and then dropped down into a chair at the table, her chin in her hand. "I told Monica I don't want to go home with her to meet her parents."

Lea almost dropped the bowl of batter but she recovered quickly. "And?"

"She ... said she didn't want to see me anymore."

Danica typically didn't talk much about Monica. Didn't let on how much she cared about her, but Lea knew, in the way Danica pressed her lips to the shorter girl's forehead, in the way she looked at her, brushed her silky hair off of her shoulder. "And?" Lea said again, looking up.

Danica shrugged and picked at her nails. But her face was etched with sadness and it broke Lea's heart. "Dan—"

"I just don't want to do it, okay? I don't want to meet her parents so they can act all weird but yet tell all their friends how accepting they are of their lesbian daughter's *lifestyle*." She spit the word out of her mouth like it was poison. "I don't want this expectation that because I met her parents, we're going to be together forever. I just don't want any of it."

Lea leaned on the counter. "That's a lot of assumptions there." Danica didn't answer, so Lea continued. "Right? That's what you're doing is making assumptions about people, which isn't fair, because you don't want them making assumptions about you. How do you know her parents aren't genuine? How do you know Monica has long-term relationship expectations?"

As she turned and popped the cupcakes in the oven, she heard Danica mutter.

"What was that? I couldn't hear you."

Danica shot her a glare. "I said, 'I don't know.' "

"And if you're stress-baking and wearing your mean apron, then clearly you're upset about the breakup."

Danica straightened. "Okay, fine, I'll call her and talk it out, all right? Now let's talk about you and why I found a condom in the bathroom trash Friday morning."

Lea froze, her fingerfull of batter halfway to her mouth. Couldn't Max have been uncaring about the status of her plumbing and flushed the damn thing?

She sucked the batter off her finger, crushed a chocolate chip between her molars and turned to Danica. It was hard to talk to her roommate about guys. Danica didn't see their appeal to begin with and despised Max. And Lea sometimes had a hard time standing up for herself in the face of Danica's domineering personality, because Danica could be persuasive. When shopping for the apartment, Lea, in a rare moment, put her foot down about that vulva-like pillow and the three Georgia O'Keeffe paintings.

Looking at Danica now, she decided to get it all out quickly, like ripping off a Band-Aid. "It was the best date ever and then we slept together and then the next morning I kicked him out," she said in one gust of breath.

Danica's eyes widened, then she blinked a couple of times. "Let's start at the beginning: What did you do for the date?"

This time Lea took her time, explaining the ice rink and decorations, and the crying on Max's shoulder. She skimmed over the sex, and then described in detail how she acted the next morning. Danica winced while she told it.

"So," Danica said. "Let me get this straight. He treated you like a queen, then you had awesome sex, and then you kicked him out."

Lea nodded.

"You know I've never been a Max fan, but . . . he really put a lot of effort into this. Did he seem really hurt the next morning when you kicked him out."

"Yes," Lea whispered.

Danica placed her hand on Lea's arm soothingly. "So why'd you do it?"

"It just felt . . ." Lea searched for words. "Too much. Too soon. How can that be possible? That we go from sniping at each other to being so into each other?"

Danica shrugged. "I think you always were into each other and that's where all that fire came from when you were at each other's throats. So when you finally stopped arguing with each other, you were then at each other's pants."

Lea rolled her eyes.

Danica laughed and scooped out some batter on her finger. "I'm serious!"

"I just don't know if I can trust him. If I want to trust him and let him in."

Danica licked the batter off of her finger. "I get that. I totally do. But you're giving up before you even got started. No one's saying you have to plunge in head first and give each other promise rings and declare your undying love and shit. Just give the damn guy a chance."

Lea chewed her lip. "But you don't even like Max."

Danica shrugged. "No, I don't. Although I'm starting to change my mind. But I think you do like him. And that's what matters."

SHE TWISTED THE plastic bag holding the shoofly pie in her hand as she walked up the front-porch steps of Max's townhome. After her talk with Danica, she'd gathered her courage and came to apologize, armed with a smile and pie. She hoped Max was back from working at his dad's. She took a deep breath and knocked.

A deep voice sounded inside and when the door opened, she first saw the side of Max's head, because he was speaking to someone inside the house.

He turned his head and jolted when he saw it was her. She swallowed and waved weakly. "Um, hi."

"Lea," he said, his voice full of confusion until he pulled down a mask of indifference.

"May I come in?" she asked.

He let go of the door and retreated into the house toward the kitchen. She followed and when she walked in, she saw Wayne hunched on the floor eating off a plate. He looked up at her and hissed. She stopped and whipped her head to Max.

He grinned sheepishly. "Oh, uh, he's protective of his treats right now."

The whole house smelled like . . . chicken. "Are these . . . the ones you made?"

He nodded, his eyes on hers. She smiled. "That's great, I'm glad he likes them."

Max shrugged but his eyes lit up when he looked at Wayne.

"Anyone around?" she asked.

"Kat and Alec just left." Max gestured toward the ceiling. "Cam is upstairs. He says he's studying, but I'm sure he's just playing video games."

She nodded and watched as Max leaned down and scratched Wayne's shredded ear. She was going to give this up? Not give a chance to a man who made treats for his cat and decorated a whole ice rink for her? What the hell was wrong with her?

She set the shoofly pie on the counter and turned to Max. Drawing up as much courage and strength as she could, she said the two simple words she thought he needed to hear most. "I'm sorry."

Max stared at her, the only movement of his body the clenching and unclenching of his fists at his sides. His eyes flicked between hers, and then he licked his lips. "What are you sorry for?" His voice was barely a whisper, a touch of raw vulnerability to it. She didn't feel like he was putting her on the spot. She felt like he really needed this answer.

"I got freaked out. The date was amazing and being with you was . . . amazing. And too much."

"What was too much?" he pressed, eyes narrowed, studying her in a way she hadn't realized he was capable of.

"You just . . . surrendered, and it was too much. I never expected that." This apology was going all wrong. Why wouldn't her mouth stop moving?

His eyes widened, and his body jolted forward, like he wanted to crowd her, but he held himself back. His voice was low, but unmistakably laced with anger. "Oh no. No you don't. Do not put all this on me. You were the one who cried in my arms and took me into your bed. You might not have expected it, but you asked for it. It's not okay to wrap your fist around my heart and squeeze and squeeze until I'm drained dry and then blame me for opening up my chest to you."

Her eyes pricked and she pursed her lips, willing the tears to stay at bay. Because Max was flayed open in front of her, those warm eyes now dulled with hurt. Sure, he'd opened his chest but she'd taken the liberty with what was inside, hadn't she?

But he wasn't done, his words like the ocean crashing the shores of her sanctuary. "That's your problem. You don't want to trust anyone. You want to live on this lonely little Lea island."

She flinched. "You don't understand—"

"You're right, I don't. Because you think it's okay to sink your claws into me while you keep on your armor."

Was that how he saw her? She didn't want to be like this. And what she learned in the days since she'd kicked him out of her apartment was that while she was scared, she wanted to try.

"You're right, Max. And I'm sorry. I've been burned in my life, and so it's not easy for me to trust. And," she took a step closer. "You make me want to trust you. You pull at everything inside of me, like you're one giant magnet and my whole body wants to give in to the pull, but my head . . . my head tells me to stay detached. I felt it all weekend and I'm tired. Tired of resisting and acting like I don't care. It's never been this hard for me before. I've never felt this pull. Not with anyone but you."

And there it was. All laid out at his feet. And she waited to see if he'd give the last tug, send out a pulse of energy and suck her in the rest of the way.

Max didn't say anything for a moment. He licked his lips, his eyes softening, and she got the feeling he was about to leap without knowing where he'd land. "Will you try to trust me?" His voice wasn't pleading, but it was earnest.

And that was the last tug she needed. The words she wanted to hear, that showed he was willing to try if she was. She took a step toward him and his hand shot out, grabbing her wrist and pulling so she smashed into his chest.

She peeked at him from under her lashes. "So, I'm forgiven?"

He shuffled closer, so his bare feet bracketed hers. "Doll, it's okay."

His thigh leaned in to her bad leg and she sucked in a breath. He looked down and grimaced. "Shit, I'm sorry."

She shook her head and reached down to rub her knee. "It's still sore from the date and . . . after."

His eyes widened and he lifted her onto the counter, his warms hands caressing her thigh. "Why didn't you say anything? Are you okay? Do you need something? I'm sorry. I didn't even think about—"

She put up a hand. "Max. Stop."

His mouth snapped shut and that grip he had on her heart tightened. "This is not your fault."

"But the date was my idea and—"

"Max. Please." She sighed at the forlorn look on his face. "My leg is also still sore from skating, which I wanted to do, and . . . ahem . . . do the other things we did. Those were my decisions and the pain is my consequence."

His mouth tightened. "Angel and the devil."

She nodded.

"But—"

"Max!" This time she shouted and he reared his head back, brows raised at her outburst. "You know, it's not always about you."

His eyes darkened, face hardened and he moved to back away, but she put a hand on top of his shoulder. "Stop, please listen."

He obeyed with a grunt of discontent.

"It's not your fault. Friday morning, I acted toward you because of *me* and what I was going through. Not because of you."

He didn't look like he was breathing, his chest still, his eyes unblinking. She raised a hand and ran it through his hair, stroking the strands at his temples. His breath hitched and he blinked, leaning in to her touch. "Max, sweet Max. You worry so much about everyone else. Just be you, okay? You can't control anyone else." She drifted her hand down and ran her fingers along his jaw. "You can only control how you let them affect you."

He shook his head, stepping into the vee of her legs. "After . . ." his voice trailed off and he looked at his hand resting on her right hip. "After what happened with Kat I told myself I'd pay more attention to how I treated people and just . . . try harder, you know?"

When his eyes met her, they were pleading. For what, she wasn't sure. Understanding? Acceptance? Reassurance?

"Max," she whispered, dragging her thumb across his chin, then tugging. And he came to her with an open, eager mouth, devouring hers, the force of his weight catching her off balance. But he caught her with a strong arm slashed across her back, keeping her upright until she grabbed his face and fought back, plunging into him, showing him she saw him just as he saw her in the best way she knew how.

And then hands were everywhere, the calluses of his palms catching on the rings in her nipples, tugging and forcing a moan from her lungs into his mouth. She tugged at his sweatpants, shoving them down so she could get two fistfuls of his high, plentiful butt that looked so amazing in the worn jeans he always wore.

She squeezed and then couldn't help but lightly smack one with the flat of her palm. He chuckled a "fuck" into her neck and then threw off her tank top and wriggled her out of her shorts.

Just like last night, Max didn't hold back, giving her whatever she asked. Harder. More.

"What about Cam?" She whispered against his mouth.

He nipped at the corner of her lips. "He always wears his headphones when he's playing games in his room."

She pulled back, shot him a coquettish look and then cupped him through the front of his pants. He groaned, grabbed her wrists and stepped back. "You better hold that thought. Hold it real hard, and I'll be right back."

He turned and walked out of the kitchen—walked a little awkwardly—and she laughed. "I'm holding it soo hard, Max!"

A grumble was her only answer.

She stripped while he was gone, down to her white lace underwear, which she always loved in contrast to her tattoos.

He was back in under a minute with a condom and stepped out of his sweatpants in the doorway so he stood in front of her naked. Naked and hard and bold and so gorgeous, it took her breath away. And his gaze on her was hot, so hot she was surprised her skin wasn't on fire.

"Fuck me, doll."

She reached forward and gripped his hip. "I think it's the other way around."

He grinned and pressed his lips to hers and she wondered how she even went two days without a kiss from Max. Without feeling those full lips on hers and his tongue in her mouth and those sexy noises he made in the back of his throat.

She pulled back and flipped open the lid to the shoofly pie.

"What is that?" Max asked as she reached down, slid a drawer open, and retrieved a knife.

"Shoofly pie." She cut a small slice and pulled it out with her fingers. "Open."

Max jerked his head back and eyed the treat. "I need some more details other than a weird name."

She giggled. And she wasn't a giggler. But everything about Max brought out an inner confidence.

"Trust me. It's sticky and sweet."

Max pressed his lips together in a closed-mouth smirk. She giggled harder and pressed the pie slice against his lips. She kissed the corner of his mouth. "Come on," she whispered, lowering her voice to a purr. "Open."

Max's lips softened, and he slowly opened his mouth, baring his teeth for a bite. While he chewed, she took a bite of her own, moaning as the taste hit her tongue.

"Good, right?"

He swallowed and licked his lips. "Delicious."

She smiled and fed him the rest of the slice. He nipped her fingers before she could take them away and she giggled (again!). He laughed, both of them spewing shoofly pie at each other.

"Ew, gross!" she said, swatting at him. He laughed harder and grabbed her around the waist. Then their lips met and it was a delicious mix of Max and sugar and carbs and she wanted to overload on all of it.

Amid sweet kisses, Max rolled on the condom and entered her on a shudder. In this position, clinging to his shoulders as he pistoned his hips, she could feel him more, every ridge, every pulse of his delicious length as he moved inside her. His strangled breath on her shoulder and hisses through gritted teeth told her it felt just as good for him.

And after she threw back her head on a climaxing moan, and he buried his face in her chest with a last grunt, neither moved. She laid her cheek on the top of his head while his breath misted between her breasts.

He shifted his hips back, slipping out of her body. She closed her eyes, stroking his hair. She was wrong Friday morning. Her souvenir from this date wasn't just the pain in her leg and the memories. It was him, those eyes and that smile and that surrender he gave her so easily, squeezing her heart.

Chapter 14

MAX HAD NEVER been a "meet the parents" type of boyfriend. Hell, he rarely even held the boyfriend title, to be honest.

It's not like he didn't know how to make a good impression if he put the effort into it. But he'd never been this nervous. He'd never felt this pressure for someone to like him so much.

He rubbed his palms on his jeans and took a deep breath, staring out of the windshield of his truck at the Hot Cakes Diner.

Lea was inside. Right now.

With her father.

He dropped his forehead onto his steering wheel. He breathed in and out slowly, trying to calm his racing heart and supply oxygen to his brain to stave off the light-headed feeling.

This was ridiculous. He was Max Payton. The Confident One. Making parents love him since 2006.

He rolled his eyes at himself and stepped out of his truck, shutting the door behind him. He ran a shaking hand through his hair, took a deep breath, and walked into the diner.

It was a Friday afternoon, so the diner was crowded. He looked around and spotted Lea in a corner, facing him, sitting across from a man with his back to Max.

After a nervous bite to the inside of his cheek, he squared his shoulders and strode across the diner, dodging a waitress with a loaded tray.

Lea's eyes lit up when she saw him. "Max!"

And the smile on her face, the flush of her cheeks, made him remember why he agreed to do this in the first place. Because whether she knew it *or* not, he'd do whatever he could for that look on her face.

He gestured for her to stay seated and pressed a kiss to her temple. "Hey, doll." Then he sat in the booth beside her and looked across the table at the man who could ruin this all for him.

"Dad, this is Max. Max, this is my dad."

"Carl," her dad corrected, reaching across the table so Max could shake his hand.

"Nice to meet you," Max said. Lea inherited her big, dark eyes from her dad, although he had a lot more wrinkles in the corners. Laugh lines, they looked like, because of the way they crinkled as he smiled at Max. A large knapsack was perched on the bench beside Carl, a ball of yarn peeking out with hooked needle stuck in the strands.

When Max raised his gaze back to Carl, he expected wariness from the older man. A "don't hurt my little girl" and "I own a gun" speech. Instead, Carl took a sip of his coffee and leaned in toward Max. "La-la told me about the date. I want to thank you, because that was really thoughtful. Can't imagine how much planning it took."

A curl of warmth tickled Max's chest and spread out to his limbs, something that felt a lot like pride. He clasped his hands together on his lap so he wouldn't fidget. He wasn't as good at reading people as Cam, but even he could see Carl's posture as inviting, nonthreatening. What would it have been like to grow up with a parent like that?

He wished his father could see him now. He'd done something right. Something someone else valued.

Max looked down at Lea and gripped her hand, flashing her a wide smile. She beamed back. "It was a perfect date." Her voice lowered to a whisper and she leaned in to Max. "Even though I panicked the next morning." Her cheeks colored in a blush, and she clapped her hand over her mouth, eyes darting to her father. Max groaned inwardly and closed his eyes.

Carl cleared his throat, his voice coming haltingly. "Um . . . well, I mean, just the date. I know nothing about the . . . um . . . next morning . . ."

Lea's cheeks colored more. "I didn't mean to say that," she said through closed teeth.

Max looked at Carl to see the man tugging at the collar of his shirt. "The public date. That's all I'm referring to."

"Dad—" Lea said.

More throat clearing. "I mean, I support the women's movement and their sexual revolution."

"Oh my God," Max said, unable to look anyone in the eye at this table because for fuck's sake, why was this the first conversation he was having with his girlfriend's father? And what kind of family was this? All open and sharing and caring. Max searched the diner for their waitress, because he needed some ice-cold water to dump over his head.

"Dad," Lea said more urgently.

"I even championed the local school board for a better sex ed class that didn't focus on only abstinence—"

"Oh my God," Max said again under his breath.

But Carl kept talking, looking like his mouth was moving before he could clamp his lips shut. "And as the father of a daughter, I'm an avid supporter of feminism, which means accepting women's sexuality . . ."

"Dad, oh my God, please stop," Lea said on a groan, finally silencing her father and descending the entire table into awkward silence.

Put me out of my misery, Max thought.

Carl looked just as uncomfortable as Max with the turn of the conversation. "Right." He fidgeted, his gaze bouncing around, avoiding Max and Lea. "Um . . . want to see what crocheting project I'm working on?"

"Yes, please," Max answered, way too cheerily and excited about a blanket or scarf or whatever the hell was in Carl's knapsack. But he was saved from having to make another awkward conversation about knitting when the waitress finally arrived at their table.

Max wanted to order about three shots of vodka but settled for a coffee.

While they waited for their food, Lea cut through the awkwardness with ease, telling her father about how she introduced Max to the wonders of shoofly pie. He managed to keep himself from blushing, glad that Lea conveniently left out how they ate half of the pie in bed together, naked, with Wayne scarfing up the crumbs left on the navy comforter.

After a brief explanation about the origins of Lea's nickname, La-la, Carl turned to Max. "And what do you want to do after graduation?"

It was a question everyone asked but it was so loaded for Max. Because what he planned to do and what he wanted to do were miles apart. Ever since he'd started helping Lea with the self-defense classes, more and more he began to feel like his true calling was teaching and coaching. He'd already looked into changing his major, researching at night on his computer, casting furtive glances at the door like he was watching porn and his father was going to come in at any minute. Hell, if he got caught watching porn, his father would probably say, "That's my boy." But researching changing his major? That was grounds for disownment.

Max twisted an empty sugar packet in his hands. "My major is business and after graduation I'm going to help my father with his mechanics business. My brothers work there, too."

It was amazing he got the words out. Because his voice sounded flat and vaguely pissed off. He stole a glance at Lea, who studied him with furrowed brows.

"And is that what you want to do?" Carl asked softly.

He didn't want to have this conversation either. He shrugged. "It's okay. Doesn't really matter, since that's what I'm doing."

The man hummed under his breath, which set Max's teeth on edge. But Lea's hand slipped onto his thigh and he relaxed, turning to her with a smile. She returned it, but it didn't reach her eyes.

"La-la said you've been a big help with the self-defense classes," Carl said.

Max's smile felt genuine now. "Your daughter's pretty tough."

Carl laughed and nodded. "Yes, yes she is."

MAX TOSSED HIS wallet on his desk and sat on the edge of his bed while Lea sat cross-legged at the head of it, petting Wayne.

"I like your dad," Max said, taking off his boots.

"Me too," Lea said, flashing him a smile.

Max took off his shirt and crawled toward Lea, laying his head on a pillow near her hip. "Think he likes me?"

Wayne's purr vibrated the bed as Lea scratched under his chin. "Yeah, I think he did."

"You *think*?"

Lea rolled her eyes and stretched out beside Max, propping her head in her hand. "I can't read his mind, but yes, I think he did."

Max chewed his lip. Lea reached over and pulled the skin free of his teeth. "Stop that," she said softly.

He pretended to bite her finger and she giggled.

"Thanks for meeting him. Were you nervous?"

Max pshawed. "Nervous? Me? No way."

She shoved his shoulder gently. "You were too nervous. Shut up."

"I was cool as a cucumber."

Lea laughed and flopped onto her back, staring at the ceiling. "We could have brought up our grocery-story cucumber discussion too, just for a total trifecta of sex-pie-vegetable awkward conversations."

"I'm pretty sure listening to your father talk about the 'women's sexual revolution' shriveled my balls."

Lea cackled and rolled onto her side. "Aw, poor Max."

"I think they need to be held and stroked and maybe fondled a little."

"Do they?"

Max nodded gravely. "Soon, too. Or I think they'll stay shriveled."

Lea rolled her eyes and ran her fingers over his bare chest. "So . . . when do I get to meet the rest of the Paytons?"

He didn't think it was possible for his balls to shrivel more. He hadn't thought this through. Meeting Lea's dad seemed like a natural step, but his dad? Fuck, she didn't know what she was asking. "Uh . . ."

Her touch vanished and her lips turned down. "I guess . . . I just thought . . ."

She was inching away, not just physically, but her eyes were darkening. Shit.

He reached out and laced his fingers with hers. "Of

course I want you to meet my brothers and . . . my dad."
If she noticed the crack in his voice on *dad*, she didn't
show it. How to stall . . . "But they're really busy. They
work a lot."

Her eyes lightened a fraction. "Oh, okay. Well, I'd like
to meet them when they have time."

He could have told her right there. Pieced together the
clues he'd sprinkled in during conversations with her so
she saw the whole picture. But he didn't. Because maybe
he could just keep putting it off until he could figure out a
way to make sure his dad wasn't an asshole to her or said
something obnoxious.

"I'll talk to them, okay? Just give me some time."

A smile now, a bigger one. "Okay, Max." And then
those dark eyes drew closer and those full lips touched
his and then he forgot all about families and dads and
unwanted futures. Because it was the present and he had
Lea under him and in that moment, it was all that mattered.

MAX STARED AT the front window of his dad's shop,
watching the cars drive by on the busy road outside.

He glanced at the clock for the ten millionth time that
day and sighed. He still had another hour and a half to go
before he could leave. And go to a party with his friends
and Lea. A *beach-themed* party. Which meant Lea is some
sort of revealing clothes. And that made his face heat.

Cal walked into the shop, a plastic bag dangling from
two fingers. "Dinner!" he called into the garage, then

slapped a sub down on the front counter for Max. "Extra onions."

Max grabbed the sub and broke the tape so he could peel back the paper wrapping his cheesesteak.

He took a bite and raised his eyes to see Cal squinting at him. "What?"

Cal swallowed his Italian sub. Extra oregano. The thing reeked. "You ask that girl out yet?"

The cheesesteak settled into his gut like lead. "Why?"

Cal shrugged. "Just curious."

Max picked at his sub, pulling out a long string of onion, then dropping it into his mouth. "I did."

Cal brightened. "Yeah?"

"Are you trying to live vicariously through my social life?"

Cal shoved his shoulder with a laugh. "Fuck you."

"We had some dates." Max took a bite of sub and avoided Cal's eyes. Keep it simple. The less information, the better.

"You going to keep seeing her?"

Max opened his mouth but a booming voice cut him off. "See who?"

Max winced, and Cal rolled his eyes.

Jack's grease-stained hand grabbed his sub. He ripped the paper off one end and took a bite out of it while standing up, icy eyes on Max. "You got a girl, again?"

Max wanted to chuckle. Did he have a girl? No one really had Lea. If anything, Lea had a boy. Him.

"She anything like that exotic one you had last year?"

Exotic? Max guessed it was an upgrade from "foreigner," a reference to Kat's Brazilian heritage that his father had used to describe her after Max showed him a picture on his cell phone.

He couldn't imagine what his Dad would say about Lea's limp. He'd be a dick about it, for sure.

It felt weird to think about Lea in his dad's shop. This place was grease and noise and metal.

Lea was clean and soft and gentle.

How the hell was he ever going to introduce her to his family? His brothers . . . okay, that could work. But his dad? Jack Payton already owned his future. Max wanted one thing that was his— all this—and that was Lea. He wanted to keep her separate from all of this until he could figure out how his two worlds would mesh.

And so he blew the question off to get his dad off his back and prevent further questions. "Just some girl I hung out with. No big deal. I'm gonna break it off before she gets too attached."

Lies.

Jack's eyes narrowed, like he was feeling his son out for the truth. Max resisted squirming.

Brent walked in, breaking up the tension of the moment, and the attention shifted away from Max to talking shop.

Max stayed silent, picking at his sandwich, glad he'd shut down the conversation. But an odd sensation rippled over his skin and a weight settled in his gut that felt a lot like guilt. Had he done the right thing? Or should he have told his dad the truth?

Brent and his dad returned to the garage to start shutting down for the night. Cal threw his sub wrapper in the trash and then turned to Max. "You fed Dad some bullshit about that date being no big deal, didn't you?"

Max looked him in the eye, took a bite of his sub. And gave his brother nothing.

But Cal's narrowed eyes let Max know he wasn't fooling him.

Chapter 15

LEA ITCHED HER hip, tugging down the grass skirt so it fit lower over the waistband of her leggings. Max stood next to her, in a pair of faded hibiscus-patterned swim trunks and a shirt with painted-on pecs and abs. Alec wore a pair of short, snug swim bottoms and a button-down Hawaiian shirt, so he looked like Elvis Presley right out of *Beach Hawaii*. Like Lea, Kat wore a bikini top and a grass skirt over leggings. Lea felt a little naked but she had a cardigan draped over her shoulders. She thought they looked like beach rejects.

But Max had talked up his friend Tanner's parties and swore his annual beach-themed one was the best. He lived in a big place on the outskirts of Bowler with a couple of roommates. Tanner's parents were some rich surgeons and bought the house so Tanner could live there, then rented out the other rooms. Tanner's parties were legendary, because he had an huge living-room area with a high ceiling up to the second floor. Lea looked down at the sand squeezing up over the soles of her flip-flops. She wondered what it cost to bring in all this sand and who was responsible for cleaning it up. Inflatable palm trees strung with Christmas lights glowed from the corners of the room. People had already started sticking the drink umbrellas in their cleavages and pants. Max rolled his in his teeth, the umbrella spinning back in forth in front of his mouth. He looked over at her and winked.

She looked back down at her feet, then shifted her gaze to Kat. She shimmied and danced along the wall, her untouched rum punch sloshing over the rim of the cup she held in her hand. Alec finally took it from her and nudged her to readjust her top. She blushed and kissed his cheek.

This wasn't Lea's scene. She partied enough in high school. Sowed her wild oats. She entered college like a sixty-year-old sniping at the youths to get off her lawn.

But Max was alive in this setting, feeding off the energy of others. She wasn't sure she'd ever met a true extrovert until him.

He wrapped a hand around her shoulders, and she took a sip of her rum punch. She barely tasted the alcohol. "Is there rum in here?"

Max frowned. "That's what Tanner said."

She eyed her cup. "Pretty weak."

Max fluttered his lips and straightened off the wall. "Fucking Tanner."

"Fucking Tanner is awesome?" The man himself said, sauntering toward them. He eyed Kat, who ignored him, dancing with her body plastered against Alec.

"Did you put grain in this?" Max said, drawing Tanner's attention.

"What?" Tanner wasn't necessarily good-looking. His face was a little narrow, Lea thought. And smarmy charm eased from his pores like oil. But he was rich and threw a lot of parties and got girls drunk, if Max's glare was any indication.

"You know what I'm talking about. I told you last time—"

"Chill, Patyon. Chill. I swear there's rum in it. No grain."

Lea had grain alcohol once in high school. She and her friends had tried to make sangria with it. It was dangerous because it was hard to taste and the effects hit you like a train. She'd been standing one minute, and then hugging the toilet, heaving her guts out, the next.

She shuddered, and Max stepped closer to her.

Which drew Tanner's attention. Those watery blue eyes took her in from head to toe and back again.

If Lea was a cat, she would have hissed a warning.

Max laid his hand on the small of her back. It didn't feel like he was trying to act possessive or protective, but like he was letting her know he had her back.

Recognizing she wasn't some weak little girl.

She wanted to press her lips to his and suck his tongue into her mouth.

"I'm Tanner."

"Lea."

His eyes floated to Max's arm disappearing behind her back. Then he grinned and Lea wanted to wrinkle her nose.

"So what you have planned for tonight?" Max said. Lea knew he tried to hide the underlying irritation in his voice, using his question as a diversion from Tanner's leering eyes.

Tanner didn't know Max as well as she did, because he looked at Max with glee.

"Well, I think we're going to do a limbo competition. And of course, karaoke." He clapped Max on the shoulder. "I mean, what's a party where Max Payton is in attendance without a little karaoke?"

Max's eyes cleared and he laughed. "Man, that's some pressure."

Tanner shot him a grin and then with a wink to Lea, he walked away.

"What's his major? Car salesmanship?"

Max threw back his head and roared with laughter. "He's so oily, right?"

"Like bad margarine."

"I know, but he throws good parties."

"He likes you, though. He wants to impress you."

Max frowned. "Me? Nah."

She raised an eyebrow. "He gets a karaoke machine just because you're coming to his party?"

Max waved his hand. "That doesn't mean anything."

"You like doing that?"

"What?"

"Singing cheesy songs in front of people."

Max chuckled again. "Yeah, it's fun. People laugh and clap."

"Yeah, that's how people react. But do *you* like it?"

He stopped and his smile faded. "What do you mean?"

"Do you do it because you like it or because you like how people react to it?"

He scrunched his lips and his eyes floated over her shoulder before meeting her gaze again. "I do it because I like it how it makes me feel, to get lost in a song."

His answer made her so happy. He needed to start doing more things for himself. "Good, can't wait to hear you then."

He beamed. "I think I have the perfect song."

Two girls in bikinis and heels held the limbo stick. They were gorgeous and giggly and Lea sort of envied that they were so comfortable standing there in practically nothing.

Max rubbed his hands together and looked at her. "You know this won't end well for me."

She eyed the limbo stick, then him. "You're kind of bulky."

"Bulky?"

Lea puffed out her cheeks and braced her fists on her hips, elbows out, in a bodybuilder pose.

Max gestured toward her with his hands. "And is this supposed to be me?"

She raised one arm into a bicep curl and lowered her voice. "Welcome to the gun show."

Max threw back his head and then stepped forward, squeezing her bicep. "You do have some guns, doll."

She waggled her eyebrows. "Yours are bigger."

He grinned.

She raised up on her tiptoes. "Size matters, you know."

He laughed again and wrapped his arms around her waist. She squealed as he lifted her off the ground. "You drive me crazy, you know that?"

She nodded and bit her lip.

He rolled his eyes and placed her gently on the ground. Drunk party goers stumbled into line, ready to fall flat on their backs under the limbo stick, Lea was sure.

"Jump in the Line," by Harry Belafonte, blasted over the speakers. Kat squealed and raised her hands in the air, like Winona Ryder in *Beetlejuice*. Alec laughed and mimicked Kat's actions. Max picked Lea up and she wrapped her legs around his waist as he shook his hips.

"*Okay, I believe you!*" Max yelled the lyrics out loud and Lea, Kat, and Alec screamed it on the next verse.

"Time for limbo, baby!" Kat hollered and jogged to the end of the line, still shaking her hips, her arms over her heard, rotating her wrists to the beat. Alec and Max followed her. Lea hung back.

Max stopped when he noticed Lea wasn't at his side. He turned around to face her. "You coming?"

She could do a lot of things—martial arts, ice skating but limbo while she was slightly intoxicated? No way. Her leg couldn't handle that.

"No, I'm just going to watch."

His eyes flicked to her leg. He opened his mouth, surely to protest, then stopped himself. "Okay, doll. You okay if I do it?"

She wanted nothing more than to watch Max do the limbo. "Please, I want you to."

He smiled, "All right."

He turned and walked to the end of the line, and she was so grateful he hadn't argued with her. No one knew her body and her limits but her.

Half an hour later, she was in tears of laughter. Ninety percent of the competitors had fallen on their asses after two limbo-stages. Five percent knocked the limbo stick on the floor. And about three percent had said, "fuck it," and poured themselves another rum punch.

The bikini-clad girls were drunk and had about a five-inch height difference between them so the limbo stick wasn't level.

The whole thing was the funniest sight Lea had seen in her life. Why had it taken her so long to get her ass out of her apartment?

Kat was still in the competition. She was small and surprisingly limber. Most of the guys couldn't take their eyes off of her but her focus was on Alec and his was on her, like no one else really existed. He cheered her on every time and rewarded her with a kiss when she did a crazy back bend shimmy, her chest centimeters below the wobbly limbo bar.

Max was up next. Lea couldn't believe he'd lasted this long because of his . . . "bulk."

"Come on, my big man," she called. "You can do it!"

He glared at her, and she bent over with laughter.

Max and Alec bumped the sagging limbo stick on the next round, and Kat ended up winning. Tanner presented her with a palm-tree beaded necklace. He asked her to flash him for them and she told him, in his dreams.

Kat fiddled with her necklace as she and Lea stood off

to the side. Max and Alec were helping Tanner set up the karaoke equipment.

"How are classes?" Lea asked.

Kat groaned. "You want to talk about school? Now? You're a buzzkill, MBF."

Lea rolled her eyes with a snort. Kat had started her calling MBF—major best friend—last year when Kat changed her major to education. Lea protested the acronym. Kat didn't care. And because Lea adored Kat, she let her get away with it.

"I know you had that test Friday. Quit being annoyed. I'm asking because I care, silly."

Kat grinned at her from under her lashes. "I know. And it went okay, I think."

Lea smiled. After obtaining a dyslexia diagnosis last year, Kat's academic life still wasn't easy. But she got more support and had a ton more confidence and her grades had improved because of it.

"Hey sexy ladies," drawled a voice that made Lea grin. She turned her head and almost swallowed her tongue.

Danica was a beautiful girl, but sometimes Lea forgot that, distracted by the clothes and wigs and contacts.

But this Danica had gone all out—looking sexier than Lea had ever seen her. A real-life Ariel. She wore a long, lush red wig that fell in waves down her back and over her shoulders. Her eyes were a vivid green and her ample breasts were covered by a seashell bikini top. She wore an emerald iridescent mermaid-style skirt and the whole look made Lea think that if she dove in water, she'd actually swim.

Danica would reel in any sailors who saw her. Too bad she wasn't interested in seamen.

A whistle sounded from across the room and Danica turned her head, her hair swishing around her upper body. Alec sauntered over. "Well, damn, Dan. You clean up nice."

She narrowed her eyes and punched his shoulder. "I told you before. That's not a compliment, Stone."

Max appeared at Alec's side, eyes wide on Danica's boobs. "Fuck, you look hot."

Her eyes narrowed on him. "Quit staring at my cans."

He shifted his eyes to Lea, and stuck his lower lip out. "Can I look at your cans instead?"

Lea laughed and shimmied her shoulders. "Go right ahead."

"Good, Danica won't let me touch hers anyway."

"Damn straight," Danica muttered.

Alec laughed and threw an arm around her. "For real, Owens, looking hot. Who you trying to impress? You bring Monica?"

Danica tossed her hair. "I'm single tonight."

Lea stopped making eyes with Max. "What?"

Danica shook her head. "I don't want to talk about it. I want to get sufficiently drunk and do things I'll regret tomorrow."

Kat wiggled her hips, swishing her skirt. "Oooh, that sounds like a blast."

Alec slipped his hand into hers. "Just don't leave without me, all right? Drink what you want but stay where I can see you. Tanner's a dick."

"Okay," she said, leaning into his arm and stretching up on her toes to kiss his cheek.

Max leaned in to Lea, his eyes filled with concerned warmth. "You gonna drink a lot?"

She shrugged. She liked to drink but she didn't like to be so drunk she didn't have her wits about her. Plus, she wanted to make sure Danica got home okay. "A little."

Max looked relieved. "Okay, just let me know if you need anything. And . . . uh . . . I know you can take care of yourself." He pointed to his carotid artery, and Lea threw back her head and laughed. "I sure can," she said, then beckoned with her finger. "C'mere."

He took a couple slow, sauntering steps toward her. "I'm here."

She grabbed the hair at the back of his neck and tugged him down until his lips met hers. She teased them, slowly nipping along his bottom lip, then swiping her tongue across it. When she pulled back, his eyes were half closed, his whole body lax with pleasure.

"Wow, that was sort of hot if I pretended Max was a girl," Danica said.

Lea sighed and Max pulled back. "Hey. Was it that easy to pretend I was a girl?"

Danica waved. "The facial scrub ruined it for me. Shave next time, okay?"

He frowned and rubbed his chin. Lea replaced his hand with hers. "I like it," she whispered. He grinned.

"Okay!" Danica clapped. "Where's the fucking booze?"

Chapter 16

TANNER WAS TALKING to him. Something about the bikini limbo girls. Alec had disappeared, probably in the bathroom.

But Max's attention was on the girls.

Specifically Danica.

Okay, so specifically Danica's hand on Lea's bare knee poked up through the strands of her grass skirt.

They sat on stools at one of the bar tables Tanner lined the room with opposite the karaoke stage.

And they were close. Kat sat across from them swaying to the beat but Danica and Lea were sitting with interlocked knees, laughing and touching.

Lea's cheeks were rosy and her laugh louder than normal. She was on her way to drunk town and Max didn't mind that. He'd take care of her.

He'd always thought two girls making out would turn him on. That was hot, right out of every straight man's fantasy. Danica looked smoking and Lea looked gorgeous.

As Tanner droned on, Max sipped his beer and watched. Danica turned her head, looked right at him and then slid her hand a little higher on Lea's knee.

Max tensed.

He was a little bit turned on but the overriding emotion was . . . was . . . what was this? Jealousy?

Max swallowed. He was jealous. Jealous of someone else putting the moves on his girlfriend.

He wondered if he'd be as jealous if it was Kat—a straight woman—feeling up Lea. Maybe, maybe not.

All he knew was right now, he didn't like the smug look Danica was shooting him, a curl to her crimson-tinted lips. And he didn't like how Lea leaned in to Danica. He definitely didn't like how Lea's breasts brushed Danica's arms. Because he remembered those metal-tipped breasts brushing *his* skin. That was the way it should be.

"Dude, are you even paying attention?"

"What?" Max turned to look at Tanner's exasperated face.

"What's with you?"

"Nothing, I—"

Tanner waved his hand. "You can stand here by yourself if all you're gonna do is stare at your girl all night." And then he walked away.

Max flipped him off behind his back.

"Sorry, man," Alec said, walking up beside him. "Couldn't deal listening to that guy talk anymore. Made myself scarce."

Max shrugged. "I just tuned him out. Hey, what do you see over there?" He pointed to Danica and Lea.

Alec raised his eyebrows. "The girls getting drunk?"

Max shook his head. "No, between Lea and Danica."

Alec cocked his head. "Um, they're talking?"

Max speared Alec with a glare. "They're doing a lot more than talking, don't you think?"

Alec's eyes widened. "Are you jealous of Danica?"

"I don't know!" Max threw up his hands. "Do you know if anything's ever happened between them?"

"Seriously? I don't know. Danica isn't exactly open about her sex life."

Max looked back at the girls. "I don't like it."

Alec stepped in front of him, blocking his view. "You, Max Payton, are not happy about two girls getting a little touchy-feely?"

Max clenched his jaw and crossed his arms over his chest, swirling his now lukewarm beer in his cup. He stayed silent, figuring that was the best course of action with Alec's intelligent eyes trying to read his mind. The genius bastard.

"Well, fuck me sideways," Alec said. "Max is jealous of a lesbian. Well then go stake your claim, buddy." Alec moved to the side, and Max's eyes met Danica's.

Lea's head was turned, talking to Kat, as Danica inched forward, eyes still on Max. He began to walk toward their table and Danica's lips parted. She grabbed the back of Lea's head, pulled her forward and Max started walking faster. Danica's lips moved and he wasn't a lip reader but the mouthed word "kiss" was unmistakable and then Danica's lips were on Lea's.

He knew the taste of Lea's lips, the feel of them all soft and firm at the same time, the slide of lip gloss, the bold way she used her to tongue to tangle with his. He wanted that to be his hand on Lea's knee, his mouth on hers.

His lips tasting her cherry lipgloss.

Danica's hand that wasn't on Lea's head was on Lea's knee, and Lea's hands gripped the sides of her stool. Her eyes were half open.

When he reached Lea's side, Danica pulled out of the kiss and opened her blurry eyes, swiping her tongue across the bottom of her now glossy lip.

Lea laughed and turned to Max, her dark eyes glazed, her face flushed, and Max didn't like it. It wasn't funny, because he wanted to put that color on her skin. He wanted to be the one to give her kiss-swollen lips.

He wanted to be the one who Lea wanted to be with.

He gripped the sides of her head with both hands, closed his eyes and pressed his lips to hers, wanting to replace the taste of anyone else with his own.

While Lea might have been passive with Danica, she was anything but with Max. She gripped the back of his head and tugged on his hair, mashing their faces together and stroking her tongue into his mouth. There was no one else. No sound. Nothing. Just the feeling of Lea's lips and the scent of her in his nostrils and the feel of her skin on his palms. He curled a hand around to her ponytail and tugged, angling her head up so he could get further into her.

He might have started out this kiss wanting to replace Danica's lips with his own, but now Lea's roommate was the farthest thing from his mind. It was all about Lea and him and this energy between, currently strumming through his body, like he was one giant Lea tuning fork.

The kiss went on indefinitely, until Max registered the pain in his scalp and the tight grip he held on Lea.

He slowed the kiss and rested his forehead against hers. They breathed in each other's breaths as the rest of the room slowly came back into focus, as Max registered they weren't alone.

Lea's lashes fluttered against her cheeks, burning hot beneath Max's palm. She didn't laugh after this kiss. She looked drugged.

"Don't kiss anyone but me," Max whispered, his voice barely above a growl.

Lea's eyes blinked open and those dark orbs met his. Her mouth hung open, lips slack. She licked them. "I'm agreeing to your command only because you wiped out some of my brain cells with that kiss."

Max grinned. Lea smiled back and he pressed his lips to hers in a firm, deal-sealing kiss.

"Whoa," said a voice and Max pulled back, lifting his eyes over Lea's head. Kat stared at them, mouth open and Alec stood beside her, arm around her shoulders, his mouth also slack.

Alec gestured toward Danica, Lea and Max. "You take that show on the road?"

Max growled and Lea shoved her face into his chest, giggling.

A throat cleared, and Max directed his glare at Danica. Her smirk was gone, but a soft smile graced her lips.

Without taking her eyes off of Max's, she reached into her seashell bra, pulled out a ten dollar bill and slapped it in Kat's outstretched hand.

"What's that?" Alec pointed at the money as it disappeared into Kat's cleavage.

Danica was silent, her eyes still on Max.

Kat turned to her boyfriend. "Danica bet me that Max would be turned on if she kissed Lea. I bet that Max would be jealous."

"I overestimated the power of a girl-on-girl kiss." Danica shrugged.

Max shifted his weight and ran his fingers through the silky strands of Lea's ponytail. She sighed and leaned in to him. He pressed a kiss to her forehead. "I'm just as surprised by my reaction as you are."

Danica's smirk was back. "So you were jealous?"

Lea straightened. "Wait a minute, I was just a pawn in a bet?"

Danica was unashamed. "Yep."

Lea narrowed her eyes. "Jerk."

Danica smiled and shifted her gaze to Max. "Yeah, well, your boyfriend passed."

THE LAST TIME Max had sung in front of Lea was in the supply closet of the rec center on campus. He'd pitched his voice high and intentionally sang off-pitch just to mess with her and make her laugh.

He licked his lips and gripped the microphone of the karaoke machine tighter in his hand. At Bowler, Max was known for belting out classic rock, getting the crowd excited. But Lea had never seen him.

She watched him now as he stood on the makeshift stage. A smirk to her mouth, beautiful dark eyes sparkling, like she couldn't wait to laugh while he made a fool of himself.

Max curled his lip into a smile, feeling a little devilish. He'd show her.

The familiar guitar rift surged through the speakers. Max grinned and Lea returned it.

Alec's whistle drew Max's attention and he gave his best friend a chin nod. Kat was already bouncing around, hands in the air.

Max rocked his hips, shimmied his shoulders, then raised the microphone to his mouth and started singing the classic Bon Jovi song.

The emotion in "Livin' on a Prayer" always warmed him from the inside. The song was friendship and love and celebration. He lost himself in the words and the beat, belting out the chorus with fist pumps, playing air guitar. The crowd clapped and hooted and sang along with him.

When he sang, "*we got each other,*" he stole a glance at Lea. She stood out in the crowd because she was the only one not moving. She watched him, her lips parted, her eyes wide and unblinking. He shouted into the microphone, "*we'll give it a shot!*" and she jolted at the words, then came out of whatever trance she'd been in, cupping her hands to her mouth and hollering. Then a huge smile stretched over her face and she began dancing to the song.

When the music faded, Max tossed the microphone to Tanner and hopped off the stage. He went right to Lea, grabbed her face, and stole another kiss. Because he was so fucking grateful that he could, that she returned his kiss and clutched his biceps like she didn't want to let go.

When he pulled back, she licked her lips. "Yeah, let's give it a shot."

He smiled.

After grabbing another drink, Max relaxed on one of Tanner's couches with Lea.

He doubted the couch was sanitary, but he was too tired to protest. He wanted to relax with Lea, enjoy this moment where he felt like he had control of his life. The party swirled around him and he cradled Lea in his lap, protecting her from whatever diseases lived in the fibers under his ass.

She ran her fingers through his hair and he wanted to purr like Wayne. "Why do you always smell like coconut?"

She smiled. "It's coconut oil."

"Coconut oil?"

She nodded. "Yeah, I use it like lotion."

And there went every rational thought in his head. "Are you telling me you cover your body in oil every day?"

"Max—"

He cut her off, closing his eyes. "No, don't ruin my fantasy. Okay, so you step out of the shower and drop your towel. You are naked and wet and then you rub—"

She pushed his shoulder, laughing. "Max! Stop!"

He opened his eyes grinned. "I'll cherish that mental image for the rest of my life."

She rolled her eyes and kissed him, a slow teasing swipe of her lips. "If you could do anything after graduation, what would you do?" she asked, her musical voice trickling into his ear.

He could barely keep his eyes open, a result of too much rum and the warmth of Lea's lips on his cheek. Oh, now they were traveling down his neck.

"Max," she whispered below his ear.

He was in that buzzed place where the alcohol in his veins was like a truth serum. And Lea was a pint-sized superhero, coaxing the words from his lips.

"I loved helping teach that self-defense class, you know?"

Lea pulled back, gripping the sides of his neck. She nodded. "I know."

He rolled his lips between his teeth and admitted to her what he'd barely admitted to himself. "If I could do anything, I'd want to teach gym class at a middle school or high school and coach hockey."

She licked her lips and rubbed the base of his neck with her thumbs. "So, you wouldn't help your dad at the garage."

He clenched his jaw. "I hate it," he whispered. "And it kills me because it's a family business. And Dad helps pay for my school. And the money I earn there helps pay for the rest of it. And I love my brothers." He paused and gulped. "But doll, I hate it."

He expected sympathy, a whispered, I'm sorry. But instead those thumbs got up the soothing rhythm, like she was urging his vocal chords to release all the words

MAKE IT RIGHT 201

they'd suppressed for so long. And her brow was furrowed in curious determination.

"Why do you hate it?"

"I don't care much about cars. I don't feel . . . fulfilled."
God, had he ever uttered that word in his life? "I don't
think I have any purpose."

"So why don't you tell your father that? He might understand."

Max snorted. "No."

"What? Why?"

"You don't just . . . tell my dad anything. He tells you
how high to jump and you better double that height."

She scooted closer, the grass of her skirt rustling. "But
have you tried?"

He looked into her eyes and saw the fear in his own re-
flected back at him in her dark depths. "No," he whispered.

"Do you plan to?"

She didn't understand. "No."

Confusion passed over her face before the determination set in. "Promise me you will."

The alcohol didn't let him lie, even though he wanted
to. "I can't make that promise."

"So you're just going to be miserable?"

He shrugged weakly. "You don't understand . . ."

"No, you're right, I don't."

He closed his eyes and when he opened them, hers
were still on him, imprisoning him, challenging him.

"Can I promise to think about talking to him?"

Her lips twisted and her eyes narrowed slightly. "Okay.
I'll accept that." Her begrudging tone made him smile.

He slipped his fingers past the grass skirt and bur-rowed under the waistband of her leggings so he could feel the soft skin at her hips. He loved knowing about the tattoos that were there. "You're tough, you know that?"

Her lashes dipped and a smirk curled her lips. "I do."

He nuzzled into her neck, opening his lips at her skin and stealing a taste with the tip of his tongue. "I like it."

A tremor traveled down her body. She leaned in, her lips at his ear. "I like your limbo skills."

He threw back his head and laughed and she dissolved into giggles in his arms.

A half hour later and two more rum punches later, they collected a drunk, dancing Kat and Alec and headed home. Kat rarely drank and in her drunk state, her mouth moved a mile a minute, interspersed with giggles. Max had no idea what she was talking about but he heard "Segway" and some other randomness and shook his head. Pure Kat.

He called to Alec in front of him, who gripped the hand of a rambling Kat so she didn't wander off. "Dude, I want pancakes."

"Seriously?" Lea looked at him like he was nuts. "It's three A.M."

He rubbed his stomach. "Your point? That's the best time to eat pancakes."

She rolled her eyes and Alec shot him a thumbs-up over his shoulder. "Onward to the Chipped Plate, my king!" he called, gripping Kat's hand.

Max held his hand out in front of him like he held a sword. "Onward, my knight!"

Lea huffed beside him. "You two are so weird."

Max opened his mouth to answer, when he spotted a spring rider standing alongside a house. It was one of those playground toys with a large coiled spring stuck in the ground and a metal purple unicorn sitting on top.

"Oh shit, I love those things!" He let go of Lea and jogged over. He knew the toy wasn't made for his six-foot frame but he didn't care. He sat on the metal saddle, which froze his ass through his thin swim trunks, and gripped the handlebars, propping his feet on the foot rests.

"Yee haw!" He yelled and pitched forward, then waited for the spring to throw him back.

But it didn't. One shift of his weight and the whole thing gave way. He plunged face forward, slamming his chin into the cold ground, the horn of the stupid unicorn jammed into his groin. He rolled and watched as his three friends blinked at him in surprise.

He groaned. "The fucking unicorn bucked me off."

They erupted. Alec roared with laughter, doubled over, clutching his stomach, and Lea and Kat clung to each other, giggling hysterically over his epic fail in the face of a metal unicorn.

He rose to all fours and glared at it. "That is not cool, putting this here without securing the spring into the ground. There's probably a hidden camera around here somewhere. Preying on stupid drunk college students."

"Like you!" Alec yelled, dissolving into another fit of laughter.

Max grumbled and he heard a snap. He looked up and Lea held her phone in front of her, eyes bright and wet.

"Did you just take my picture?"

She nodded, biting her lip, but her shoulders shook with restrained laughter.

He lunged toward her. She squealed but before she could take one step, he scooped her up and hauled her over his shoulder, smacking her grass-covered butt. "Let me down, Max!" she hollered but the laughed.

"Nope, I want pancakes."

Chapter 17

THEY SAT IN the cafe at three A.M. Max crunched three strips of bacon on top of his stack of pancakes, covered it in a layer of syrup and then methodically devoured it. Lea ate a bagel with cream cheese while Kat and Alec shared an order of cheese fries and chocolate shakes.

Lea tongued the corner of her mouth, chasing an errant smear of cream cheese, and thought about Danica's kiss.

When Danica had leaned in and said, "Let's get Max hot. Give me a kiss," Lea hadn't had much time to react or brace before Danica's lips were on hers. She'd never kissed a girl before and Danica's lips were soft, her scent pleasing, her hands at the back of Lea's head and on her knee tender.

But at the same time, Danica held back as much as Lea did. It was all for show. Both of them keeping the important pieces of themselves.

Lea missed the roughness of Max's lips and stubble. The way he crowded her with his big shoulders, at the same time giving everything of himself to her.

Max didn't hold back.

Lea reached over and wiped a smudge of dirt from Max's chin. He grinned at her and then returned to his pancakes.

She'd never forget the sound of his voice on that stage, the way he moved his body to the music. He could have been a front man for a band, that's how much charisma he'd shown. She hadn't expected that.

And then his face when he'd fallen off that toy. All tonight, he'd shown a side of himself, more carefree and happy, than she'd ever seen him. Based on what he'd told her of himself on their date, she wondered how many carefree moments he'd had like that growing up.

The vision of his large, muscular body on that child's toy before he fell off flashed in her head again. She giggled just thinking about it.

"What?" Max asked, licking syrup from his lips.

"You and that unicorn."

Max narrowed his eyes. "Bruiser."

"Huh?"

"That's what I'm calling him."

"You named the unicorn."

"I named him because he nearly broke my ass."

Lea leaned closer and lowered her voice. "I can check for bruises later."

Max stopped mid-chew and turned his head slowly, meeting her eyes. "Are you propositioning me?"

Lea just smiled.

He leaned in. "You can check my bruises anytime you want. Hell, you can give me new ones."

Lea laughed and Kat spoke up. "Alec and I are still here, you know?"

"Hey, I've had to listen to your lovey-dovey bullshit for months now," Max protested, pointing his fork at Kat.

She pressed her lips together and didn't protest.

Alec threw his arm around her shoulders and leaned back. "Tonight was awesome."

Kat snuggled into the crook of his arm. "Very awesome."

Alec grinned at Max. "Missed your singing, man. You were on top of your game tonight."

When Max had held her in the closet of the rec room and sang, he'd pitched his voice high and it'd sounded awful. But tonight? He'd belted out that song in a deep, gravelly voice that did something to her insides. His voice was strong, notes in tune. It surprised her and turned her on a little.

Max reached over and squeezed her leg through her skirt and leggings. "Ready to go?"

She nodded.

Max paid and held her hand as they walked back to her apartment. Danica's door was closed and Lea pressed her finger to her lips to keep Max quiet.

"You shushing me again, doll?" he teased.

She rolled her eyes and opened her bedroom door. Max walked in ahead of her and then as she shut the door, he turned around and pressed her against the door, his head bending to hers for a kiss. Max's arousal was evident and pressed into her belly as they tumbled to the bed.

He rolled on top of her and she arched up with her hips. "As much as you drank, I'm honestly surprised you're that hard."

He raised his eyebrows, his beaming smile proving she'd just complimented his manhood. "Oh doll, a little liquor can't knock me down. I'm always ready for you."

He kissed her, starting out slow but gaining speed, and Lea could feel his excitement in the kiss. She squeezed her eyes shut, tamping down the anxiety of what she was about to do. But the kiss proved to her all along that Max trusted her. And it was time to repay him with her own trust. "Max," she whispered, licking his bottom lip before pulling away a fraction. "Your turn."

His eyebrows dipped. "What?"

She took a deep breath and raised her hands above her head, gripping the headboard. "Your turn."

His eyes traveled up her arms, lingering on her hands where they white-knuckled the spindles before returning to her face. He trailed his fingers down the side of her neck, right over her carotid artery and her lips parted as his tongue followed the path of his fingers, igniting her blood.

. He gripped the side of her neck, pressing his thumb into the indent at the base of her throat then he licked the spot.

He took his time touching her, paying extra attention to the rings in her nipples and the ink on her hips. He nipped her skin with his teeth and caressed her inner thighs, his thumbs moving in a circular pattern that drove her crazy. She wanted to tell him to get to it already, give in to what they both wanted.

But she'd given him control.

So she closed her eyes and gave in to the sensations of his talented tongue and hands and lips.

She opened her eyes when his weight settled full on her. His face was inches above hers and he nudged her nose with his own. "You drive me crazy," he whispered, echoing the words he'd said earlier in the night."

"You drive *me* crazy," she whispered back.

His thumbs pressed into her neck, moving across her skin, leaving goose bumps behind. Every so often he added a scrape of a thumbnail and the sensation went straight to her toes.

"Been on campus over three years. Three fucking years. Took me this long to find you," he mumbled and she didn't know if he was talking to her or to himself.

"But we did now, so that's all that matters, right?" her voice was faint, barely a tone as she concentrated on speaking the words over the rush of arousal spreading through her body like wildfire.

"Yeah," he whispered.

Then his thumbs were gone, and he rolled on a condom and slowly, oh so slowly that she thought she'd come out of her skin, he entered her.

She released the headboard and wrapped all her limbs around him. He started out slowly, gliding in and out of her as he touched every inch of her face with his lips, whispered words like, "beautiful," and "doll," and "finally."

But she wasn't able to speak because her heart was beating and her ears were ringing and she worried she'd floated away, disconnected from her body.

Her orgasm hit her like a shot, and she slammed back into herself, crying out, clutching Max as hard as she could as he exhaled her name into her neck and came with a moan.

She didn't let go of him for a long time, not until he pried her arms and legs from around him, pressing a kiss to her forehead as he crept to the bathroom and then back into her bed.

She lay with her head on his chest, their breaths mixing in the air above them. She trailed her fingers through the sparse hair on his chest, loving the strength and solidity of the body under hers.

"Max?"

"Yeah."

"Thank you."

His breath stuttered but he didn't answer as he carded his fingers through her hair.

And she knew that while she might hold his heart, he held hers too. Like they both kept the other beating, the symbiotic relationship necessary for them both to survive.

She didn't know when this happened, maybe it was seeing him singing in front of strangers. Maybe it was watching him eagerly climb onto a child's toy. Maybe it was listening to the crunch of the bacon as he broke it into small pieces on top of his pancakes.

All she knew was that Max had burst his way into her

heart with his warm eyes and big smile. She'd let herself trust, and she hoped this time it was right. That this was the time it didn't backfire.

LEA STOOD BESIDE the TV with her hands on her hips. Danica and Monica cuddled on the couch watching *Kissing Jessica Stein*. The current on-screen kiss between two girls was kind of hot. And reminded Lea of her kiss with Danica. She ducked her head to hide her blush, hoping Monica wouldn't see, because Danica's girlfriend had only just forgiven her for kissing Lea. She hadn't thought their "break" at the time was definite enough for Danica to go around in a bikini and lip-lock other girls.

But they'd made up, and Monica wasn't glaring at Lea, so she figured all was well.

Lea turned away from the screen. " So, I need help."

Danica raised her eyebrows into the bangs of her pink wig. "What's up?"

Lea shifted her weight from foot to foot. "I want to . . . bake something."

"Okay . . ."

"Well, that's not really my thing. My mom bakes. I don't. But I want to surprise Max and take him something at the garage. I know he hates his job and . . ." she waved her hand, realizing Danica didn't need to know all the details about Max's life and probably didn't care. "So can you help me?"

Danica cocked her head, studying Lea. It made her uncomfortable.

Monica clapped her hands and then gripped Danica's thigh. "Snickernoodles. We can make snickerdoodles."

Danica wrinkled her nose. "What are those?"

Monica's mouth dropped open. "You bake and you don't know what snickerdoodles are? Oh honey, we are definitely introducing you to these treats." She turned to Lea. "Have you ever had them?"

Lea scrunched her lips to the side. "Aren't they sugar cookies rolled in cinnamon and sugar?"

Monica nodded. "Pretty much."

"I think my mom used to make them," Lea said. "So good."

Monica smiled and hopped to her feet, tugging on Danica's arm. "Come on, let's check to make sure we have the ingredients. I love to bake!"

"But I wanted to watch this movie," Danica grumbled.

"We can watch it later. It's not going anywhere. I own it." Monica tugged again. Come on."

Danica shot Lea a dark look, which made Lea smile, then followed her girlfriend into the kitchen.

Monica flitted about the kitchen on silent feet, her gauzy shirt flowing behind her, checking the cabinets for supplies while Danica listed them from a recipe she'd searched for on her phone.

Lea stood at the counter, enjoying watching the ease and happiness of her roommate together with her girlfriend. Lea was proud of Danica, because she'd finally got over herself and agreed to meet Monica's parents.

Monica was good for Danica. She didn't try to change her. She condoned Danica's crazy looks every day and with every shift of her eyes in Danica's direction, Lea could see affection.

Danica was the same, her cheeks rosy under her pale blush as she watched her girlfriend grab bowls out of a cabinet.

Lea thought Max would appreciate the cookies, since she knew he did most of the cooking for his dad and brothers. In the week since the beach party, he'd let her in a little more about "growing up Payton." He talked about his brothers a lot, to the point she felt like she knew them. But he never mentioned introducing her to them. That dug under her skin like a splinter. While Danica moaned about meeting Monica's parents, Lea was envious. Didn't Max want her involved in every aspect of his life?

Well, she'd beat him to it and surprise him, armed with cookies. His brothers and dad would have to like her if she had cookies.

"Hey, Lea, get over here. You're not getting out of helping," Monica called her over with a wink.

Lea measured the sugar while Danica softened the butter in short bursts in the microwave.

After the first batch of cookies were in, Lea's cell phone rang. She glanced at the caller ID. "Oh hey girls, it's my dad. I gotta—"

Monica swallowed a hunk of batter and waved her off. "Go, we'll make sure the cookies don't burn for the grease-monkey love of your life."

Lea shot her a thumbs-up and answered her phone. "Hey Dad."

"La-la," her dad's husky voice came over the line. "How are you?"

"Good, how are you and Mom?"

"Better than good," he said, his common answer making her smile. A clatter sounded from the kitchen, like a dropped cookie sheet, followed by a cackle of laughter.

"What was that?"

"I'm making cookies to take to Max at work and Danica and Monica are helping me bake them. I think they might have just ruined a batch."

More laughing from the kitchen.

"Well, I'm calling for another reason, which is not happy."

"Oh?" Lea sat up.

"I'm sure the university will be notifying the students soon, but I just heard on the news that there was another assault. And the witness reported seeing one of the assailants with a gun."

Lea sucked in her breath as ice slid down her spine. "No. Why?"

"I don't know. Some people don't have motives for the things they do and . . ."

"But this is horrible, Dad. Assaults are bad enough, but a gun? What are they thinking?"

"I don't know. But please warn your friends. No walking by yourself anytime, but especially at night."

Lea wanted to cry. She hated the level of fear that had been pervasive on campus since the first reports of the assaults. Bowler campus was known for its fun, carefree atmosphere. No one wanted to watch their back in fear of landing in the hospital.

It wasn't fair and it made her want to hurt someone. Preferably these jackasses. Armed jackasses.

"Thanks for letting me know, Dad. I'll give everyone a heads-up. I'm sure the campus will be sending e-mails out soon."

"I'm sure. Tell Danica hello for me and take care, sweetheart, okay?"

"I always do, Dad."

Danica and Monica looked up from a lip lock as Lea entered the kitchen. Their smiles dropped off when they saw her face. Danica skirted the counter and walked right to Lea. "What's wrong?" She grabbed Lea's shoulders and looked into her eyes. Lea realized Danica didn't have any contacts in today, and her gray eyes were clouded with concern.

"So, I'm sure the campus will let us know soon, but there was another assault. And apparently these dick-wads have stepped up their game. The victim reported a gun."

Monica gasped and Danica closed her eyes. Her fingers curled into claws, squeezing Lea's shoulders until Lea grunted from the pain. Danica's eyes flew open and she released Lea's shoulders. "If I get ahold of these guys—"

Lea shook her head. "You're going to get away how I taught you and cry for help."

"But—"

"Danica, do not stand your ground and try to beat up people with a gun!" Monica said, slamming her hand on the counter. "Why do you have to be so stubborn?"

Danica rounded on her girlfriend. "I'm not stubborn!"

Monica threw up her hands. "Denial isn't just a river in Egypt."

Danica's eyes narrowed. "Don't spout overused quotes at me, Mon."

"Then don't act like you can take on three guys with a gun, you idiot."

"Ladies!" Lea clapped and stood between them. "Stop fighting over this." She turned to Danica and pointed a finger at her chest. "You will avoid running into these guys at all costs, but if you do run into them, you will get away as fast as you can and call for help." She pointed to Monica. "And you, quit riling Danica up. Because you know if you ask her to walk, she's only going to run faster."

Monica clenched her jaw, then turned her attention back to the cooling cookies, arranging them needlessly on the foil lining the counter. "Excuse me for caring."

Danica sighed and stepped around Lea, then wrapped her arm around Monica's waist and rested her chin on the smaller girl's shoulder. Murmurs of apology followed before the two turned back to her.

"Sorry for yelling," Lea said. "This whole situation has me on edge."

Danica kept her arm around Monica's waist. "Me too," she said, as Monica nodded.

"So, we're all cool? Everyone's happy again?"

Danica smiled. "How about we get these cookies finished so you can surprise your man?"

Lea picked up a hunk of dough, rolled into a ball of cinnamon and sugar, then popped it into her mouth.

She grinned around the treat. "Okay."

Chapter 18

CAM TAPPED AWAY at his phone, booted feet propped up on the table of magazines in the shop's office.

"Will you get your feet off the table?" Max scowled. "People read those, you know."

Cam raised an eyebrow, tapped another minute on his phone, then shoved it into his pocket. "Oh yeah?" He leaned forward and grabbed a magazine off the table. "You get a lot of demands for . . ." He held up a coverless magazine and peered at the spine. "*Entertainment Weekly* from February of last year?"

"It's vintage," Max muttered.

Cam's truck was currently in the garage, getting inspected by Brent. Cam could have gone to a garage closer to campus but he said he'd rather give Max's family the money.

And family was the one thing that meant the most to Cam.

"How's your mom?" Max asked.

Cam's gaze shot to Max's face. He swallowed and ran his tongue over his teeth before answering. "Fine."

Cam had been raised an only child by a single mother. He'd joined the Air National Guard out of high school so he could afford school and wouldn't be a burden on his mom.

"Why'd you say it like that?" Max asked.

Cam tapped his thigh with the side of his thumb, a nervous gesture he had. "Just, money stuff. It's tight."

"Fuck, I'm sorry, man."

Cam shrugged but it was jerky and he hadn't met Max's gaze.

"Well, when you graduate and get a job, you can help, right? I mean . . ."

Cam's eyes swung to Max and his face hardened. "It's not that easy to find a job, Max. I can't pull one out of my ass."

Max frowned but held back his own temper. "I know that. What's with the attitude?"

Cam closed his eyes like he was in pain. "I'm not sure what to do. She needs help with the house and money. I want to be there for her but finding a job in my field in my shit-hole town is pretty much impossible. And I just . . . don't want to be back there. With . . . everything."

He looked out the window again and Max winced. He knew what it was like to feel like your future choices had been taken from you. Cam had fought and clawed, got his ass kicked in basic just to keep his options open. But his love of his mom warred with that.

"I'm sorry, man. If there's anything I can do . . ."

Cam waved his hand and let out a sigh, like he was ridding himself of the negative conversation.

"So what's up with you?" Cam asked. "Turning into Zuk?"

"What?"

Cam's lips curled into that-bad boy smile with the dimples, the one Kat said got him the ladies. "Lea. Am I the last man standing? Holding strong and single?"

Max shrugged. He didn't want to get into it with Cam. He didn't want to explain how he felt stronger because of Lea, that he'd found there was strength in being vulnerable.

He knew Cam didn't want to hear it. Because he'd been vulnerable once too, and he'd been burned.

"I'm okay with being hooked." Max shrugged.

Cam smiled knowingly.

Brent walked into the office and handed Cam his keys, letting him know his truck was parked in the lot, good to go for another year.

Cam thanked him and waved off to Max, letting him know he'd see him later that night. Cam had already paid, so Max waved back as Cam walked out the door.

Brent gave Max a nod and then walked back out in the garage to finish a tire rotation.

Max went back to filling out inspection paperwork, but his mind wandered.

He had done what Lea had asked. He'd thought more about talking to his dad about changing his major to something he actually wanted to do. The thought of confronting his dad made him break out in hives. But he couldn't imagine sitting in this office for the rest of his life. He couldn't imagine working for his father, having to see him every day. Would he turn into him eventually? A bitter, jaded man without a wife and with three boys who avoided him?

Max didn't want that for his life. He wanted to do something with purpose.

And it was time to let his dad know he'd met someone. Even if he no longer needed or cared about his dad's approval, he was still his dad. He deserved to know Max had something special in his life.

Because Max planned to bring her by to meet his Dad and brothers next weekend.

That made his palms sweat. Because none of them were couth. They'd lived without a woman in the household for too long. They let the belches and curses fly.

Max cringed. He'd have to somehow hint to his dad that vacuuming might be a nice thing to do every once in a while, too.

He glanced out into the garage. There was a lull in the work, so maybe he could talk to his father now. He couldn't wait until they got home and his father had a six-pack in him. That wouldn't end well for anyone.

The door opened and Brent walked in, his thick-soled boots clomping on the stained carpet.

Max scribbled some numbers on the sheet in front of him so it looked like he'd been working rather than daydreaming about his girlfriend and leaving the family business.

"Hey, can you call Mr. Walker and tell him his car is ready?" Brent asked.

Max nodded and grabbed the paperwork on top of his pile. Once he called the car owner to let him know he could pick up his car, he turned to Brent, who stood at the counter filling out some paperwork.

Max licked his lips and spoke before his brain could catch up with his mouth. "Did you ever think of doing anything else?"

Brent jerked his head up, the pen frozen over the paper. "What?"

Max wanted to grab his words back and shove them in his mouth until they puffed out his cheeks like a chipmunk. Brent had been a gear head for as long as Max could remember. He'd always wanted to work at a shop. Maybe not with dear old Dad, but no way in hell would Jack let him work for someone else.

"Never mind."

The pen clattered onto the glass countertop. "No, what do you mean? Not work here? Another shop?"

Max stared at his hands. "No, I mean, like, do something else—"

"Not work for Dad?" Brent asked the question like he'd probably ask, *Dogs can talk?*

Because it was a ludicrous for a Payton not to work at Payton Automotive.

Ludicrous, Max. You're an idiot.

"What the hell else would you do?"

Max told himself to stop talking but his mouth

flapped open despite his common sense telling it not to. "I was thinking maybe teach," he mumbled.

"Teach?" Brent squeaked, then started laughing. In that mean cackling way he had that Max hated.

"You? Teach? Max are you even allowed on school grounds anymore? Didn't you get caught painting a crooked pickle on the front doors of the middle school on senior skip day?"

"It was a dick," Max mumbled.

Brent ignored him. "You were every teacher's nightmare and you think you're a good role model for kids?"

He did think so. Because he knew all the tricks. He knew why kids acted out and acted like little assholes. Because he'd been one. And he could help them snap out of it. At least he thought so.

But Brent's sneer heated his face. If he couldn't even stand up to Brent, the least threatening of the entire Payton clan, how the hell was he going to eke out one word of this to the patriarch?

Brent spread out his arms. "Get used to this place, little bro. Because there's no way in hell you're leaving."

"Leaving what?" His dad's voice boomed across the office. He'd stepped in, Cal at his heels, and Max had been so absorbed in his conversation with Brent, he hadn't heard his father's heavy tread.

Brent shot him a smirk and then walked back into the garage, whistling like an asshole.

Max stared at his father, into those hard and cold slate-blue eyes. The same eyes both his brothers had. But not Max. He'd inherited his mother's eyes. And he wondered if that was the reason Jack hated him the most. Because he looked at Max and saw the wife who'd left him.

"Leaving what." This time it wasn't a question. It was a declaration. Or more like a challenge.

Max's chest felt tight and his head swam. He could do it right now, tell his dad he wanted to change his major. Tell him he was dating a girl who made him want to hold on to his dreams.

Those eyes bored into him and his dad took a step closer; his shadow thrown by the overnight bulb above his head fell over Max.

And he was an eight-year-old kid again. On beat-up skates, bulky pads, and an oversized jersey.

He'd just been elbowed in the face. His lip burned and he tasted iron on his tongue. The pain throbbed all over his face and the telltale prick behind his eyes told him tears were imminent. And his dad had grabbed him and shook him so badly, his skates scissored on the ice. "Who are you?" He'd boomed in Max's face.

"A Payton," he'd mumbled, his words muffled as his lip swelled.

"Right. And Paytons aren't whiners. Now get back out there."

And that was that. Paytons weren't whiners. They didn't cry. They played through the pain and did as they were told and what was expected of them.

Why couldn't he just be strong and accept his future?

LEA PICKED THE container of cookies off of the passenger seat and stepped out of her car.

The garage didn't look much different from any auto shop she'd ever been to. PAYTON AUTOMOTIVE in steel block letters hung above several garage bays. A sign in the front window advertised a free oil change with any state inspection.

She took a deep breath and smoothed her khaki coat down over her skinny jeans. She felt out of place here in the cracked parking lot, a little overdressed as her boots clicked on the pavement.

Max had said he'd introduce her to his brothers and dad eventually, so she didn't think he'd mind if she dropped by. She was tired of him stalling. Plus, she wanted to tell him about the escalating assaults. He often came to her apartment late at night and sometimes had to park several lots away.

A fluorescent Open sign buzzed as she swung open the door, a bell tinkling overhead.

She took one step inside and the door shut behind her, blocking the rush of cold air.

The first thing she saw was a man standing with his back to her. He was tall and broad shouldered, in stained jeans and massive boots, with unkept salt-and-pepper hair. Then he twisted at the waist to face her and she looked up into a face that would have frozen her in her tracks if she wasn't already frozen in place.

Cold gray-blue eyes squinted and lips thinned in his lined face. "We're full up."

What? "Excuse me?"

"Ain't got no time for your last-minute oil change or whatever you need, girl. You can head on down to Quick-Lube down the road and see if they're still open—"

"I—"

"Always the girls coming in last minute on a Saturday," he muttered.

She clutched the cookies tight to her chest, thinking this had been a horrible idea. A terrible mistake. This is what Max grew up with?

"Dad, Jesus," a familiar voice said from behind the boulder of a man and Lea closed her eyes, thinking this was going to be awkward for all of them.

When she opened her eyes, the boulder had moved and Max stared at her, eyes wide, mouth open, all color drained from his face.

Mulligan! She wanted to yell. Just, mulligan this whole scene. Do it over. With her back home. Eating cookies and watching lesbian romance movies with her roommate and her girlfriend. Forget this drive and forget this garage even existed. Forget this *man* existed, who somehow had swimmers intelligent enough to produce the man she l . . .

No, not that word.

Not now.

"I brought cookies," she mumbled and then felt her face flame. She brought cookies. The only word more silly than *cookies* was *cupcakes* and thank God she hadn't made those. And thank God she didn't actually say the word *snickerdoodle*. It would have been out of place in this office, with grime on the walls and stains on the carpet. Like a couch on a front lawn. Couches were meant to be inside, in living rooms. And words like cookies and cupcakes and snickerdoodles didn't belong around this hard shell of a man currently glancing between Max and Lea.

"Hey," Max finally said, his voice oddly low, like he was trying to lower it. He sounded like a prepubescent trying to talk like a man.

She'd never thought about how Max would act different around his dad. Around his brothers. A man shifted in the far corner and she glanced at him, quickly realizing that he must be one of Max's brothers.

It seemed ages ago when all she knew was the cocky, arrogant, rude Max. Because she'd finally seen the real one. The caring, funny, sincere, trusting Max.

It hadn't occurred to her that there could be a third Max.

This was so wrong.

"You two know each other?" Max's dad said. And Lea wanted to shout No! Because how many more Maxes she hadn't met yet were inside that one body?

Max cleared his throat. "She's friends with Kat."

That one sentence could have been a punch in her gut. She looked down to see if there was a fist slammed into her flesh. There was nothing there but the container of cookies, but she felt the punch all the same.

She was just Kat's friend? That's all he planned to introduce her as?

She steeled herself and met his eyes, daring him to not call her his girlfriend.

His eyes flickered. Something. But then it was quickly gone and this weird, impassive Max with a deep voice jerked his chin toward the boulder. "This is my dad."

She met his eyes and all she got out of him was a head bob.

What was with this family?

Her father hugged her. And knitted her socks. And called her La-La and brought her pie and held her when she cried.

This . . . this family she didn't understand. And every cell in her body told her this was how they always were. This wasn't some fluke.

And Max sat behind that desk, still as a stone, just like his father, staring her down.

She didn't belong.

Max's dad turned to his son and pitched his voice low. But she still heard every word in his low rumble. "Thought you wanted to break it off before she got too attached," he said. "Woman tip: cookies mean attached." And those two sentences were an uppercut. Right to the chin. Her head whirled. TKO.

She tried to think rationally despite the pain in her stomach and head. Max had told his father he planned to break up with her before she got too attached? Too attached? She was so attached she didn't know if she'd be able to leave this office without leaving half of her bleeding heart on the table covered with ripped and stained magazines.

So he was a liar. This is what happened when she trusted. She'd dropped her gloves, exposed her tender areas and he'd taken the shots.

Fine. He won. He could have the gold belt. She'd go home and lick her wounds and learn her lesson for next time.

"Excuse me," she mumbled, fumbling behind her for the door.

She wanted nothing to remember this weird, horrible moment by. She tossed the cookie container on a table covered in magazines. "You can have those," she said, avoiding eye contact with either man.

There was a whispered curse and a creak of a chair but she was already out the door, pushing against the wind. But she didn't feel it because her whole body felt numb.

And right before the door closed, she heard the deep rumble of the boulder. "Something wrong with her leg?"

And that's when the tears came. She felt those through the numbness, tracking in hot streams down her face. But she kept her head up.

They wouldn't see her fall.

They wouldn't see her stumble.

And they most certainly wouldn't see her cry.

Screw Max and his thousand personalities. He could live with them, because she was done with dating several guys at once.

She was halfway home before she realized never once had he even said her name.

Chapter 19

HIS DAD KEPT him late at the shop, like he knew Max was miserable and wanted to torture him more. Max wanted to throw a tire iron at him, scream about how he was done with this. Done with this garage and this life and everything that took him away from Lea.

He wanted to live his life for himself.

But he didn't. Because his sole focus now was getting back to Lea.

As soon as the garage was closed, Max ran to his truck and fired it up, wheels screeching as he took off toward Lea's apartment.

All the visitor spaces in her parking lot were taken and he slammed his hand against the steering wheel, waiting for his headlights to find an open space.

No dice.

He growled and wrenched his truck out of the parking lot, heading to the nearest lot, which was on campus.

He'd have to cut through, between a couple of dorms, but it didn't matter.

He parked his truck haphazardly, not caring he wasn't between the white lines, then took off across campus, shoulders hunched, hands shoved in his pockets.

Staring at his feet as they crunched on the cold ground, Max thought of what he'd say to Lea when he reached her apartment. If only she'd understood he'd done it to protect himself. And her.

He ran through lines in his head wondering if he was going to have to camp out at her door when she refused to open it.

Just as he was thinking maybe he should have gotten some flowers or something a blow hit him from behind.

He grew up with two older brothers. He knew what a punch from a fist felt like. And this wasn't a fist. This was something hard and cold, and pain laced through his scalp. His head rolled and he stumbled to one knee and a palm. He fought to keep his wits about him, shaking his head, pretending this was a hockey game and he'd been checked into the boards. He couldn't lose consciousness. He had to figure out what the hell was going on and how to get out of it.

Get up, Max. Get up and get that puck.

He struggled to his feet and arms immediately clamped around him, pinning his arms to his sides. He blinked blearily into the dark, head swimming from the blow.

"Hurry up and help me!" A muffled voice yelled by his ear. "He's a strong fucker!"

A strong fucker. He was a strong fucker, and big, yet right now he couldn't do a thing. He couldn't get out of the iron grip around him. He heard more footsteps.

This guy had backup. And that's when it finally hit him, like whatever that had been to the back of his head, that these were the guys. The ones who'd been preying on the campus and town.

The ones who hurt Nick.

"Stop struggling." That voice rasped in his ear, like gravel scraping open his skin.

The fear paralyzed him. He was fucked.

He'd been so focused on getting to Lea. To apologize, beg, whatever it took to get her back that he hadn't watched his six. He hadn't paid attention to shadows in the dark.

The footsteps grew closer. Murmuring voices.

Grunts sounded in his ear as he renewed his efforts, wiggling and squirming, trying to break free.

No luck. This guy had a vice grip around his middle.

He wanted to pound these guys into the ground. That's what his dad would do. That's what his dad would *want* him to do. Stay and fight and make them pay for all the pain and fear they'd inflicted in this community. For landing Nick in the hospital. For making Lea cry.

Lea.

And then her voice pounded in his brain, breaking through the pain fog like a beacon.

Create a diversion and get away.

He shook his head again. *Think, Max. Think.*

In this position, heel stomps didn't work. But grabbing this guy's junk would

His arms were pinned at his sides, but he slipped his right arm back. The guy stiffened and Max had his shot.

He took it.

He grabbed a hold of something he never wanted to touch ever again in his life and squeezed and yanked.

The arm prison around him dropped and a male howl sounded in his ears. Max slumped into a crouch.

The footsteps grew closer, and Max saw two figures materialize out of the dark in front of him.

He paused. He could turn around and kick this guy in the ribs. He could take on his two friends. Two against one wasn't so bad. He was a "strong fucker" after all.

But then Lea's voice again.

Life isn't a Jason Statham movie.

He knew where the emergency phones were and if he made it out from between these two dorms, he could reach one in seconds.

"Hey asshole!" Called one of the dark figures. "Oh shit, he got Ray—"

And Max didn't stay to hear the rest. He took off like a sprinter out of a starting block. His head pounded as he pumped his arms. He stumbled. That guy probably gave him a concussion, but he couldn't worry about that now.

His focus was getting to that phone under a bath of streetlight.

He tripped over the sidewalk, his depth perception fucked, and fell on his hands and knees again, this time knowing he tore open his jeans as gravel dug into his skin. But that pain was nothing compared to the pain in his head. He got back up and didn't stop running until he was right in front of the phone. His body slammed into the pole holding the call box, and he ripped the receiver off of its hook. As he raised it to his ear, he heard one ring and then, "Bowler police."

Relief washed over him. "The guys. The assaults. I'm Max Payton. They just attacked me and I got away. I hurt one of him, between Macon and Dorset dorms."

The voice was saying something in his ear but he couldn't concentrate because there was something trickling down his neck. Something warm and wet. What the . . .

He reached up with shaking fingers, realizing his whole body was trembling. And then the pads of his fingers touched something sticky. He drew his hand away and saw the red and smelled the iron. How . . .

The voice in his ear was more urgent now. But he couldn't make out the words. Something about staying put or . . .

He looked at the phone but it was no longer in his hand, it was dangling by its cord beside the box. His vision blurred, his head rolled, and the ground rushed up to meet him.

LEA IGNORED HER ringing phone for the third time. She didn't even look at the display. She figured it was Max, calling to officially end it.

And she didn't want to hear it because her gut still churned, and she was still too raw. She needed her wounds to heal, scab over, develop scar tissue because she needed protection from Max.

What did more scars matter? Inside and out. She matched now.

She heard the ringing of another phone out in the living room and hoped Max didn't start calling Danica, too, because she'd staple his balls to the wall.

She heard Danica's voice answer her phone, her murmurs too low to decipher even through their thin walls.

Then the volume of the TV stopped, Danica's voice rose higher. Lea thought maybe she should get out of bed and walk out there, take the phone from Danica and end it with Max once and for all.

Because Danica hadn't been amused by Lea's retelling of the scene at the shop. In fact, she'd been furious.

No one messed with Danica's people. And Max had just been dropped as one of Danica's "people" and shoved solidly into enemy territory.

There wasn't a gray area with Danica.

But then there was a crash. Followed by a curse. And then bare feet ran down the hall and Lea's bedroom door flew open, slamming back on its hinges.

Danica's face was white, her lit phone held out from her ear. "Lea," she gasped.

Lea raised to a sitting position, bracing her arms behind her. "What's going on? Are you okay?"

"It's Max," Danica whispered.

Lea frowned. "What's Max?"

Danica looked at her phone and Lea could hear a tinny male voice through the speaker. "I don't want to talk to him, Dan—"

"He was attacked."

Lea's body flushed numb. Like someone had stuck a needle in her spine and injected some serum right into her marrow.

The gun. She hadn't told him about the gun. And then that needle was yanked out and in its place was a bone-deep chill. She wrapped her arms around herself, in a lame attempt to warm up her body temperature, and rocked forward. "The gun. Oh shit, Danica, *the gun!*"

Danica nodded. Then slowly raised the phone to her ear. "I'm back, Stone."

Lea closed her eyes, not even wanting to hear the words, the words that despite her anger at Max, despite the fact that minutes ago the sound of Max's name had made her want to spit fire, were words she didn't want to hear.

Max with his arrogance and his eye-for-an-eye-justice bone. *Oh Max, what happened?*

Danica said, "Well keep us updated," and Lea raised her eyes because updates were good. Updates meant there was something to update. Updates meant there wasn't an end.

"How bad is it?" Lea whispered. She remembered Nick lying in the hospital bed. Swollen eyes. Casted arm.

And that was before these assholes armed themselves. She looked around for her trash can in case she needed to hurl.

The guilt was . . . overwhelming, thickening her blood in her veins. She clutched her chest as the pain splintered out from her heart into all her limbs. If only she'd calmed down, taken a minute to forget her anger and warn him about the gun. She knew he often came back to his town house Saturday nights. She knew and yet she'd let her emotions take over.

She'd lost control.

And she hurt Max.

Danica walked over and lifted up the covers, crawling into bed beside Lea. They sank down onto their sides, sharing a pillow. "Alec said Max's brother called him. Max is at the hospital. He was taken by ambulance when they found him collapsed at a campus emergency phone."

Campus? What the hell had he been doing on campus? His town house was in town.

Danica brushed Lea's bangs off of her forehead. "Lea, he was bleeding. From the head."

"Oh my God," Lea groaned, knowing the only reason she wasn't throwing up now was because her stomach was empty. "Was he shot? Was—"

Danica shook her head. "I'm sorry sweetie, but all Stone knows is that Max is alive." The *for now* hung in the air between them.

Lea yanked on her hair. "This is my fault, I—"

"What?" Danica gripped her wrist and tugged so Lea let go of her hair. "In what world is this your fault—"

"I didn't tell him about the gun—"

"It's not your fault they had a gun! Lea—"

"I know, but I should have told him!" Lea shouted, and Danica's face fell. Lea had never seen Danica cry, but now her face was flushed, her eyes wet.

"Honey . . ." Danica started.

And then Lea broke down in sobs. "I should have told him. He would have been more careful, then. I know it."

Danica grabbed Lea's head and tucked it under her chin. Lea nuzzled into her roommate's soft skin as tears soaked Danica's shirt.

"Even if you told him, this still could have happened . . . Max isn't always the most careful person. I think he thought he'd be untouchable to these guys . . ."

But Lea didn't believe that. Max would have listened to her. If she asked him to be careful, he would have.

Or . . . the Max she thought she knew. The one who took her on dream dates and sang karaoke and kissed her until she didn't know her name.

She had no idea which Max was real. And if she'd ever get back the Max she fell in love with.

So all Lea did was sob until she couldn't anymore, until her pillow was soaked and her body ached and until she fell asleep with Danica smoothing her hair.

Chapter 20

WHEN MAX WOKE up, he swore he had an axe embedded in his skull, splitting it in two. His palms and knees burned, and his whole body ached.

He remembered a little of the night before. Reclining in an ambulance, wheeled to a bed in the hospital. Poking and prodding and a thermometer in his mouth and a blood pressure cuff on his arm.

Nurses disturbing his precious REM sleep throughout the night to complete the same routine over and over again. He'd tried to bribe one to leave him alone and she'd rolled her eyes at him.

He guessed his charm didn't work with a head injury.

Max reached up and gingerly prodded his head, feeling a bandage behind his right ear. It was sore as shit and he winced and dropped his arm back to the bed, noticing the additional bandages on his hands.

He wore only a hospital gown and other than that, he

was naked. His knees and palms were bandaged, probably where he fell, and his arms were bruised. He wiggled his toes under the thin hospital sheet.

His room was small, with a couple of chairs and a TV bolted to the wall across from him.

Fumbling for the remote to the bed, he raised it to a sitting position so he could check out his surroundings.

A snuffled sound drew his attention. Cal was slumped on a chair beside the bed, snoring softly. His boots were untied, his fly was down and his shirt wasn't buttoned right. A baseball cap was pulled down over his eyes, arms crossed over his broad chest.

"C—" Max said, then swallowed thickly around his dry, swollen tongue. He tried again. "Ca-al." The word was rough and broken, the two syllables snagging on the sandpaper of his tongue.

Another snuffle, then blinking slate-gray eyes appeared below the brim of the cap.

Cal gasped awake, bolting upright on unsteady legs like a newborn colt. "Bro." He gripped Max's chin in the palm of his calloused hand. He didn't say another word, just searched Max's face and roamed his eyes over Max's body.

"Cal." Max said again. This time one syllable. "I'm thirsty."

Cal nodded abruptly and pressed the nurse button on the bed remote. A male voice answered seconds later. "Can I help you?"

"He wants water," Cal said bluntly.

A pause. "I'll be there in a minute." Then a click.

Max squinted at Cal. Which made his head throb more so he quit doing it. "You couldn't say please?"

"You're thirsty. We need water." Cal said, as if that explained his rudeness.

Max sighed.

Cal pulled the chair over beside the bed and sat down. "How ya feeling?"

"Like shit."

"You look like shit."

"You're a ray of sunshine. They ask you to visit the pediatric wing to give a pep talk?"

Cal shot him the finger, and Max laughed, then winced and clenched his jaw as pain pierced his skull and ripped down his spine. "Fuck, don't make me laugh," he said through gritted teeth.

Cal looked down and rubbed his hands together. "Good to hear you laugh," he said quietly.

Max rested his head on the mattress behind him and rolled to look at Cal to his left, fortunately on the side without his bandage. "What?"

Cal looked up but his eyes skittered around the room. His jaw ticked before he finally locked eyes with Max. "They had a gun."

"A gun?"

Cal didn't answer.

Max fingered the bandage behind his ear again. "I thought . . . I thought it was just a crowbar or a pipe or something. Those fuckers had a *gun*?"

Cal nodded.

"When the hell did these guys get a gun? I don't remember that on any of the news reports."

Cal sighed. "They apparently attacked someone the night before your attack. The victim reported seeing a gun. It hit the news while we were working, and the university e-mailed late that afternoon." Cal shrugged.

"Do they know you're supposed to shoot it, not fucking whack people in the head with it?"

"Not. Funny."

"I'm just saying—"

Cal's eyes flashed. "We just got a call that said they found you bleeding from the head by the campus phone. I mean, what the fuck, Max? Dad went into shut-down mode, and Brent wouldn't stop rambling. I almost had to thunk their skulls together to get them to focus and get in the fucking car to come to the hospital."

"Are they here?"

"Brent's in the cafeteria eating. Because that's all Brent ever does. And Dad went home to get you some clothes. You had blood on the ones you wore here and they had to cut the shirt off of you.

"They cut my shirt?" Max whined.

"Bro, they didn't want to move your head too much." Cal said.

That made Max more upset than anything. This would require mourning. He'd been wearing his special Cross Keys bowling shirt he got last year at Kat's surprise birthday party. It was the only time he could get away with wearing a graphic that looked as close to a cock and balls as possible. "Damn it, I'm gonna need Kat to get me a new one."

"That shirt was stupid," Brent said.

Max turned his head and ignored the pain because his brother had just insulted his favorite shirt. "No, it wasn't. All you wear is flannel. Don't try to talk to me about clothes."

"I like my flannel shirts!"

"Just saying—"

"Can we not argue about this right now?"

Max chewed his lip and fell silent, his thoughts drifting to the stress his hospital stay would place on his family. But it's not like the Paytons didn't know hospitals. Or injuries. "Look, I'm okay. I mean, we got hurt as kids all the time, I don't—"

Cal talked over him. "This isn't a fucking game, Max. You got jumped."

Max bristled. "You think I don't know that? I'm the one who got hit in the head. I'm the one who ran like a fucking bat out of hell to get away from those punks."

Cal shook his head and smoothed the corner of the blanket on the bed. "They got 'em."

Max relaxed his shoulders. "What?"

Cal met his eyes. "The police. There was a cruiser driving nearby when you called. So they radioed him to swing by and got all three guys."

Max turned his head and stared at the white cinder-block wall in front of him, a riot of emotions curling in his stomach like smoke.

Part of him regretted the thought of those guys sitting in a cell now, because Max had wanted them to pay for the pain they gave to others with pain of their own. Instead, he sat in a hospital bed. He was angry.

But at the same time, he was relieved. He was proud. Because his actions were the reason those guys would hopefully pay—legally—for what they did.

He straightened his spine. "I did that."

Cal looked at him silently.

"I did that," Max said again. "I got away, I called the cops and now those fuckers are in cuffs."

Cal's smile was slow, but it ended with a blindingly white grin. He reached out and squeezed Max's shoulder. "You did. Proud of you, bro."

Cal had always been the serious brother. The one with the common sense, always thinking of the family unit. The one who held them together when Dad didn't.

So his approval flushed through Max like a breath of fresh air. "Thanks," he whispered.

The door of his room swung open and the nurse walked in with styrofoam cup of water and a straw.

He handed Max a cup, and he sucked down the water greedily, despite the nurse's commands to sip slowly. Fuck that.

The nurse—Jeremy—then took his vital signs and told him a doctor would be in soon. Max would need an MRI to check for any swelling in his brain, which is why they'd kept him overnight. Then Jeremy left him alone with his brother.

Cal shifted in chair. "Why were you on campus?"

"Huh?"

Cal squinted. "You were attacked on campus and called from an emergency phone near a dorm."

"What are you, a cop?"

"Just answer me."

Max tensed and immediately regretted it as his head throbbed and muscles screamed. The whole reason he was in the hospital now was because he didn't open his mouth when it mattered.

He didn't stand up and be strong when it mattered.

He'd kept silent and he hurt Lea. Probably beyond repair.

It'd been a dumbass idea to try to chase after her last night. He should have called her or something rather than racing across campus at dark o'clock only to get his ass jumped.

Did she know? Did she care?

She was the reason he got away. She'd given him that strength and that knowledge.

And now it was time to be honest.

"I was on my way to see Lea."

"Who's Lea?"

"My . . . well, she was my girlfriend." Max moved his toes under the sheet. "I think she's pretty pissed at me right now but—"

"That was her."

Max looked up. "What?"

"That was her. At the shop. The one Dad was a dick to."

Max hated when Cal did this all-knowing omniscient shit. "How do you know that?"

Cal snorted. "Maybe Dad's too old to see it but I could tell right away something was up between you. I'm not an idiot."

"Yeah, well—"

"You sure fucked that one up, then." Cal leaned back and linked his hands behind his head.

Max glared. "A little support maybe?"

Cal shrugged. "You didn't even say her name."

Max opened his mouth and then shut it. Shit. He hadn't. He hadn't even said her name. She'd stood in that shop with the container of cookies clutched to her chest, chin raised at his bear of a father, not backing down.

And Max hadn't even acknowledged he knew her name. That was kind of fucked up.

"Prepare to grovel," Cal said.

"Again, are you rubbing this in? Enjoying it? I have a massive head wound because I got pistol-whipped. Would it kill you to be nice to me?"

Cal smiled, but then as quickly as it came, it faded. He brought his hands down and fisted them at his sides. "I'm joking with you because I'm glad I can."

Max let his anger fade. "Yeah, okay. I can deal with that."

Cal nodded and then rose. "Gonna go get Dad and Brent, okay?"

Max nodded. Cal made it to the door and placed his hand on the lever, but he didn't move.

"Cal?"

A pause, and then he twisted just at the hip. "Brent told me what you said to him. And . . . you need to get honest with yourself. And then you need to get honest with Dad. All right?"

Brent and his fucking big mouth. "But—"

Cal shook his head. "Step up, Max. You're not weak just because you don't wanna do what's expected of you."

And with that, he jammed the lever down and slipped out the door.

THE BOOK SPINES usually felt soothing in her hands, the familiar letters and numbers making her feel at home.

But this morning her leg hurt and her head ached and her eyes were raw.

She'd almost stayed home from work but then thought that lying in bed and wallowing wasn't such a good idea. So she was here. Distracted.

Out of her mind with worry.

She'd woken up to an empty bed. Alec hadn't called again before she had to drag her carcass out of bed to get to the library on time for her shift.

Despite everything, she wanted to be at the hospital. She needed to see for herself that Max was okay. But she had to work before visiting hours started and she didn't know if Max could even have visitors right now.

She shelved another book with a sigh. Then growled at herself when she had to pull it back out and reshelve it because apparently she didn't know the difference between a three and a five.

Stupid curly numbers.

"Lea," a voice breathed behind her, and she whirled around to see Alec standing behind her, hands in his pockets, hair unkempt. His eyes were red behind his glasses.

"Alec?" His name a question on her lips, because she wanted to hear news. That was it, news about Max.

"He's okay."

She closed her eyes and gripped the book in her hands so hard that her fingernails cut grooves into the soft leather binding.

"Oh, Lea." And then he was in her space and she was in his arms. She breathed him in, smelling soap and hair product and leather jacket and everything that was Alec.

But he wasn't Max. Only Max got to wear the stains of her mascara-laced tears on his shirt like a souvenir.

She let Alec hold her because she appreciated the warmth and the comfort of his hand moving up and down her spine. When he stepped back, he gripped her shoulders and bent his head so he could look in her eyes. "I didn't get a chance to talk to him. His brother Cal called me and told me Max was sleeping. But he'd been awake and talking. And made a couple of jokes, so we got our Max back.

Which Max? she wanted to ask, but instead she whispered, "Okay."

Alec glanced at his watch. "You wanna hear what happened from me or wait to talk to Max?"

Dread dripped down her spine like acid. Alec didn't know. He didn't know about what had happened at the garage. About how Max had treated her. He didn't know about how she'd failed Max by not telling him about the gun.

So she ignored the question, glad they were in a secluded alcove in the library. "How bad is he?"

Alec ran his fingers through his hair, a gesture she'd never really seen him use. "He doesn't have a lot of injuries, just a rather serious one to his head—"

Head injury. That tap controlling the acid burning down her spine opened wider.

"—but they are monitoring him and the swelling is going down, so everyone is optimistic."

She gritted her teeth. "And how did he get the injury to his head?"

Alec blinked. "Oh, right, well apparently these assholes decided to step up their game and found a gun. One guy came up behind him and hit him with it. Cal told me the doctors were surprised he didn't lose consciousness with the blow. It wasn't until he was on the phone with dispatch that he went down. He had on his favorite shirt—that stupid bowling one—and they had to cut it off, so he's been bitching about it."

She sucked in a breath. Relief warred with guilt. They'd used it on him. They'd smashed a gun on Max's head. He would have had blood in his beautiful, thick hair. And on his clothes. And . . .

"Why was he on campus?" The words left her mouth as soon as they entered her brain, like there'd been no filter.

Alec frowned. "What do you mean? He parked in the campus lot and was coming to see you, wasn't he? Why else would he have been between Macon and Dorset?"

Lea reached out for a shelf. Her knees threatened to give out. This is what happened when she trusted. She got hurt and she let other people get hurt.

None of this would have happened if she'd kept her distance. And with that guilt came anger. Now that she knew he was okay, that anger was directed at Max. Because he was the one who'd flayed her open, then walked away so she now writhed in agony.

"We . . . we're not together. I'm not sure why he was on his way to see me."

Alec stared, then his face twisted in confusion. "Come again?"

She straightened her spine. "We saw each other for a couple of weeks but I went to see him at his shop and he made it clear in front of his dad and his brothers that I'm not welcome in that part of his life. That he only let me get to know one version of Max. And that's not okay with me."

Alec stared at her, blinking his pale green eyes behind his frames. "Wait, I need an explanation here, because—"

"There's nothing to explain—"

"But Max's family—"

"I know!" she shouted, then lowered her voice. "I know his dad is . . . whatever he is . . . but at least he was honest, letting me know Max planned to break up with me."

Alec's eyes widened. "What? He was on his way to talk—"

"Or break up with me—"

"No. No, Lea. You gotta believe he cares about you. You have to let him explain—"

"There's nothing to explain. Because I left before I could tell him that those guys had been reported as armed. I forgot. And that's on me." Her voice cracked at the end, and she looked away, unwilling to meet Alec's eyes.

"Lea."

She shook her head, but Alec wasn't going away quietly.

"You can't possibly blame yourself for that."

She pursed her lips and still refused to look at him, letting her eyes drift down the long shelf of books. She saw one spine upside down and she glared at it, her fingers itching to fix it.

But then Alec stepped into her line of vision, forcing her to stare at the zipper on his leather jacket or up into his eyes.

She chose the zipper.

"Lea, no one could have predicted those guys would have been there. But do you know how he got away?"

The zipper blurred a little and she raised her eyes to Alec's. Max had gotten away, that's how he'd reached the phones . . .

"He did what you taught him. He got away and he didn't stay and fight and he called for help. And Lea, because of that, the police got all three guys. They're in jail now."

Her mouth dropped open as warmth surged through her body, healing the damage caused by that acidic drip of dread. "He . . . he did?"

Alec's jaw clench and he took a step back. "Yep, he did. So he might have fucked up at the shop, I get that. But he was thinking of you when those guys attacked him. So before you write him off, remember that."

And that was Alec's parting shot, because he turned on his heel and walked away.

Chapter 21

LEA SAT ON her bed, fingered the neckline of the T-shirt she'd just driven a round-trip of three hours to purchase.

For a boy.

A boy who infuriated her, yet still held her heart.

A boy who sat in a hospital bed with a head wound because he'd done the right thing. The hero thing.

After talking with Alec, she asked her coworker at the library to cover for her and left early to buy him a new shirt. The bowling pin and balls on it looked . . . well . . . rather phallic and Max laughed every time he put it on.

And now she sat on her bed, paralyzed, staring at the clock as the time wound closer to the end of visiting hours.

He'd been on his way to her apartment for closure, she was sure. And so she'd provide her own closure. The shirt would be her parting gift.

Lea heard a knock at the door. Out in the living room,

Danica's voice mixed with a male one and Lea assumed Alec had come over to study or something.

But then heavy footsteps sounded down the hallway and stopped outside her door.

Lea looked up. Nick stood in the doorway. He'd recently gotten his cast off and the only remnant of his run-in with the assaulters was a small scar on his chin.

She smiled weakly at him as he sat down beside her on the bed and took the shirt from her hands. "What's this?"

"A shirt."

"No shit, Sherlock. Looks a little big for you, though."

She bit her lip and looked at him from under her lashes.

His eyes softened. "For him?"

She took it back and ran her fingers over the lettering. "Alec said they cut his other one off. Blood and stuff."

"So you drove an hour and a half away to get him a new T-shirt?"

She'd called him on her way to work that morning, bright and early and hysterical. She'd told him about what happened, and texted him later when she found out Max was okay.

"So you're heading in to visit?"

She nodded.

"I hope you're going to give him a chance to explain."

Her body felt loose and fuzzy, like it was stuffed full of cotton balls. She was exhausted. "Nick, you weren't there. You didn't hear what his dad said. You didn't see me walk to my car, alone. Max didn't come after me. Or call me."

Nick shook his head. "Look, I'm not saying any of that

didn't happen. I just think there's more to it than that. We all saw how into you Max was."

"Oh, so now you're a Max apologist," she hissed.

His jaw ticked. "You're just being stubborn."

"You're not my dad, Nick."

"No, I'm not, but I'm family. And I'm telling you that you're so fucking scared to trust again that it's crippling you from having a real emotional connection with new people."

She stood up and rounded on him as he rose to face off with her. "Because when I let someone else have control, I get hurt. *Other* people get hurt."

His eyes widened. "Wait, what?"

She let her eyelids droop and hung her head, pissed at herself for saying what she had. It'd been fine all tucked inside, but Nick had rubbed and rubbed and rubbed the bottle until she let out the genie of fury.

"Max did get hurt—"

"No, no no no." Nick took a step closer. "I'm going to need you to back up. We're not talking about Max here. What are we talking about?"

Her eyes dipped to his wrist, the one he'd broken in the accident, and he must have caught it, because he sighed. "You can't be serious."

She bristled. "I should have known—"

"Are you carrying around guilt for that? Seriously? You were thirteen, Lea. Thirteen years old."

Her eyes pricked. "But I was old enough—"

"The only one responsible for what happened to us was Trent's mom. That it's. She's the only one. She got behind the wheel impaired and ran the red light. I wasn't even hurt that badly!"

"But you were hurt!"

Nick ran his fingers through his hair and tugged. "I was, okay. And so were you. But none of that was your fault."

"But Max had been—"

"Lea, you really need to let go. You're not so all powerful that you can control everything around you. Shit happens. And if you blame yourself when something bad happens to someone you care about, you're going to be buried under guilt. For no reason."

His words penetrated through the small crack in the pile of guilt remaining. Like a blinding ray of sun, she blinked at it, wondering how it had gotten this bad—when she had let this all pile up so she could barely see out.

Nick swiped the shirt off the bed where she'd dropped it and draped it over her shoulder. It was stiff and had that not-yet-washed cotton smell. "And once you let go of thinking you're responsible for everyone else, maybe then you'll be able to trust someone with your heart."

"I did trust Max," she whispered.

"I know you did. And I know he let you down. But I think you owe him a chance to explain."

He kissed her forehead, waved good-bye and she watched the second man she disappointed that day walk out of her room.

She didn't know what her options were. She couldn't

move forward. And she couldn't go back. Because she'd let Max in, she'd learned what it was like to trust someone. To have someone.

But what if he only wanted closure?

THIS TIME THERE was no dirty blanket. There was no soft, deep voice or guiding supportive hand on her lower back.

There were no deep brown eyes in the soft light of the street lamp.

There was only Lea. And the shirt in a white-knuckled grip as she rode the elevator to the same floor Nick had been on.

That felt like ages ago, when it had only been several weeks? A month? She shifted her weight and eyed the glowing numbers above the metal doors.

The elevator reached her floor and she stepped out, studying the plaques on the wall to make her way to Max's room, which she'd learned from the help desk in the lobby.

When she reached his door, she stopped in front of it, staring at the sliver of light peeking out from the crack in the opened door.

She closed her eyes, inhaled through her nose and blew it out of the mouth. Once. Twice.

She could do this. She'd visited Nick in the hospital and she hadn't broken down.

Max was strong. He was tough.

He was okay.

She raised her hand, ignoring the trembling limb, and pushed gently on the door.

It opened and she stepped inside the small room.

Her eyes took in the prone figure on the bed, the only other person in the room besides her.

Lea gripped the shirt in both hands and brought it up to her chest, like a shield, and walked forward.

Seeing Nick in the hospital hurt her because she loved him like a brother.

But seeing Max? She loved him with a bone-deep ache, she now recognized, because the sight of him in a hospital bed, injured, buckled her knees. She sank into a chair that fortunately had been placed beside the bed and breathed deeply, blinking back tears.

Max was asleep, his face slack. He looked so young without the cocky smirk and squinted eyes. In sleep, he was almost boyish, those beautiful eyes hidden from view, his long, thick, dark lashes resting on his cheeks.

He lay on his back, shirtless, with the thin blanket twisted around his hips, and that made her smile through her tears. She imagined him bitching about wearing a gown, teasing the nurses about showing his ass.

She placed a shaking hand on the bed and leaned closer. There was a bandage behind his ear and bandages on his hands. Bruises darkened his face, highlighted with abrasions.

When the tears threatened again, she dropped her eyes to his chest and watched his chest rise and fall.

Inhale. Exhale.

Inhale. Exhale.

He was breathing. He was okay.

She ran a finger down that vein on his bicep, the pulsing of blood a physical reassurance he was alive.

She wanted to rest her head on his chest and listen to the beat of his heart until it was the only rhythm she could hear, until she heard it in every song.

She licked her lips and opened her mouth, words . . . some words on the tip of her tongue.

But nothing came out and she looked at the shirt, now a wrinkled mess in her lap. She unfolded it and laid it flat on her knees, smoothing out the creases, picking a piece of lint off the sleeve.

What would he say if he woke up? Would he thank her for the shirt and for the good time? Would he seek closure?

Movement drew her eyes back to the bed. Max had shifted; his head rolled toward her, eyes blurry and half open. "Who . . . ?"

His gravelly voice wrapped around her heart and squeezed.

Max's eyes drifted shut again and his face twitched, like he was fighting sleep or the drugs, whatever was pulling him under.

She leaned forward, needing to touch him now. She cupped his cheek and brushed a thumb along the corner of his mouth. His skin was hot, the stubble on his cheek a welcome sensation on her palm.

"Max," she whispered.

His eyes fluttered again and his mouth opened.

Deep voices outside the open door drew her attention. She whipped her head around because she recognized that one voice.

Max's father.

She looked back down at Max, whose eyes had closed again, but his hands grasped the sheet, like he was reaching for something.

The voices drew closer and even though every part of her body wanted to stay in that chair with Max, listening to the beat of his heart and feeling the echo in her own veins, her head took over. Lea pulled her hand away from his face, recognizing this would most likely be the last time she touched Max.

She shoved the shirt in his grasping hand and with a quick peck on his forehead, she hopped up from the chair and slid behind the door.

Seconds later Max's father walked in with another man, who she assumed to be one of Max's brothers.

With their backs turned, she slipped out from behind the door and trotted down the hallway to the elevators.

She stabbed the DOWN button once. Then double-stabbed it. And then smashed her palm on it repeatedly, wanted to get out of this hospital and away from Max's dad and away from the feeling that she was going in the exact opposite direction she should be.

She looked up at the display, saw the elevators were at the stupid basement and huffed.

But when she tried to resume her assault on the elevator button, a hand covered up her plastic victim.

She looked up and froze.

Because his face sent her brain mixed signals. He had those slate-gray eyes of Max's father, but he had Max's nose and mouth.

He was a little shorter than Max but no less attractive. And her feet felt rooted to the floor as his gaze took her in.

She tried to hide her recognition, because while he must be one of Max's brothers, he couldn't know who she was. Lea cleared her throat. "Sorry," she mumbled.

He took his palm off the button and leaned back on the wall, arms crossed over his chest. "So you're Lea."

What? "How do you—?"

"I was at the shop yesterday."

She flashed back and remembered another man standing in the garage office while her relationship crumbled around her.

"I'm Cal. The oldest." His voice was so like Max's, not enunciating the *t* in *oldest*.

She clenched her fists and raised her chin. "Well, you know who I am, then."

His eyes drifted behind her and then met her eyes again. "You visit Max?"

She swallowed. "He was sleeping."

Those icy eyes narrowed. "So he didn't know you were there?"

She shook her head. "I don't think so. He kind of woke up but . . . he didn't seem to know what was going on. And I left when I heard . . ."

Cal closed his eyes and took a deep breath. When he opened them, he looked pained. "Look, my dad—"

Saved by the bell. The doors dinged open and she quickly slid inside. She didn't want to hear him make excuses or explain how she couldn't be with Max. She knew.

She jabbed the CLOSE DOOR button, but Cal slapped a hand on the elevator doors so they sprung back open. "Lea—"

"I'm sorry, I need to go. Please let the doors close." Her voice cracked. Oh God, she was going to cry. In front of Max's brother.

He seemed to fumble with words. "Do you want me to tell him you were here?"

Did she want Max to know? She jabbed the CLOSE DOOR button again and met Cal's eyes. "Do what you need to do."

The doors slid closed, and then the tears flowed. Was getting closure supposed to feel this painful?

Chapter 22

VOICES FILTERED IN through the haze of sleep and pain. He searched for that musical voice, the one he wanted to hear more than any others.

He swore he felt the touch, heard his name from those beautiful lips. But when he blinked awake, all he heard was a football game on TV. His dad and Brent faced away from him, drinking coffee and watching the game. Cal sat in the chair beside him, reading a magazine.

Max's one hand rested on the thin, scratchy hospital blanket but the other hand gripped something soft.

He blinked and raised his hand. Wrinkled fabric fell to his chest and he frowned.

Cal leaned over, grabbed it and unfurled it.

Max's eyes widened. It was a Cross Keys bowling shirt. Max reached out and grabbed it. He brushed his hands over the fabric and the smell of coconuts overwhelmed the cotton smell.

Lea. He hadn't imagined her voice after all.

He raised his eyes to Cal's. "She was here." He didn't phrase it as a question because he knew. It was her scent on the shirt and the tingle on his cheek where she'd cupped his face and the sound of his name echoing in his ears in her musical voice.

She had come.

Despite everything that had happened, she'd cared enough to visit and buy him a new shirt. A shirt she hated and rolled her eyes at whenever he wore it.

She cared.

His whole body flushed hot. He had a chance.

"Hey." Max's father stood at the end of the bed, drawing his attention away from the shirt. "How's the head?"

Max was too tired to act macho. "Hurts like a bitch."

His dad blinked at him, his gaze lingering on the bandage Max was sure was visible behind his ear. But something else worked behind those cold eyes, something Max couldn't read. And his dad's body language was all wrong. He was always tense, but confident. And now his posture radiated an odd anxiety.

"They had a gun," his dad said. The word *gun* said with so much venom, it hit Max in the chest like a bullet. "They whipped my kid with a *gun.*"

His tone was all wrong. His words were all wrong. Max couldn't remember the last time his father even acknowledged Max was his kid. Or had ever been a kid. He was always supposed to be a man.

But he kept talking, his eyes burning into Max. "You

didn't stay and fight. Always told you never back down until the whistle. But you ran and called for help."

It was a statement of fact, and for once, Max couldn't determine the meaning behind the words. Was he ashamed of Max? Cal stiffened beside him and Brent came to his feet, standing on the other side of Max's bed, his gaze darting between Max and his father.

They were a triangle of Paytons, Max's father at the end of the bed and his sons making up the base.

Max remembered his dad's words, that he'd take on all three guys. That he'd stand his ground.

Life isn't a Jason Statham movie.

And this time, Max spoke up. "It wasn't a game, Dad. There was no ref. There was no whistle. I—"

"*I know that!*" his father roared, the sudden emotion like a blast of hurricane-force winds, rocking all three of his sons back. Then, like his shout had weakened him he sank into the chair at the end of the bed, rested his elbows on his knees and thunked his head in his hands.

Max had never seen his dad in this position. The man before him now was a stranger. A stranger who radiated uncertainty and maybe a little bit of regret.

Brent sank down onto the bed beside Max and they all stared at the hunched broad shoulders of their father.

Finally, Cal cleared his throat. "Dad?"

He raised his head and those eyes were right on Max. "You did the right thing."

Max sucked in those words on a sharp inhale and then held them there, letting them swirl around in his head, pump through his veins and feed his body, because he didn't know if he'd ever hear them again in his father's voice. When he needed to breath again, he exhaled roughly. But those words, he'd kept them. They weren't escaping.

"Dad—"

The big man shook his head. "They had a gun." He repeated again. This time drawing out the word on a groan. Max bit his lip so he didn't talk as his father continued. "Thought I'd been teaching you boys the right thing all this time. I thought fighting, eye for an eye, was right but . . ." He closed his eyes slowly and then popped them back open, zeroing in on that bandage on Max's head. "They coulda killed ya."

They could have. Max knew that. They hadn't killed anyone yet, and they might not have wanted to. But accidents happened. Fingers slipped. Bullets hit flesh.

His dad shook his head, visibly shuddering. This wasn't the response Max expected. He thought he'd be called a coward. He thought he'd be told to get out of bed and take it like a man.

He hadn't his father to practically break down at the foot of his bed while all three sons watched.

As much as he told himself that he hated his father, he didn't. It was his dad who'd raised him with his brothers when his mother bailed. Sure, he bitched but he did it. He kept them in a house and fed and clothed.

And he'd tried.

That was better than what Jill did.

Jill bailed. Jack and Jill went up the hill but only Jack

came back to take care of his family. His dad wasn't a quitter in things that mattered. He just had to know when quitting was the smart thing to do.

Brent's eyes were wide and Cal gripped the sheet near Max's hip with white knuckles. Max took a deep breath. "Well, they didn't, Dad. I'm here. I'll be okay."

He hoped, at least. His head hurt but he was alive and he remembered everything and knew the year and the president so it couldn't be too bad.

His dad nodded toward the shirt. "What's that?"

Max folded the shirt carefully on his lap. "My girlfriend brought me a shirt."

"Girlfriend?"

Max raised his eyes. "The girl who came into the shop last night. The one you were an asshole to? Yeah, that's Lea."

His dad frowned. "Why didn't you say anything?"

Max shook his head. "I was an idiot. She surprised me, and then you brought up the lie I told you, about how it was just a one-time thing. And I froze." Max took a deep breath. "I was on my way to apologize to her when I got jumped. I care about her and I'm a lot in love with her and now I feel like I have at least a slim chance of getting her back if she cared enough to visit me."

Max's dad rubbed his palms together. "And her injury . . ."

"Childhood car accident."

He nodded. "I guess I owe her an apology then, too."

Max ran his tongue over his teeth. "Yep, I think you do."

"I can do that," he said quietly.

THE NEXT MORNING, Jeremy woke up Max, telling him it was time for his MRI. He helped Max into a wheelchair, and Max let him because no one was around to make fun of him for being a baby.

The MRI showed he still had some swelling in his brain. And for a split second, Max wanted to go give those fuckers some swelling in their brains. The cops had talked to him yesterday, asking him questions and letting him know about the charges against the three criminals. So that thought calmed him down. Jeremy let him eat, and Max fell asleep again.

He woke up on his own this time, and his dad was beside him, elbow propped on the arm of his chair, chin in his hand, watching Sports Center.

"Dad," Max said.

He jerked his head up and then grabbed a cup of water off of Max's side table. "Thirsty?"

Max nodded and took the proffered cup. "How long have you been here?"

His dad shrugged. "Hour? Two. I think I fell asleep for a little."

"It's quiet here during the day."

"Yeah, it's not the maternity ward. Loud as shit there."

Max shifted to face his father. "Yeah?"

His dad kept his eyes on the TV. "Cal and Brent both had colic, so the hospital stays were a blur of screaming. But you . . ." he cleared his throat, "you were a really good baby. Slept well, ate well. Being in the hospital with you was like a vacation."

"Really?" He never heard much about when he was a

kid. His mom had left shortly after and it always seemed like his dad blocked out that part of his life.

"Yeah, I let your mother sleep because she was always so tired from the boys and . . . you slept in my arms on the pullout couch in the room."

"I slept on you?"

His dad looked at him. "You slept the best on me. Your mother said she thought I made you feel more secure than when she held you."

How had he gone twenty-two years and never heard any of this?

His dad waved his hand. "Good thing, because when she left you didn't seem too bothered by it. As long as I was there." He sighed. "You got really dependent on me. So I tried to break you of that."

Max never remembered feeling dependent on his father. But looking back, he'd always felt safe.

So if his father didn't want him to feel dependent on him anymore, then it was time to break free, wasn't it? Time to be honest.

All this time he'd thought his desire for something different for his future meant he was weak. That if he could just buckle down and stay strong, stay the course his father had set for the family, that he'd be rewarded.

Then he'd be a real man.

But now, every throb of his head was like a lighthouse beacon, shining into the recesses of his heart.

His dream of teaching, of coaching, of making a difference in people's lives in the way he wanted to wasn't a weakness. It was only weak if he didn't stick up for himself.

And as he gazed at his father, sitting beside his bed with his arms crossed over his chest, he knew he was done being weak.

Because the longer he suppressed himself, the more he'd atrophy, until who knew how much Max would actually be left.

If his dad truly wanted Max to be an independent man, then this was the right decision.

"I don't want to work at the garage after I graduate," he said.

His dad jerked his head toward him, then moved the chair so it faced the bed rather than the TV. "What did you say?"

"I want to change my major. I want to teach physical education and coach."

His dad was eerily still. Max braced himself because his dad definitely had a "calm before the storm" mood. Or more like the eye of the storm. Because no matter which way you turned, you hit the swirl of temper.

"I'm sorry, Dad. I'm just being honest," he whispered.

Slowly, his dad ran his lips over his teeth and studied his hands. Full of callouses and grease permanently worked into his nail beds. His whole body showed a life of hard work. Six days a week. Sunup to sundown.

"What do you want to coach?"

Okay, so he wasn't yelling. So far, so good. His dad didn't give two shits about creating a scene in public so Max didn't expect their location was in his favor. "Hockey."

His dad's gaze trailed over his face, stopping on the

scar above his eye, caused by a hockey stick when he was little. If they wanted to go through the injuries Max had suffered, they'd be there all day.

"How long have you been thinking about this?"

Max licked his lips and went with honesty. "A long time."

His dad nodded and looked back down at his hands. "And you didn't tell me because . . . ?"

Max picked at the blanket pooled at his waist. "I thought you'd quit helping me pay. I thought you'd disown me. I thought you'd flip your shit."

A lip twitch. "Flip my shit."

"Come on, Dad, you know—"

"I know. I know."

Max tapped his fingers. "So, are you going to flip your shit? A warning would be nice. I might need more pain meds."

"I guess I didn't give you the impression I won't flip my shit, did I?"

Who was this guy? "Dad, who are you? I didn't have a near-death experience. I just got hit in the head. And all of a sudden you are . . . I don't know . . . diffcrent . . . and I—"

He held his hand up and Max snapped his jaw shut.

"Brent flapped his gums," his dad said.

"What?"

"I heard him talking to Cal and Cal was angry that Brent discouraged you. And I . . . I realized that Brent did that because he probably thought that's what I would do. But Cal said he was proud of you for wanting something different and I . . . I realized that it was unrealistic to keep all of you in that shop with me. It's hard work. Your brothers and I like it. But I can't make you do something you don't want to, can I?"

Max nodded. "Actually, yeah, yeah you can."

"Okay, but do I want to?"

Max squinted. " I don't know. Do you?"

He shook his head, but Max could see the sadness lingering in his eyes. "No," he said quietly. "I realize I didn't make it easy on you to tell me."

This was the first honest discussion he'd had with his dad. Ever. Was he dreaming?

"I need to check in at the shop, so I gotta get going."

"Okay, Dad."

He leaned in and gripped Max's shoulder. "We'll talk more later."

MAX SAT ON the end of his hospital bed, humming to himself and tapping his feet. His brain was "A-OK" (that wasn't the medical term, but he stopped listening when they used Latin words) and so he'd been discharged. And now he was waiting until Cal could pick him up and drive him home.

He wasn't allowed back at school for a week, which was going to be hell on his classes, but at least he could e-mail his advisor to get an appointment to switch his major.

And then he needed to phone Lea.

Or bet at her doorstep.

Anything, really.

His door opened and Max looked up, expecting to see his brother, but instead a pompadoured head peered in.

"Zuk!" Max cried, thrilled as hell to see his friend. Cal said he'd talked to him and Max had been sad he'd been conked out and missed him.

"Hey, man." Alec smiled and walked forward with a container in his hand.

Max eyed it. "What you got there, Zuk?"

Alec set the container down on the bed and stood in front of Max. "I come to drive you home from the hospital after you got pistol-whipped and you only care about what treats I brought?"

Max reached for the container. "That's old news."

"Max." His voice was pleading.

He met his best friend's gaze, noticing his eyes were bloodshot behind his glasses, his skin pale. "How about you never do this shit again, okay? Because I . . ." Alec shook his head and looked at the floor.

Max's stomach dropped. Alec lost his father as a kid. He didn't have a huge circle of friends but the ones he cared about had his whole heart. And Max was lucky to still be in that circle.

"Hey, dude. I'm all right. It sucked but I played it smart, didn't I?" Max asked.

Alec looked up with a wry grin. "Yeah, you played it smart. Proud of you for not trying to be a hero. Because you were a hero. Your brothers tell you they got the guys?"

Max nodded.

Alec nudged his shoulder. "Good job, man. So, how's the head?"

"All right. Just got a killer headache. Happy to be heading home.

"Good."

"Okay, enough chitchat, what's in the container?"

Alec rolled his eyes and plopped it in Max's lap. "Danica, believe it or not, felt sorry for your ass and made you muffins."

Max peeled off the lid and popped one in his mouth. "Oh wow, apple cinnamon. These are fucking great." He stopped chewing. "Did Lea help her?"

Alec's smile froze and then faded. "I don't know."

Max swallowed his lump of barely chewed muffin that wasn't so tasty anymore. There was something in Alec's posture, like he knew something he wasn't telling. "Have you talked to her?"

Alec blew out a breath and looked out the window of the hospital. "Uh . . ."

"Please just tell me whatever—"

"I think you need to talk to her." Alec met Max's gaze.

"Well, no shit."

"I don't know everything that happened but—"

"You probably heard it, what, like third or fourth hand by the time what happened made it to Kat's ears and then yours? Who knows what you heard."

Alec chuckled. "A dragon swooped in and threatened to burn down the garage, but Lea tore off a helmet and said, I'm no man!'"

Max glowered. "There was no *Lord of the Rings* reenactment. But that would have been fucking awesome."

"I talked to her, asshole. And, basically, you didn't

acknowledge you knew her and stood there like a lump when your dad was a misogynist dick."

The bit of muffin churned in Max's stomach. "That sounds really bad."

"I think it was pretty bad, Max."

"Like you've never fucked up—"

"Don't make this about me. I have fucked up. But then I fixed that fuckup."

Max smashed his fist down on the mattress. "I was trying to fix my fuckup, but then I got jumped by some pistol-wielding kleptomaniacs. And I've been in a hospital since then. What am I supposed to do?"

Alec shift his lips from side to side. "You could call her."

"I'm not calling her to grovel. She has to see my puppy-dog eyes. And maybe I'll flex a little and try to look handsome at the same time."

He expected Alec to laugh and assure him he'd get his girl, but Alec didn't look very confident.

Max reached over to his side table and grabbed his shirt. "She visited me while I was sleeping and brought this."

Alec reached for the shirt and held it out in front of him, a small smile on his lips as he took in the logo. He dropped it back onto Max's lap. "How do you know Kat didn't bring it? Or me?"

Max narrowed his eyes. "Don't try to confuse the head-injury victim. I know it was her, okay? I know. I heard her voice, and I felt her touch, and I can smell her scent on this shirt. It's driving me fucking crazy and giving me a hard-on which is super awkward because my nurse is a dude."

Alec reared back in his seat and put his hands up. "Max, swear to God, I didn't need to know that. At all. Fuck, man."

"That's what you get for trying to mess with me."

Alec rolled his eyes. "So you're not giving up?"

"Fuck no."

Alec let a small smile through. "She's got her armor back on. It's gonna be tough to climb that wall with her again."

Max knew that. It hadn't been easy to conquer "Mount Lea." He didn't know if he had it in him again but he sure as hell was going to make the trek again. He hoped the altitude didn't kill him.

While they waited for a nurse to bring his discharge papers, Max told Alec all about his conversation with his dad. Alec was surprised that Max stood up to his dad, but he was proud of Max for finally standing strong.

They talked about what it would take to change his major and estimated Max would have to attend another full year. He hated the thought of sitting out of graduation when Alec, Cam, Lea and Danica graduated but at least he'd have Kat to keep him company next year, when she'd be a senior.

And in the whole picture of his life, one more year in college was worth it to get the degree he wanted, to do what he wanted.

When Jeremy brought the discharge papers, he also brought a wheelchair.

"Seriously?" Max whined.

The nurse patted the padded back. "Sorry, it's policy."

Max rolled his eyes and plopped down onto the seat while Jeremy opened up the leg rests.

"Zuk can roll me out," Max said to Jeremy, and the nurse nodded and led the way to the lobby.

Max tapped his fingers on the armrests and said over his shoulder to Alec, "Can you make zooming noises?"

"Absolutely not."

"Come on—"

"No."

Max pouted, and then when they went around a turn at the end of the hallway, Max made a high-pitched screeching sound out of the side of his mouth.

"Seriously?"

"You're no fun."

Chapter 23

LEA DOUBLE-CHECKED THE meeting time with her advisor and then closed her browser, slinging her bag over her shoulder.

She'd received an e-mail earlier in the week from him, requesting her at his Wednesday office hours. Dr. Mayberry didn't say why, but she assumed it had something to do with her student-teaching assignment next spring.

She glanced at her phone, which had been abnormally silent today. In the last week, she'd had all kinds of phone calls and texts—from her parents, sister, Alec, Kat and even Danica when she couldn't corner Lea in their apartment.

The name she both loathed and loved to see never showed. Part of her wanted him to fight for her. And every time she thought of him in that hospital room, she wanted to throw up.

Which told her she wasn't over this. Over them. Not even close.

When she reached Dr. Mayberry's office, she knocked lightly and the door gave way beneath her knuckles.

She stepped into the office, smiling at Dr. Mayberry and then froze in her tracks when the door opened the rest of the way to reveal Max.

Max Payton. Lounging on a chair in front of Dr. Mayberry's desk looking not at all surprised to see her.

In fact . . . was he smirking?

Dr. Mayberry stood behind his desk, and Lea tore her gaze from Max before she tore out his throat. What was he doing here?

"Lea, this is Max Payton, although he said you know each other."

Lea didn't trust herself to look at Max, but she swore he snickered.

"Anyway, Max has just changed his major to secondary education."

Lea flinched at the words. Was she the one with the head injury? Did he just say Max changed his major? She slowly turned to Max, sure that confusion was written all over her face. He stared back, smirk gone, a slight challenge in his eyes. Was this a joke? Did he really . . .

"And since he's making the change senior year," Dr. Mayberry continued, "he suggested another student help with the transition. And he mentioned you helped one of his friends, Kat Caruso. So, if you're willing, I'd like you to give him a little guidance."

Her ears burned. She clenched the strap of her book bag until she was sure the nylon pattern would be etched into her palms. Max had engineered this. He'd kept silent for a week, letting her think he was fading into her past when really he was plotting a way to sneak into her future.

The jerk.

Dr. Mayberry cocked his head, confusion passing over his face. She loved her advisor. He'd been wonderful and supportive since she was a freshman, so she didn't want to let him down.

And Max knew she wouldn't say no, pass off a responsibility. Even if she thought it was stupid and unnecessary.

The jerk.

She cleared her throat and eased up on the death grip she held on her bag strap. "Yep, I'd be happy to help."

Dr. Mayberry clapped, clearly happy to have passed off this duty. "You can start with showing him around the education building. You two can exchange numbers and if you have any problems, please see me." He turned to Max, who stood beside her, and the two men shook hands. "You're in good hands."

"I know I am," Max said and the grin in his voice made her see red.

They walked out of the office side by side. And Lea hated that part of her that wanted to lean into Max's warmth, wanted to feel his arm around her shoulders, his breath on her face, his lips at her ear. She wanted to touch him back, run her hands over his head and down his arms, to verify tactically for herself that he was healthy and in one piece.

She stared at the tile of the hallway. She stopped at a door and gestured inside. "This is one of the computer labs for the Grove Education Building. The other one is on the second floor, at the opposite end of the hallway."

Max stood in the doorway, facing *her*, his eyes boring into *her*. "I don't really want a tour."

She ducked her head and kept talking. At the set of double doors at the end of the hallway, she pointed inside. "This is the faculty room, as we call it. It has all the office-type supplies the school provides us, like the copier and—"

"I don't give a shit about this room, Lea—"

"—and a soda machine and this is where all the posters are hung for clubs or whatever on the bulletin board over there—"

"Lea, damn it—"

"—and a small kitchenette so it's a nice place to hang out and socialize."

"Fuck it," he growled and then she was crowded into the empty room, the door shut behind her, and then Max's body was pressing hers against the door. His breath was on her face and his lips inches from hers. His one hand on the door near her shoulder, his forearm braced above her head.

"Why are you avoiding me?"

"Max—"

"You gotta talk to me eventually—"

And that snapped her spine straight. "Oh? Do I? And why's that?"

His eyes narrowed. "You're still my girlfriend."

"Well, that's news to me."

His voice lowered even further. "We never broke up."

She leaned forward now, taking the offensive. "I'm not interested in being Max's girlfriend only on campus. You met my dad. And then I go to visit you, and your family doesn't even know who I am. Or wait, they did know me as the girl who got too attached and made you cookies—"

"You didn't give me a chance—"

"There were plenty of chances there, Max. Plen-ty. But instead your dad treated me like a twelve-year-old and—"

"God, I know!" He yelled, pushing off of the door and tearing his hands through his hair. "I know. And if I could do that day all over again, I would."

He linked his hands on top of his head and watched her. She had to look away before she was dragged back into the warm brown depths of his eyes. She didn't want to let her heart be that open with him again. She couldn't deal with that and him getting hurt . . .

"I want to," he whispered.

She snapped back. "What?"

He lowered his hands and stepped forward hesitantly. "I want to do it over again. Don't you see? I'm making changes. I'm trying to make it right. I told my dad. And my brothers. I told them everything. About changing my major. And coaching." He licked his lips. "And you. I told them a whole lot about you."

She could already feel herself weakening. "I can't do this."

He grabbed her hands and she didn't protest. "You can't do what?"

The words scraped into her throat like barbs as she croaked them out. "I can't let myself be weak and trust you again."

Max froze, his eyes flickering as he processed her words. She bit her lip and tugged her arms so he let go of her wrists. Closed his eyes slowly and looked down at his feet, hands on his hips, and then he raised his gaze to her. He swallowed, his Adam's apple bobbing under his skin. "You think trusting someone else is a weakness?"

Her hackles went up. "Don't act like you're better than me. You didn't trust me to meet your family—"

"No," he cut her off. "That's not why I didn't want you to meet my family. At the time you were the one thing in my life that I truly wanted. I was facing a future I hated, and my dad was breathing down my neck and, fuck, you met him! You gotta understand why I was hesitant to take you to meet him. Because your dad is love and pie and laughter and mine is hard and cold and . . ." He paused and shook his head. "It had nothing to do with not trusting you. I do trust you. With my heart. Do you think that makes me weak?

He had her cornered in this conversation. "We're talking about me, not you."

"Right." He nodded. "But that's your logic. That I'm weak because I trust. You're strong because you don't trust."

Well then her logic was flawed. Because nothing was stronger than the sight of Max grabbing the headboard, closing his eyes, and trusting her with his naked body and naked heart. "I don't think you're weak."

His exhaled with relief and stepped closer, brushing his fingers over her bangs, eyes watching the hair fall back into place. Then he met her gaze. "I don't think you're weak either. I know you have it in you to trust. Is it me? You can't trust me?"

Everything in her heart screamed she could but her head didn't want to admit it. "It's not you," she whispered. "I don't see myself as broken or hurt or weak. And I've never trusted another person, other than my family, to feel the same way about me. To see me as an equal and not a fragile doll."

He laughed softly, cupping the back of her head, thumb rubbing the shell of her ear. "I call you doll because you look like one. But you sure as hell aren't broken."

She gave in to the feeling, the weight of his hand on her, the caress of his thumb. He took another step closer, so her chest brushed his. He cupped the side of her neck and tilted her head up with his thumb on the bottom of her chin. She had to look at him. There was nowhere else to look. A soft smile played on this lips. "That's what you've taught me, even if you don't know it yourself. I've never felt stronger than when I decided to open up to you. When I decided to surrender my heart to you."

He tore down that wall, brick by brick with his bare hands, that she'd so painstakingly put into place since that day at the shop. She opened her mouth but didn't know what to say, which was good because Max kept talking.

"I thought keeping my distance from everyone and sticking with the family business was strength. I thought working out at the gym was all it took to call myself strong. But, you . . . fuck, Lea, you showed me how liberating it was to let all that go—how it was stronger to put my heart on the line and fight for the future I wanted."

"But . . ." The guilt welled in her throat, cutting off her words. She swallowed and tried again. "But I made you weak."

"How?" he challenged quickly.

"I . . . I knew about the gun. I had planned to tell you at the shop when I visited, but then . . . and I was the reason you were on campus. That's what happens when I open up and trust. I get hurt." She exhaled roughly. "And other people get hurt."

Max looked at her with a wry twist to his lips. "Are you serious?"

She smacked his chest. "Don't make fun of me, asshole. Yes, I'm serious." But her resolve was weakening, because Nick had told her the same thing.

He shook his head. "Look, we can't change what happened. I was there and so were they, and so . . ." He shrugged.

"But I didn't tell you about the gun and—"

"Is that what you're upset about? What, you feel guilty?"

She nodded and his face relaxed. "Oh doll, it wouldn't have mattered. And you know what happened, right? You know I got away. Because of you. Because of what you taught me. I got away and those assholes are gonna sit in a cell now."

"Yeah, but—"

"No buts. And no guilt." He said each word with a

slight shake of her shoulders, like he wanted to imprint it in her brain. And each shake rattled that pile of guilt until the small ray of sun peeking through was a wide beam. Soon, it'd be the whole sky.

"Max . . ." She reached up and wrapped her fingers around his wrist, closing her eyes.

"You're not weak. Not at all."

She opened her eyes and fell into his.

"You wanna know what I told my dad and brothers about you?"

She nodded.

"I told them you're funny. And smart, so fucking smart. And I told them you can kick my ass . . . they really loved that and Brent wants you to do some moves on Cal. And I told them you're beautiful. I told them you're the strongest person I know."

She sucked in a breath when his voice caught on *strongest*.

"And," he continued, "I told them you're the girl I fell in love with."

That was it. Max stomped the wall beneath his boots into dust. But she stood behind that wall, not weak or defenseless, but strong because being with Max made her stronger.

He was right. In his Max way.

Neither of them was weak.

She flung her arms around his neck and pressed her lips to his. His arms were around her back, lifting her up so he could wrap her legs around his waist.

He opened his mouth and she took what she could,

showing him how he was the the cause for the strength pumping through her veins.

He pulled back, his breath coasting over her lips, and sat her on the counter of the kitchenette, keeping his place between her thighs. "I don't think we should make out here."

"Yeah, probably not."

He rested his forehead on hers and she ran her hands through his hair, pausing at the stitches on his scalp behind his ear. Her stomach twisted. "I'm so glad you're okay."

He didn't say anything, just watched her eyes.

"I thought about you every day," she said.

He fingertips slipped under the hem of her shirt and skimmed the skin at her hips. "I know it was you who brought me the shirt."

She leaned in to his touch, unable to resist rolling her hips against his. His breath caught in his throat. "Cal told you it was me?"

He leaned in to her body, his hands roving now, around to the small of her back, his fingers dipping beneath her waistband. His lips were at her ear. "No, he didn't."

She crossed her ankles, locking herself around him, and pressed a kiss to his jaw. "How did you know?"

He pulled his head back to look in her eyes, his whole hands down the back of her pants, kneading her butt. "I just knew. I heard your voice in my head. And I felt your touch. And I smelled you. Everywhere in that room and on that shirt. Still haven't washed it."

She dropped her forehead onto his shoulder.

"Why'd you leave?" he whispered.

She closed her eyes. "I heard your dad's voice. I left before he came into your room."

He stroked her hair. "I'm sorry about him. Look, I'm not going to lie. I told him I was going to break up with you. But it's because . . . you were the one thing in my life that was mine. What I chose. I didn't know those words were going to come back and bite me in the ass. I never intended to break up with you, for what we had to be a one-night thing."

She bit her lip. "I wish I would have trusted you enough."

"We'll work on it," he said, brushing her bangs back and forth on her forehead with his fingers. "We got time. We were just interrupted a little."

"You really changed your major?"

"I did."

She pecked him on the nose. "I'm proud of you."

"Proud of me, too, doll." He gave her a peck on the lips. "Anyway, your presence has been requested at the Payton household for Thanksgiving. Now, I can't promise mashed potatoes that aren't lumpy and I can't promise the green beans won't be steamed into mush, but I can promise a hell of a turkey because Cal has perfected the art of the turkey fryer. He only burnt down our back porch once."

Her eyes widened at the mention of fire. "Are you serious?"

Max's eyes twinkled. "If you come to Thanksgiving, I'll tell you all about it."

She twirled the hair at the nape of his neck. "Okay, if you promise to go shopping on Black Friday with me and my mom at midnight."

Max's mouth dropped open in shock and she threw back her head and laughed. When she looked back at him, his eyes were narrowed. "You're kidding, right?"

She grinned. "Yep, but you do have to come with me to my parents' on Friday."

"Deal," he said on an emphatic nod.

She pushed on his shoulders so he stepped back, and then he helped her down off of the counter.

"This was pretty clever," she said, twirling her finger. "Cornering me in my professor's office and everything."

He leaned back, bracing his arms on the counter, and his shirt stretched across his broad chest. "Yeah? I thought of it all by myself."

"You want the rest of the tour?" she said, sauntering toward the door.

He pushed his lips out and cocked his head to the side. "I want *a* tour."

"What tour do you want?"

He pushed off from the counter and prowled toward her. "Your apartment. Your room. I'd love a tour of your bed, specifically between the sheets."

"That's a really specific tour."

He grabbed her around the waist. "I'm a Lea-specific kind of guy."

Chapter 24

The pie was still warm and it heated Lea's thighs despite the thermal bag she'd placed it in. Which was nice because despite the heat blasting in Max's drunk, it was still wasn't very warm.

Danica had helped her with an apple crumb pie, and it smelled divine when they'd baked it that morning, along with the pie Danica planned to take with her to Monica's house for Thanksgiving.

Lea checked her phone. Danica had finally texted back in answer to her inquiry. *Just got here. It's all good.*

Lea smiled.

"What are you smiling at?" Max asked, glancing at her briefly before returning his eyes to the road.

"Nothing, just a text from Danica."

"She still hate me?"

Lea turned to Max. She knew he meant the question to come off as a joke but there was a hint of vulnerability in his tone. He didn't want her roommate to dislike him. "No, she doesn't hate you. I don't think she ever hated you. She just didn't care for you. And actually, she's more mad at me for leaving the hospital without talking to you."

He thought for a minute. "You know I was a little mad at you, too. I was laid up and I wanted to talk to you and apologize. But looking back, maybe we both needed that time. I needed to get my shit together and you needed to . . ."

He let his voice trail and she nodded. She had to let the past go and trust again.

"I wish it hadn't had to happen that way, though."

He reached for her hand. "But it did. And we're stronger for it."

She twined her fingers with hers and leaned back in the seat, closing her eyes and humming along with the radio.

"Meoooorrrrwwwww," Wayne called from the backseat, where he was secure in his crate. He had such an odd-voweled meow. Max said he must have led his pack with it. When Lea explained stray cats weren't really pack animals, Max hadn't wanted to hear it.

Lea's eyes popped open. She rolled her head to the side and smiled. "I think he's had enough of the trip."

"Quiet down back there!" Max scowled in the rear-view mirror, then winked at Lea. He'd been adamant about bringing Wayne. Even though they'd only be gone a couple of days, Max worried about Wayne being alone in the town house, even with an automatic feeder and water bowl. Lea secretly thought it was cute but outwardly rolled her eyes at him.

Wayne let out another cry.

"You know," Lea said, twisting with a knee up on the seat so she could face Max. "Pretty sure when I saw you trying to coax the injured cat to trust you is when I knew you'd get to me."

"Oh yeah?" Max raised an eyebrow, keeping his eyes on the road.

She leaned closer. "I think that's when I knew I'd fall in love with you."

Max whipped his head to look at her.

"Eyes on the road, Max," she said in a singsong voice. He straightened his head but his hands clutched the steering wheel in a white-knuckled grip.

It'd been weeks, and he hadn't said the words since that day in the faculty room on campus. And she hadn't said the words at all. Not that she didn't know—because she did— but because she didn't know when to say it. And now, on the way to see his family while her nerves tickled her belly, she wanted to walk onto his home turf with full disclosure.

"I love you, Max," she whispered.

And now he turned his head to her again, a scowl on his face, which was the last thing she expected to see.

"Seriously?" he said incredulously.

"What?"

"You tell me that now? While I'm driving?"

She threw a hand in the air. "Well I don't know! Did you want, like, candles and rose petals in a bath?"

"Maybe, if you were in there naked!" He fired back.

"Are we seriously fighting about where I told you I loved you!"

"Yes!"

"Why!"

"Because I don't want to tell you that I love you back when I'm not able to kiss you!"

The irritation drained out of Lea's body in a rush. Max looked so adorably miffed that she had to tuck her lips between her teeth to stop from laughing.

Max glanced at her out of the corner of his eye. "Doll, this isn't funny."

"Mims a mimble mummy," she mumbled through closed lips.

"What?"

She opened her lips and a giggle burst out. "It's a little funny."

His death glare was the last straw, and she burst out laughing as Wayne let out another meow.

And then the car jolted and the tires spun as they careened into gravel on the side of the road. She grabbed the handle on the door as the truck came to an abrupt halt.

Then Max's seatbelt pinged and so did hers. She had the presence of mind to set the pie on the floor at her feet before she was hauled across the bench of his truck seat onto Max's lap. The steering wheel dug into her back and the gear shift jabbed into her knee but she didn't even feel it once Max's lips were on hers.

She grasped his hair and he cupped her neck, his thumbs at her jaw, tilting her head so he could direct the kiss.

And she let him. She let him control this kiss and manipulate her legs until she straddled his hips. And she let him show everything he could physically in a way that made the words they had just said pale in comparison.

The kiss slowed and then Wayne meowed again, clearly impatient in his crate and urging them to get back on the road. Max rested his forehead against hers, his full lips wet and a little swollen. She leaned back against the steering wheel and grinned. "You still mad?"

He narrowed his eyes at her. "Yep."

"No you're not."

He barked a laugh. "Fine, I'm not, but unless you wanna screw in the car, I suggest you get back over on your side."

"Such a gentleman."

Max smirked.

"And you brought me over here, so you put me back."

He rolled his eyes and encircled her waist with his hands. With a grunt, he deposited her back onto her side of the car. "Happy?"

"I think so."

He started the car and then waited.

"Why aren't you driving?" she asked.

He nodded at her seat. "Put your seat belt on."

"Meooorrww!" Wayne echoed.

"See, he agrees with me."

Lea buckled her seat belt and then looked at Max expectantly.

Once they pulled out onto the highway, Lea hid her smile behind her hand. "Max?"

"Yeah?"

"I love you."

He growled.

HALF AN HOUR later, Max turned onto a tree-lined street full of small ranch and split-level-style homes. He pulled into a driveway and a man on a ladder, fiddling with a light fixture over the garage door, turned around.

Lea recognized Max's dad instantly and her gut tightened.

Crap, in the excitement to come home with Max, she hadn't let herself think about this confrontation. Or how awkward it was going to be. She gripped the pie in her lap and willed her nerves to settle.

She broke her eye contact with Max's dad and turned to Max, opening her mouth to ask if she could stay in the truck. Or maybe ask him to drive her back home. Or maybe just shove him out and she'd hightail it out of there herself.

But Max apparently could read minds, or at least emotions, because he held up his hand. "He wants to talk to you."

She bristled. "Well good for him, but last time—"

"I know," Max said wearily. "You know it's just us, right? Dad and my brothers?"

He didn't tell her who was missing. He told her who was present. She didn't miss that. "Yes," she said quietly.

"So Dad doesn't have an excuse for being an asshole, but I just ask you to have a little patience with him."

She pressed her lips together. "I think I can do that."

"You feel uncomfortable for a second, just say the word, and we'll go to your house."

A bubble of laughter burst between her lips. "Okay."

A knock startled her and she turned to her window to see Max's dad's lined face peering through the dirty glass. He motioned his finger in a circle, asking her to lower her window. Max gestured to the manual crank in the old truck and she turned it, lowering the window and letting in the chill air.

She straightened her spine and met the man's eyes. He had those gray-blues she remembered in a face lined with life. When those eyes met hers, something shifted and she finally got a glimpse of humanity.

"Got off on the wrong foot," he said through a tense jaw, and she knew this wasn't something he did a lot. Do-overs. Apologies. Conversations. He reached a weathered hand into the truck above the half-lowered window. "Jack Payton. Call me Jack."

His voice was a rumble, like once it made it past all the crags on the way, it had lost a lot of its tone. She reached up and shook his hand. "Lea Travers."

"Teacher?"

"Huh?"

"You wanna teach?"

She blinked at the question. "Yes, my major is education. I also want to get my master's in library science."

He squinted his eyes at her, shifted them to Max behind her and then back to her. "Maybe you can find jobs near each other then."

"I—"

"Sorry about that day at the shop."

This man really had crappy conversation skills. "Um ..."

He waved his hand. "Bad day and ... yeah." He tapped his hand on the side of the car and stepped back, his face closing down, signaling the end of the conversation. Lea had no idea what happened but she figured that was his peace offering.

It was better than nothing.

"Get her inside, Max, before Brent burns the house down." And then he walked away, climbing back up the ladder to continue doing whatever he was doing to the light.

She looked at Max and he shrugged. He grabbed Wayne's crate out of the cab and propped a foil-covered casserole dish on his hip.

"Hey, what's that?"

"My specialty," Max said.

"You're not going to tell me?"

"Nope."

When they walked by his father toward the front door, Max called, "Dad, Brent said he'd do that."

"Well I'm doing it," he said without looking back.

"You fall and break your neck, I don't wanna hear bitching." Max yelled.

Jack mumbled something but Lea assumed it was cursing.

Max opened the front door for her and ushered her inside.

The curtains were drawn closed and Lea made out a hallway ahead of her, lined with dozens of crooked pictures. As she followed Max down the hall, she twisted her head to look at them, all shots of the boys in various sports uniforms and positions of mischief—climbing trees, jumping in lakes.

There was no *Jill*.

Only Jack and his three boys.

The home reeked of masculinity. It was dark and could use a deep cleaning but was surprisingly clutter free. Lea wondered if Max had anything to do with making sure the place was clean for her visit. She knew Cal and Brent didn't live at home.

"Taste this. Am I the boss or what?" They heard as they stepped into the kitchen. The room was a mess, food and dishes everywhere. Cal and another man whom she assumed to be Brent stood beside a mixing bowl. Brent held his finger toward Cal's face, a lump of mashed potatoes on the end.

"If you think I'm licking that off your finger, you're fucking crazy," Cal said.

Max clapped. "Hey."

Both boys looked toward them. Cal's gaze zeroed in on her as Brent stuck his mashed potato covered finger in his own mouth. "Hey," he mumbled around it.

Max introduced Lea to his brothers and she greeted them. Brent eyed the crate. "What is that?"

"Wayne," Max answered, setting the crate on the floor.

"Who's Wayne?" Cal asked.

"My cat."

"You have a cat?" Brent craned his neck over the center island.

Max opened the front of the crate, but Wayne didn't venture out.

"I'm not sure I believe there's a cat in there," Cal said.

"I'm telling you—""

"Meeeeeooooorrrrrrrwww," came the battle cry and then a streak of black flew out of the crate and took off down a hallway.

Cal jumped back, covering his face with his arms while Brent cowered behind him, gripping his shoulders.

Max laughed. "Dudes, calm down."

Brent peered from around Cal's shoulder. "What the hell was that thing, a bear?"

"I told you I had a cat."

Cal glared at him. "If that thing eats my face in my sleep, I'll never forgive you."

Max waved a hand and set the crate by the back door. "Oh, he's harmless. Probably sleeping on my bed right now."

Neither brother looked appeased.

"How's the food coming?" Max asked leaning on the counter.

Brent straightened and returned to his place by the mixing bowl. "Cal won't try my mashed potatoes."

"I didn't say I wouldn't try them, I'm just not sucking them off your finger, dickbag."

"Then get a spoon!"

Max swiped his finger in the bowl and tasted the mashed potatoes. "More salt."

Brent whirled on him. "What? No. No way."

Cal pulled a spoon out of a drawer, made to dip it into

the mixing bowl, then paused. He looked at Lea. "Here, you be the judge."

She took the spoon from him and then scooped out a mouthful of potatoes. She stuck the spoon in her mouth. They were good, maybe a little thick, but fluffy and buttery. She placed the spoon on the counter and realized all three boys were staring at her expectantly, with baited breath, like she held the key to the meaning of life. "They taste great. Just the right amount of salt," she declared. Brent whooped and Max grinned despite her disagreeing with him.

Cal rolled his eyes and went back to the sink.

Brent hummed happily and began dishing the mashed potatoes into a slow cooker.

"I thought they were done, why are you putting them in there?" Max asked.

"Keeps 'em warm and fluffy. I saw it on TV."

Lea turned to Max. "Do you guys always cook Thanksgiving dinner?"

Max poked at a bag of rolls. "We used to go to our grandparents' and then they passed away. We've only cooked at the house here the last couple of years. We're getting better every year though."

"Hey, my turkey was amazing the first year. It was you dumbasses that screwed up everything else."

"I disagree with that. My stuffing was amazing." Max puffed out his chest.

Cal turned and stared at him thoughtfully. "Okay, I'll give you that." He turned to Lea and winked. "Max makes a mean stuffing."

She smiled at Cal. "I'm looking forward to eating it."

Cal returned her smile. "Glad you're here to eat it."

She turned to Max. "Is that what's in your dish? Stuffing?"

"Yep."

"That's really not that secretive of a dish to make on Thanksgiving."

"I know. I just like to keep you guessing."

CAL ENDED UP not burning down the deck when he fried the turkey. Max gleefully showed her the burn marks on the old wood where the flame and oil had gotten a little out of control. Cal glared at him, and Jack marked to be thankful the house hadn't burned down and so that had been the end of that.

During dinner, Jack was quiet while Brent chattered the most to Max about the shop and about girls and Lea listened, but really, she enjoyed a full house.

She'd thought Max's family was so different from hers and it was, because it was noisy and full of deep voices and curses. But she realized that, at the core, they all cared about each other. So in that respect, his family was just like hers.

Afterward, they sat in the living room watching football. Max helped her cut the pie and they delivered it to the other guys on paper plates with scoops of vanilla ice cream they'd found wedged in the freezer.

Jack probably ate half the pie himself and patted her shoulder, his hand heavy and calloused. "Good pie there, sweetheart."

And Max had stared at her, eyes wide, mouth. full of pie, open in shock.

When Jack left the room so use the bathroom, he leaned in to her. "I don't think I've ever heard him use that word."

Lea took a sip of milk she insisted on pouring. Because apple pie was always served with milk. "Does he date?"

Max wrinkled his nose. "Ew."

"Well—"

Max held his hand up. "Please, just stop." He fake gagged and she rolled her eyes.

"Do you have a girlfriend, Brent?"

"Huh?" His mouth full of ice cream.

"Girlfriend? Boyfriend?"

He narrowed his eyes. "I like girls and no, no girlfriend. Cal and I like to keep our options open."

Cal, who'd been intent on the game whipped his head to his younger brother. "Speak for yourself!"

"What?"

He shrugged and turned back to the game. "You don't know everything about my life."

"Whoa oh oh!" Max cried, hand over his mouth. "Cal's been keeping a secret!"

"We live together, dude!" Brent sat up in his recliner. "How the hell do I not know you have a girl?"

Cal shrugged.

"That's all you're gonna do? Shrug?" Brent exaggerated raising his shoulders in a mocking gesture.

Cal smiled and picked at the label on his beer bottle.

"Bullshit, man," Brent said, flinging himself back in the recliner. "Gotta go find a new wingman."

"What's the hollering about?" Jack said, walking back into the room and taking his seat in the other recliner.

"Cal's got a girl or something."

Jack's eyes narrowed on his oldest son, and Lea squirmed because those eyes were knowing. Then they shifted to Max, and then to her, where they lingered.

Finally, he turned to the TV and lifted his beer to his lips, taking a swig. When he lowered the bottle, he wiped his mouth with the back of his hand. "Don't mess it up if it's important."

He spoke like a man who knew what he was talking about, and his sons must have known, because they all went quiet.

And then Max looked at her out of the corner of his eye. He smiled and placed his hand on her thigh, palm up. She twined her fingers with his and smiled back. She rested her head on his shoulder and they watched the game with his family, while Wayne's broken purr sounded on the couch beside them.

Chapter 25

MAX STRETCHED HIS legs in front of him as far as the bleachers would allow and braced his arms behind him on the metal bench.

Kat looked up at the blazing sun behind wide sunglasses and fanned herself with the graduation program. "I should have put on suntan lotion," she grumbled.

Max picked at his shirt, wafting it away from his sticky skin. "It's hot as hell, and I'm hungover."

Kat grinned at him. "I know, I'm kind of enjoying your pain."

He bumped her with his shoulder. The stadium was packed, full of friends and family of the graduates. Music from the university orchestra drifted through the speakers and Max took a gulp of his bottled water, squinting his eyes at the sun. He drifted his eyes to the sea of empty chairs on the field below.

He wished he was in the gymnasium of the rec center

right now, sweating in his gown, blowing the tassel of his cap out of his face, laughing with Cam and Alec.

Shooting Lea heated looks.

But he knew when he changed his major that this would be his consequence. He managed to load up on classwork during the spring semester and was taking classes over the summer. So in the fall, he could student teach and if all went well, he'd graduate in December. Only a semester behind.

It wasn't so bad. He'd keep Kat company during her last year. He'd support her in a way he hadn't when he was her boyfriend.

"Zuk's probably pissed the cap is messing up his hair," Max said.

Kat laughed and pulled a lock of her hair over her shoulder, rolling it between her fingers. "I don't think he wanted to admit it, but yes. He grumbled a lot when he put it on."

Max smirked. Alec was probably hungover, too. And Cam. Last night was a little bit of a blur for Max. They'd gone to *Hot Spot* last night, drunk way too many mind erasers, sung drunken karaoke and then . . . well . . . the mind erasers kicked in.

He was pretty sure Lea had to undress him like a baby while he tried to grab her boobs.

God, he loved her.

He turned to Kat. "It's awesome Zuk is going to be close for law school."

Kat twisted the program in her hands and her lips turned down. "Yeah."

Her low tone bugged Max. "What's wrong?"

She shrugged. "Nothing, it's fine."

Max leaned forward, propping his elbows on his knees. "Okay, no you're not, what's up?"

She turned her head and he could see the faint outline of her eyes through her shades. "You always let me get away with saying 'it's fine.' "

"I'm not that guy anymore."

A small smile. "I guess not."

"So . . ."

She picked at the skirt of her sundress. "I don't know. I guess I'm just nervous. I know he loves me and wants to be with me, but it's scary to think of him on another campus, with all these pretty girls with massive brains and . . ." She blew out a breath and then shoved her shades onto the top of he head. Her blue eyes shone crystal clear as she bit her lip. "I'm being dumb, aren't I?"

Max would always care about Kat. She was a great girl, a beautiful girl, but they weren't right together. She and Zuk? A perfect pair.

He shook his head. "Nope, not dumb, babe. Never dumb."

She smiled, her lip popping out from between her teeth.

"You're what he wants," Max said. "He's going to miss you like crazy and he won't be far away. You can visit each other all the time. Zuk's as faithful as they come. You know that."

"I don't think he's gonna—"

Max cut her off. "I know you don't. I'm just saying. He doesn't even look at anyone else."

She shifted her lips back and forth. Then launched herself at him, wrapping her arms around his neck. "I'm glad I get one more semester with you."

Max hesitated, then dipped his nose into her citrus-scented hair and hugged her back. "Me too."

She squeezed and then pulled away and he let her go. "So proud of you, Max," she said.

He tugged the end of her hair. "Proud of you, too, babe."

They separated as a voice over the loudspeakers welcomed the crowd to the spring Bowler University graduation and then asked the murmuring crowd to welcome the graduating class.

More than six hundred students shuffled in, and Max assumed Alec and Cam weren't the only hungover ones.

They filed in alphabetically, so first they saw Danica, who wore high platform wedge shoes and lavender hair. Then Cam, who shot Max the middle finger, because he was classy like that. Kat squealed when Alec came into view and took rapid fire pictures on her phone. Max suggested she switch over to video and then she proceeded to narrate Alec's progress into her phone speaker along with the video.

Max spotted Lea easily because of her unique walk and watched as she scanned the crowd. He'd told her where he'd be sitting and he wore his Cross Keys Bowling shirt, so when he stood up and waved his hands, she waved back and blew him a kiss.

Max zoned out during the speeches while Kat listened intently, nodding along to the dean's reading of some inspirational poem. But after a while, she grew bored too and began playing some game on her phone.

They whooped loudly when their friends' names were called and they walked across the stage to receive their diplomas.

And at the end of graduation, when they turned their tassels and threw their caps in the air, Max smiled. Because that'd be him in less than a year, as long as he played his cards right.

And instead of dreading graduation, he was looking forward to it. To his future doing what he wanted, with the perfect girl.

The crowd of friends and family waiting to leave the stadium bleachers was packed. Max hauled Kat on his back and hopped down the bleachers rather than use the stairs. Kat giggled in his ear about butting in line but he didn't care. She wanted to get to Alec as much as he wanted to get to Lea.

And when they were finally on the field, Max spotted lavender hair next to a pompadour and made his way over.

He let Kat down and she ran and tackled Alec, nearly taking him down. Danica stood with her arm around Monica and Cam laughed with Lea.

Max walked up to her and wrapped his arms around

her, picking her up and swinging her into the air. "You're a college graduate now, doll."

Lea stuck her tongue out between her teeth and gave a very un-Lea-like squeal, throwing her arms in the hair. "Whoo hoo!"

He kissed her then, full on, lips moving and tongues tangling, and didn't stop until a voice cleared behind him.

He set her down gently and placed his arm over her shoulder. When he turned around, Lea's parents stood behind him.

"La-La," her dad said, holding out his arms and Lea squeezed Max's hand and then went to her father.

As she chatted with her parents, Max slapped Cam on the back. "You made it, buddy."

Cam had entered Bowler a semester late, but he'd loaded up on classes to graduate at the same time as Alec. He wore a pair of cut off camo pants and a tan T-shirt, his gown thrown over his shoulder. "Hell yeah. Sometimes I thought I'd be in school forever."

Max pointed at himself with his thumb. "Uh, that's me. Super senior here."

Cam smiled. "Hey, you got a good reason."

"What's going on with you job-wise?"

Cam blew out a breath, his lips fluttered and ran a hand through his sweat-damp black hair. "Man, I was gonna take this job up in New York, but Mom . . ." His jaw clenched. "I gotta go back home. I'll find something there."

Max frowned. He knew Cam had never wanted to return home. That was the reason he'd entered the military at eighteen, so he could afford college and a job and get the hell out of his small town.

"If you need anything . . ." Max began, but Cam cut him off with a dimpled smile and a friendly shove to the shoulder. "I'm cool, man. I want to celebrate today, not think about where I gotta be this summer, all right?"

"Yeah, man, I get that."

"Max," Lea called and he turned around. She waved him over to her parents and he joined them, shaking her father's hand and accepting a hug from her mother.

He'd met her parents a couple of times now. Her dad seemed very protective of Lea but never made Max feel uncomfortable or unworthy. He made Max want to show him he deserved Lea, to be proud of him.

"So, this'll be you next year, right son?" Mr. Travers said.

Max loved that he called him son. He gripped Lea's hand. "Yep, hope so."

"Ah, you'll make it." Her father smiled at him and Max returned it.

They held a graduation party back at the town house. By the time the sky had begun to darken, all the parents had gone home. Max sat on the recliner with Lea tucked into his side. Kat sat on the couch talking quietly with Cam, Alec's sleeping head in her lap.

Max ran his hand through Lea's hair and leaned his head back. Wayne was perched on the back cushion on the recliner, one of his favorite spots, and Max didn't mind because he made an excellent pillow. Even if the purring gave him a little bit of a headache.

"So I have an idea on where I want to go first."

"Hmmm?" Lea mumbled sleepily.

"On our road trip." They'd made plans to take some time together, just the two of them, before Max's summer classes started. Lea had been offered a job at the school where she student taught, which was about a half hour away from Bowler, so Max was thrilled she'd still be close.

She played with his fingers, running her hands over his calluses. "Okay, where?"

He glanced over at Cam, who was still in discussion with Kat. He'd noticed that while Cam had appeared happy, a gloom had settled on his shoulders, kind of a dread. And Max hated seeing that. "Let's go visit Cam at home."

"I'd like that," Lea said.

"Then . . . maybe I thought we'd go to New York."

Lea straightened so she could look him in the eye. "Oh yeah?"

He nodded. "I mean, it's not winter, but . . ."

"Can we ride the subway?"

He laughed. "Uh, sure."

"And I want to watch some street dancers."

"I'll put out an alert for them."

"And go to museums and libraries."

Max exaggerated a pained groan and Lea scowled and smacked his chest. "Oh stop."

He grabbed her hand and kissed her palm. "Okay, as

long as we can then hole up in a hotel room and order lots of room service."

She twisted her hand so she shook his. "Deal." Then she smiled slyly. "You just wanna get me naked in the bathtub so we can reenact our 'I love you's,' don't you?"

He pressed his lips to hers and mumbled against them. "Don't forget the rose petals."

The End

Can't get enough of Bowler University?

Read on for a sneak peek at

Make It Last

After Camilo "Cam" Ruiz graduates from college,
he finds himself in the last place ever expected:
his hometown. But he returns to Paradise and
picks up a job as a bouncer so he can help his
mother while he decides what to do with his life.
There's only one thing that can make his
return any harder—running into his high-
school sweetheart, Tate, the only girl he's
ever loved. And when he sees her again, he's
shocked to learn the pain of their breakup all
those years ago hasn't lessened. Not one bit.

Tate Ellison made a mistake when she was
eighteen, and it cost her the best thing that
ever happened to her. She's always regretted

losing Cam, but she'd hoped the regret would fade over time. Too bad it's only grown. She never imagined Cam would come home, and seeing him after all she sacrificed is a slap in the face. But when they're confronted with the truth of the past, they wonder if this time, can they make it last?

Coming January 2015

HE'D BEEN HOME three weeks before he could no longer avoid this place.

And the worst part was, it hadn't changed. Not one bit. Not the red pleather booths lining the wall—even the corner one still had its trademark X in silver duct tape covering a wicked tear. Not the robin's-egg-blue Formica countertops. Not the silver rotating stools at the counter. Not even the temperamental soft-serve ice cream, which a waitress currently wrestled while a salivating kid watched.

Not the flickering Paradise Diner sign out front, the second *a* blown out so it looked like PAR DISE. Which wasn't far off, in this town, where everyone blurred their syllables. *You're not from Pardise, are you?*

It was like he'd pressed PAUSE while playing Utope, freezing every character in the game into status quo indefinitely.

Cam Ruiz didn't know whether the static nature of this damn place was comforting or infuriating. Because all of it reminded him of her. Her little black apron covering little black shorts. Those damn wedge sandals that she said made her calves and ass look good so she got better tips. Her laugh when he'd sit at the counter right before she got off her shift, sucking down a milk shake while she mopped up the spills, shooting him flirty smiles.

Fuck, it'd been four, going on five years now. Why couldn't he just forget?

He had chosen a booth he didn't think he'd ever sat in back in high school, right near the front door. He sipped from his plastic cup of water and looked down at his watch, then at the door. There weren't tons of places open at noon to eat, so when his friend, Max Payton, called and asked where to meet, Cam froze. Then his mom yelled, "Pardise Diner!" in the background. Max had heard, and the meeting location was decided.

Through the dirty windows of the diner, Cam saw the rusted piece-of-crap truck Max drove rumble in. His friend hopped out of the truck, sunglasses in place as he squinted at the sign, and then helped his girlfriend, Lea, hop down out of the passenger side. She looked good, her limp slight, her dark hair shining in the late May sun.

Max held open the door and a bell tinkled overhead. Lea spotted Cam right away, and he stood as she hugged him. He greeted Max with a handshake and manly back slap. As they slid into the booth, Cam on one side and

Max and Lea on the other, a commotion at the counter caught his attention. A squeak followed by harsh whispers. He turned his head and all he saw were the doors to the kitchen, swinging back and forth. He shrugged and turned back to his friends.

"Thanks for visiting me," he said.

Max laid his arm behind Lea along the back of the booth. "Wanted to see the town that raised the great Cam Ruiz."

Cam rolled his eyes.

"It's definitely small," Lea said. "But I like it. Very welcoming and homey."

He guessed so, if moving back didn't make him feel like he was taking a step backward. Like a reset button wiping away the basic training for the Air National Guard, the weekends at drill, the three and a half years he busted his ass to graduate college early.

A waitress he'd never met came to take their orders, her eyes lingering a little long on Cam. Not in a flirty way, like he was used to. Plus, she was probably his mom's age and wore a wedding band. But she studied his face and his clothes and it made him uncomfortable. He wanted to ask if he had something on his face or in his teeth.

After they ordered, Max turned to Cam. "So how's your mom?"

She was the reason Cam had come back. The only reason he'd return to Paradise. He shrugged. "She's all right. She's just . . . tired and she's got a bad back. Every time she gets a job, something happens and she loses it."

He waved a hand toward the door of the diner. "Not like there are tons of jobs around here for her to pick from."

The waitress delivered their drinks and when she walked away, Lea placed her hand on top of Cam's where he twisted his straw wrapper in his fingers. "Anything we can do while we're here to help?"

Cam shook his head. "Nah, it's cool. I got a job and our rent is cheap."

Max took a gulp of water and crushed ice between his molars. "What job did ya get?"

Cam couldn't stop the growl in the back of his throat. He had a bachelor's degree and he was a . . . "Bouncer. At a bar in town."

Max's eyes widened, but then his face quickly shuttered, hiding his real feelings. "Bet you squeeze into a black T-shirt and let the tats peek out and all these rednecks scatter, huh?"

Cam laughed. "I just started last week. It's mostly girls from the community college looking to dance and stuff. I even have this fancy machine I run their IDs through to make sure they aren't fake."

"Why the hell didn't the bars at Bowler have that? Kat used her fake all the time." Max frowned.

"Until Alec shredded it," Lea snickered.

Max threw back his head. "Oh man. Apparently Kat and Alec are at her beach house with her family, and Alec is worried her brother is going to drown him in the ocean."

Lea wrinkled her nose. "Which is stupid because Marc likes Alec. He's just being paranoid."

The waitress delivered their food and even the sound

of the melamine plates sliding across the table as she announced the orders brought back memories.

He picked at his bun while Max demolished a burger.

In between bites, Max stole a handful of fries off of Lea's chicken-salad sandwich.

"Seriously?" Lea glared at him. "You have your own."

"But yours taste better," Max said around a mouthful of fries.

"That doesn't make any sense," she grumbled. "Don't make me kick your ass."

He grinned. "Maybe I want you to kick my ass. My favorite foreplay."

Cam groaned. "That's enough, guys, I'm losing my appetite."

Neither looked apologetic.

Cam ate his burger while he chatted with Max and Lea about their trip. They planned to head up into Pennsylvania and then Massachusetts. A road trip—just the two of them—since next year was going to be rough. Lea started a teaching job in the fall, and Max would be completing his last semester at Bowler student teaching.

Max picked up the tab, which made Cam bristle a little, but Max assured him it was just to thank him for taking them out in his hometown.

He followed them out of the diner and Lea hugged him before climbing into Max's truck. Max watched her through the windshield as she buckled her seat belt, then leaned a hand on his hood and turned to Cam. His eyes traveled over Cam's shoulder to the diner and then squinted at the sparse traffic on the street.

Finally his eyes met Cam's. "You sure this is what you need to be doing?"

No, he wasn't sure, but he'd committed now, hadn't he? "I need to help my mom with the bills. She worked two jobs while I was growing up to keep food on our table and a roof over our heads. What am I gonna do, leave her?"

Max ran his tongue over his teeth. "You could have maybe gotten a job and sent money . . ."

Cam shook his head. "I thought about that and I mentioned it to her but she asked me to come home first and I knew . . . I knew she wanted me here."

"Parents don't always know what's best, you know."

"I know that." But that didn't change his decision.

Max watched him for a minute, then gave a curt nod. He slapped Cam on the shoulder. "All right, man. You need anything, you call me or Alec, all right?"

He wouldn't. "Sure."

Max got in his truck, leaned in to give Lea a kiss on her cheek, and then they pulled out onto Main Street.

Cam sighed, feeling the weight of responsibility pressing down on his shoulders. But if he didn't help his mom, who would?

He jingled his keys in his pocket and turned to walk toward his truck.

As he walked by the alley beside the restaurant, something flickered out of the corner of his eye.

He turned and spotted her legs first. One foot bent at the knee and braced on the brick wall, the other flat on the ground. Her head was bent, a curtain of hair blocking her face. But he knew those legs. He knew those hands. And he knew that hair, a light brown that held just a glint of strawberry in the sun. He knew by the end of August it'd be lighter and redder and she'd laugh about that time she put lemon juice in it. It'd backfired and turned her hair orange.

The light flickered again but it was something weird and artificial, not like the menthols she had smoked. Back when he knew her.

As she lowered her hand down to her side, he caught sight of the small white cylinder. It was an electronic cigarette. She'd quit.

She raised her head then, like she knew someone was watching her, and he wanted to keep walking, avoid this awkward moment. Avoid those eyes he didn't think he'd ever see again or ever thought he'd want to see again. But now that his eyes locked on her hazel eyes—the ones he knew began as green on the outsides of her irises and darkened to brown by the time they met her pupils—he couldn't look away. His boots wouldn't move.

The small cigarette fell to the ground with a soft click and she straightened, both her feet on the ground.

And that's when he noticed the wedge shoes. And the black apron. What was she doing here?

"Camilo."

Other than his mom, she was the only one who used his full name sometimes. He'd heard her say it while laughing. He'd her moan it while he was inside her. He'd heard her sigh it with an eye roll when he made a bad joke. But he'd never heard it the way she said it now, with a little bit of fear and anxiety and . . . longing? He took a deep breath to steady his voice. "Tate."

He hadn't spoken her name since that night Trevor called him and told him what she did. The night his future that he'd set out for himself and for her completely changed course.

She'd lost some weight in the four years since he'd last seen her. He'd always loved her curves. She had it all—thighs, ass and tits in abundance. Naked, she was a fucking vision.

Damn it, he wasn't going there.

But now her face looked thinner, her clothes hung a little loose and he didn't like this look as much. Not that she probably gave a fuck about his opinion anymore.

She still had her gorgeous hair, pinned up halfway with a bump in front, and smattering of freckles across the bridge of her nose and on her cheekbones. And she still wore her makeup exactly the same—thickly mascaraed eyelashes, heavy eyeliner that stretched to a point on the outer corners of her eyes, like a modern-day Audrey Hepburn.

She was still beautiful. And she still took his breath away.

And his heart felt like it was breaking all over again.

And he hated her even more for that.

About the Author

MEGAN ERICKSON grew up in a family that averages 5'5" on a good day and started writing to create characters who could reach the top kitchen shelf.

She's got a couple of tattoos, has a thing for gladiators and has been called a crazy cat lady. After working as a journalist for years, she decided she liked creating her own endings better and switched back to fiction.

She lives in Pennsylvania with her husband, two kids and two cats. And no, she still can't reach the stupid top shelf.